Heather in a Tempest

Book Two of THE CHRONICLES OF AMBER LEAF

a novel by

SANDRA H. ESCH

A LAMP POST BOOK

HEATHER IN A TEMPEST
  BY SANDRA H. ESCH

ISBN 13: 978-1-60039-225-2
ebook ISBN: 978-1-60039-746-2

www.lamppostpubs.com

Heather in a Tempest

BY
SANDRA H. ESCH

BOOK TWO of
THE CHRONICLES OF AMBER LEAF

Look, the winter is past; the rains are over and gone.
Blossoms appear through all the land.
The time has come to sing;
the cooing of doves is heard in our land.

Song of Solomon 2:11-12

CHAPTER ONE

AMBER LEAF, MINNESOTA

JUNE 1916

Big Ole enfolded Gretta's delicate hand in his and wept silently as she slept. Pale and gaunt lying in the narrow hospital bed, how was it that his beautiful wife could appear so at peace?

"Mr. Harrington?" the doctor said.

Ole flinched and immediately pulled himself together. "Yes?"

"I know to lose a child is one thing, but then to lose another and yet another in as many years? You have my sincerest sympathies."

Though the doctor meant well, Ole needed strength at the moment, not pity. "It was that horse and buckboard accident," he said. "Damaged her insides."

"I understand. Leaving her all but barren?"

Ole nodded. Thirteen years of wanting, trying. Endless days of bed rest. Countless careful steps. The gait of a swan to keep from jarring that precious child within.

He looked about the pristine ward. In a nearby bed, a patient thrashed about like a fish at the end of a hook. Then came the groans … and Ole broke into shivers.

"Looks like you could use a break," the doctor said. "We'll take good care of your wife. Why don't you go and get a cup of coffee? Renew your spirits. Be strong for her. She will need your strength when she awakens."

Forget the coffee. Too hot for the stuff anyway. Ole needed to get home. Slam shut the door to the nursery. Lock it up for good. Stash the baby carriage in the attic. Give it a shove 'til it hit the far wall. That's what he'd do. The last thing she needed was another reminder of loss.

Though it grieved him to leave, he quietly rose and leaned in to kiss her forehead, but lingered instead. Don't wake her. She needs rest. Allow her a break from grief.

He donned his hat and wandered outside, but could barely draw a breath. Miserable steamy heat. Soggy humidity pasted his shirt to his chest and back.

He cranked up the Model T, but before driving off he gave the steering wheel an exasperated thump. He wanted children so badly it consumed him—the patter of tiny feet, soft giggles, wide-eyed looks of wonder. Building a tree house for a son, a doll house for a daughter. A hobbyhorse for either of them. Now what?

Minutes later, he stood face-to-face with his freshly painted back door. From the inside it would serve as a bastion, shielding Gretta from the painful sight of contented mothers and cooing infants roaming the streets of Amber Leaf.

But from the outside? The painter might as well have painted on bars. At the moment, it felt more like a prison gate. Passing through the door would only inflict him with perpetual memories of what might have been and a state of raw grieving. No paint job could fix that.

But a new home might.

He reluctantly stepped inside, walked down that long hallway, and entered the nursery. Tears mingled with sweat, he backhanded his eyes. What was done was done. No looking back. No more infants. In due time, approach Gretta with the idea of adopting an older child who hungered for parental love—nurturing parental love … the kind of love he never knew.

He considered that for a moment. How does one establish a fulfilling relationship with a father who so easily turned his back on him? Or with that elusive child who insists on remaining a pipe dream? Somehow neither seemed possible. If he wanted to maintain presence of mind, he needed to shift his focus. Tend to the needs of his grieving bride. Bury himself in work.

Unable to slam shut the door on the nursery after all, he tidied up a few things and then returned to the hospital, to Gretta's room.

"You're sitting up already?" he said. "Are you sure that's wise?"

She reached out to him with love-filled eyes. "We'll try again." Her forced tone sounded anything but convincing. "We'll get it right next time. You'll see … Ole? … Did we have a girl? … a boy?"

Pain crushed his throat. "A girl."

A beautiful, delicate little girl.

Gretta pressed his hand to her cheek, caressing it. "Please don't be sad. We'll get through this."

"I'm fine," he said though a tremor invaded his smile.

Tears glistened in her doe eyes. "Mister-I'm-fine, how about if we do things differently this time? Let's not put the baby carriage away for a while. Let's face it. Grieve properly. After all, our little girl is playing on streets of gold with her big brother and sister …"

"Where's this smile coming from?" Ole said, lovingly sweeping a light finger along the side of her cheek.

"I wonder about heaven, if the streets there are paved with fine dust or gold bricks. I don't know that anyone ever said."

"That sounds like something you'd wonder about."

"Just think." Gretta brightened. "Oliver Harrington, all is not lost."

"We're being a bit formal, aren't we?"

"One day when this short life is over," she continued, "we'll see our babies again, and we'll have all of the time in the world to get to know them."

Surely it was God's grace that emanated from his beloved bride's lips for one day soon the grieving would come crashing in.

Hard.

CHAPTER TWO

London, England

June 1916

Olivia De Haven sat in vigil, the clock on the nightstand ticking away precious seconds. Light rain splattered against the windowpanes as if rapping, begging to come in from the dreary cold.

Her grandmum Amelia was failing. Gaunt. Pale. Persistent wheezing. Constant shifting. Her flimsy pillow appeared to cut into her emaciated neck. Yet in the twilight Olivia waited in despair, hoping to get answers before it was too late.

She ran a slender finger along the tired bedding where frail bones cut against paper-thin skin. "I wish we could bare the expense of softer bedding. This must feel as though you're laying on a blanket of nails."

In a tender little old lady's voice, her grandmum said, "You need not worry about me." She drew a wrinkled hand to trembling lips and spat blood into her last clean handkerchief. A jolt. A gasp. Razor-edged pain appeared to accompany a coughing fit choking what little air she possessed from fragile lungs. She wheezed in another breath, the largest a suffering soul might manage against a fierce ache.

The angel of death hovered over the old woman now, waiting for her to succumb so he could move on to his next victim. Olivia sensed it.

Please don't die. Not yet.

Her grandmum dozed off. In the unnerving quiet that followed, Olivia padded across the aging floor of the modest two-bedroom flat. She quietly opened and closed the door to the icebox and placed a kettle on the cast iron stove. Long moments of misery drawing swiftly to a close, Grandmum's torturous life here on earth would soon pass.

No more pain.

But Olivia would then be alone.

She shuddered at the thought.

Another feeble cough resonated from the bedroom. Olivia took a reluctant glance back then scooped a ladle of broth into the kettle. During a stronger moment her grandmum had mentioned something about God. Said she'd asked Him to forgive her and sensed His fervent yes. But forgiven her for what? Olivia suspected the dear woman was seeking her forgiveness as well. Why might that be? Clearly she was holding something back.

The broth thoroughly warmed, Olivia placed the steaming bowl on a platter and returned to the bedroom. She then gathered an arrangement of heather and placed it on the nightstand where she fussed with it and lit a candle.

"Olivia?" her grandmum muttered from behind.

Olivia turned. "Look. Fresh heather."

"Oh, yes."

"Beautiful, is it not?"

"You remind me of heather … heather in a tempest. Yielding the way you do to the winds of war about us. Stalwart. You never complain. You also remind me of your father so long ago."

My father? A beautiful hurt nudged Olivia's heart. What had she missed in all this time? If only she could have known him, been blessed with the slightest memory on which to hold. But that was not to be.

War in Sudan had swallowed him up, stealing his future, his very last breath before she breathed her first. Robbing her of the beauty of the purest form of love.

Her grandmum's countenance saddened further. "You must marry, dear, and you must marry well. Nothing in this world is more wonderful than a loving relationship. You must marry young so you can build a long and beautiful life together." She paused, her tired eyes begging a question. "Why do I feel as if you've left our conversation?"

"I am to marry well, Grandmum?" Gazing about the paltry room, hope dwindled. "It is impossible for me to compete for the sort of marriage I desire. I would have need to be a debutante."

"You are more of a debutante than you know."

"Because you raised me to be rich on the inside?"

"No."

Could that be a glint in her grandmum's eye? Why did her tone sound confident? "I warmed some broth," Olivia said. "You might rather enjoy it."

"It seems you've changed the subject … you look distressed, my dear." The old woman lifted a frail wrist, but swiftly succumbed to its heavy weight.

Olivia drew the tray closer and spooned warm broth to parched lips. "You mustn't fret. I'll feed you."

Her grandmum choked down the liquid against another exhausting cough. "I presume you've heard no more talk of the bombings."

"No," Olivia said, "but we remain highly watchful. Those Zeppelins drop them by the bucket load."

A swallow of the warm liquid must have soothed her grandmum's throat for her voice cleared, and she appeared to gather strength. "You must flee England."

"I shall not leave you."

"When I'm gone …"

"No."

"You mustn't stay here. It's far too dangerous."

"I'm not fearful," she said, willing courage into being.

"I'm certain you're not, but do you wish to be a burden? If anything happens with this horrible fighting going on, you might easily become another casualty for someone else to manage. Is that what you desire?"

Olivia hadn't thought of the war in those terms before. She shook her head.

"If you wish to be of help, you would do more good from afar."

"I'm not leaving you," Olivia insisted. "I will not be forced. Besides, where might I go? What might I do?"

Her grandmum flinched then looked away too quickly.

"What is it?"

She looked up, her gaze appearing to deliberately avoid Olivia's. "You must get in touch with your father."

"My wha …"

"Your father."

A hot spoonful of liquid splattered against Olivia's thigh. She flinched then tore off her apron, wiped away the excess moisture, and studied her grandmum for a long moment. Why the pitiful look? Was she hallucinating? Or could that be … shame? "What are you implying? You told me he perished in Sudan."

"You must forgive me. I've been aching to tell you about him, but never could bring myself to do so." She reached out to Olivia. "Last I've heard, he is still amongst the living. You must get in touch with him."

Surely this must be deliriums talking, hallucinations brought on by intense pain. "What? Who is he? Why would you insist he was dead?"

"I had good reason. You must believe me."

Olivia's heart hammered. "Why would he choose not to be in touch with me after all this time then?"

"The story is long. He will understand. It's best the answers come from him." Her grandmum blinked back tears. "When he learns he has a daughter—"

"He doesn't know …"

The old woman's reticent look signaled regret.

"But why?"

Another coughing jag befell her, this one more severe. Fighting for air, she drew the blood-soaked handkerchief to her lips, crimson liquid seeping down her chin.

"Grandmum, you're hemorrhaging!"

The cough spent, each word choked out in a labored whisper. "You're going to … need family."

"No. Please. You mustn't talk. I must fetch the doctor."

"We haven't time. Your father is Oliver Harrington. He lives in America, in Amber Leaf … Minnesota. Your great uncle lives there as well. Deacon De Haven. My brother. And your great aunt. Maude Millning. You favor her so. We've remained somewhat estranged. That was my choice. I felt a strong need to protect you."

"Whatever for?"

"I do hear about them from time to time through our neighbor," she said, appearing to ignore the question. "You simply must … write to your father."

Olivia drew back, horrified by the thought. "No."

"You must let him know who you are. He will send for you. Of that I am certain. He is a … good, good man."

"Then why—"

Her grandmum pushed up with tremendous effort and then flopped back down, her light weight exhausting her. "You'll find a letter … in my upper dresser drawer. I wrote one to your father … soon after you were … born. Waited for the right time to send it, but that time … never came. It would be best if you … presented it to him in person. It should … explain … all there is to know."

"But—"

"Please … tell me you forgive me."

Tears splashed down Olivia's cheeks, her thoughts overwrought with confusion. "I know you, Grandmum. I'm sure there's nothing to forgive."

"Amber … Leaf."

Heaving with sobs, Olivia drew her grandmum into a desperate hug and gently rocked her. "Please … please don't leave me."

The wind picked up and a sudden draft flickered then snuffed out the candle's fragile flame.

CHAPTER THREE

Ole charged through the bustling law office of Addison & Crowley with its overstuffed file drawers and teetering stacks of thick manila folders. Heads turned away and pity-filled eyes cast downward, which worsened his agony. At least he was getting the disagreeable words of caring from apprehensive lips out of the way. Though his colleagues meant well, he preferred grieving in private.

He eased onto his groaning chair and fumbled through a stack of papers before him. At the moment, compelling legal proceedings seemed anything but. He set the papers aside and picked up the Sheldon file. He needed to win this case or he would never make partner.

Before he could focus, Boss bounded in and dropped an early morning paper on his desk. The man's pate wasn't plastered against his forehead as usual. He must be out of grease.

Ole swept up the file. "I was about to—"

"It's upside down," Boss said in lieu of hello.

Ole flipped the file around. "Hence the words 'about to.'"

"Seen the headlines yet? Is there no end to this madness? Italians keep advancing. German U-boat sunk another ship. Won't be long now before our boys will have to jump in, too."

Ole rested his attention on the paper, the headlines. Misery knew no bounds. But at least Boss wouldn't get sloppy on him.

Boss leaned in. "Sorry about the loss," he muttered, sounding as if he'd pulled his tie too tight. Then after an awkward pivot on a heel, he walked out.

Why did he have to say that?

Ole slumped in his chair. He knew hell. He knew war. And he knew more than he cared to know about loss—first his beloved Emily and only son back in his native England, then … He shook his head. For all he knew, it might be best not to bring a child into a war-torn world.

After flipping absently through a few more file folders, lasting all of about a minute, he thrummed his desk.

Concentrate.

You must concentrate.

He opened the Sheldon file again and drew out a summary, reading and rereading the first paragraph until it finally drew him in.

At half past two he stepped into Boss's office for their weekly one-on-one, the smoke-filled air reminding him of London fog. The man stood behind his desk playfully pulling at his suspenders while appearing full of himself. He inhaled a drag on a cigar then blew out a purposeful puff as fast as he drew it in. "Woman stopped by yesterday afternoon," he said. "Insists she needs a good attorney. Seems her husband has quite the history of misrepresenting himself."

"Why's that?"

"I'll get to that in a minute."

"Do I know her?"

Boss, appearing too excited to sit, reached across the desk and flicked a light smattering of ashes into an overfilled ashtray. "Name's Mabel Harding. You may have seen her when she came in. Attractive. Tall. Thin. Well-dressed. Slightly graying hair."

He remembered. The woman had emanated a rare magnetic quality.

"The Hardings are going through some tough divorce proceedings," Boss said. "When it comes to settling, it appears the hubby is a little too close to her money."

"I'm not sure why you'd want to involve me," Ole said. "I'm shy on experience when it comes to divorces. John Brown—"

"Yet."

"Excuse me?"

Boss stepped to the front of his desk and smirked. "I said yet. I've got a feeling this case might be right up your alley."

How could Ole get Boss to understand? Divorce proceedings didn't interest him in the slightest. Never would. Life was too short to spend precious hours braving the bitterness and wrath of shattered lives. "I can't imagine why."

The smirk still present, Boss held his gaze, playing with him. "What you lack in experience, I'm sure you'll gain in passion."

"And that would be because?"

"The hubby is being represented by ... Nelson Prixton."

Ole felt his eyes bulge. "Nel—"

"That's right," Boss said, releasing a full-on grin.

All these years later, Ole could still hear Nelson's lies that night Gretta caught the swine cheating on her while in the throes of convincing her she should marry him ... and then blaming her for his infidelity. That night she tripped and fell into the path of an on-coming buckboard because she had felt a need to get away from him. That night that all but destroyed her ability to bear children. He could still smell Nelson's oppressive breath, that sickening stench of cheap, spent booze, when hours later the man staggered, weeping, into her hospital room—weeping for himself, not for her. And that was long after Ole had rushed her there.

He drew back his shoulders and straightened his tie. "How soon can I start?"

CHAPTER FOUR

Olivia stood outside her grandmum's bedroom, reluctant to enter. In all of her sixteen years, she had never endured such intense loneliness. Opening the door might easily worsen that hollow feeling. She cringed at the thought. But the heather. Certainly it was rancid by now. She must retrieve the vase.

Hinges creaked. Aging hardwood groaned beneath her slippers as she quickly padded across the floor. But then she stopped mid step. Confused. Bewildered. Since an infant, her grandmum had distanced her from all of their relatives … on both sides. Why? True, her grandfather possessed the ability to embarrass a lamppost and pompously exercised that skill with abandon, but surely her relatives understood.

She scanned the room. What could be so disturbing that it warranted withdrawal, and an acute withdrawal at that? When she scooped up the vase, however, her eyes fell to the dresser, to the top drawer.

The letter. Might she find the answer there?

She pulled open the drawer, drew out the sealed envelope, and held it up to dim light. A name was written on the outside in beautiful feminine script—Mr. Oliver M. Harrington. However, the writing inside remained as hidden as the secret therein contained.

She hugged the letter. Who was this Oliver M. Harrington? How could he possibly not know that he had a daughter? And if he did know, why had he not sought her out?

Though desperately tempted to tear open the envelope and peruse the contents to unveil its mystery, she yielded instead to an unrelenting conscience. She refused to betray her grandmum's expressed wishes. Needing to present the letter to Oliver M. Harrington unopened, she delicately placed it back in its hiding place as though it were ancient parchment that might easily crumble, and then she closed the drawer. Seizing the vase, she returned to the kitchen where she disposed of the dying heather all the while wondering about her father, about her future, or because of the war ... her lack of future.

She considered her position around the corner at that small tailor shop. It helped pay the bills, but barely. She would love to further her education, but that remained a fanciful notion. How does one further their education without the funds to do so? Remaining a spinster sent nasty prickles down her spine. Might it be feasible to find happiness marrying within her social class? She gazed about her grandmum's aging flat and reflected on their numerous difficult times. That prospect seemed most unlikely.

But her father. Might she find a future with him? She washed the vase with care, as if wiping away the dross might clarify her thinking. How does one tell a perfect stranger 'I'm your long lost daughter?' Would he want her if he knew? Surely he must have more children. What a pleasant thought. Half brothers? Half sisters? An extended family?

Yet would they receive her with favor? And what about her stepmother? Oh, dear. Would the woman be resentful? After all, how could Olivia not be a reminder of Oliver M. Harrington's prior love?

After considering her options, the choice remained crystal clear. Her grandmum's dying request begged fulfillment. Secrets of the past were in need of revealing. But her grandmum's request was impossible.

How might Olivia present the letter to her father in person? He lived in America.

She must find a way to move forward. Whatever path she chose, she would tread carefully. Take this in small steps. If her father had slammed the door on his past, she needed to muster the courage to face rejection. But if he opened wide the door to a future with him, would that door be worthy of walking through? Would she meet with disappointment? Or would she be thrilled to enter a brand new world filled with wonder?

She plucked a bottle of ink, a quill, and several sheets of paper from the cupboard and nudged closely to the table curious about what words might pour forth.

She then stared for a long while at the blank parchment, which seemed stubbornly resistant to anything other than precisely formed words.

CHAPTER FIVE

Gretta, who always met Ole at the door with a welcoming hug, was nowhere in sight. Must be in a back room somewhere, he decided. The kitchen smelling of stovetop roast and the table set, he happily headed for the living room to peruse the daily paper.

A moment later, appearing oblivious to his presence, she strode down the hallway and into the kitchen cheerfully humming *It Is Well*.

He perked up at her tone.

Her pitch?

Perfect.

Though he doubted all could be well with her soul.

Since losing their beloved daughter, he had yet to see her grieve. Her eyes continually sparkled. She exuded a pleasant demeanor and said all of the right things, always. Other than occasionally storing fresh milk in the cupboards and canisters of flower and sugar in the icebox, she exhibited no signs of distress.

He set the paper aside and slipped up behind her, drawing her into his arms.

"Mmmm, wonderful to have you home, dear," she cooed then

returned to matters on the stove. "I didn't hear you come in. How was your day?"

"The usual. Demanding clients. Disgruntled employees. A boss who loves to reduce his workers to the status of machines. Other than that, it wasn't too bad."

Suddenly the kitchen grew uncharacteristically dark. He glanced over his shoulder then hurried to the window, drew back the curtain, and peered out toward the east. "I wonder what's going on," he said. Strangely, the horizon remained a bright azure blue. "Be right back."

From the window in the parlor on the west side of their home, however, the sky loomed black as soot.

He returned to the kitchen in a rush. "Big storm's blowing in," he said.

And with the storm came darkness and that imbecilic onslaught of claustrophobia.

Again.

That feeling that compelled him to back away from closed-in spaces, confining basements numbering among them. His heart raced. Knees turned to rubber. Try though he may, and after all of the storms they'd endured, he couldn't bring himself to admit how debilitating that overwhelming fear made him feel.

Gretta peered out the window and glowered at the menacing clouds that rapidly overtook the sky. The wind picked up and thunder grumbled. "You're right," she said. "It is blowing in with a vengeance. We need to get down to the basement."

The air in his lungs locked. "You go. I'll stay by the doorway the way I always do."

"Ole … this one is way too bad. What if it drops a tornado? Why do you … you aren't … if anything ever happened …"

Though it grieved him to disappoint her, he held his ground.

Bolts of lightning danced in the inky sky. An ear-splitting thunder-clap vibrated the floor and rattled the windows. Branches of trees blew sideways, breaking off, skipping across the road like tumbleweed. From the front yard the limb of a giant oak cracked sickeningly in the fierce wind, further jarring his jumpy nerves.

He stepped back, clearing a path for Gretta. "You'd better get down there. If it gets too bad, I'll come, too."

"If that tree falls on the house, you'll be ..."

Great! Go down into a basement? Dark? Dingy? No doors to the outside?

Air emptied from his lungs. Sweat seeped from his palms. He wobbled like a drunk on his size twelves. "I'll be fine. You go ahead now," he said. "Please."

She plucked a thick candle and a box of matches out of a cabinet drawer and then pulled open the basement door. "Just in case the electricity goes off," she said. "I don't want to get stuck down there ... alone ... in the dark."

While he knew she meant no malice, the alone word walloped him with guilt.

"Promise me you'll come down if it gets too bad," she said.

When donkeys yodel.

She flew down several steps then stopped and looked back with concern-filled eyes. "Sweetheart, what made you this way?"

"You'd better light that candle. Electricity does go off, you'll be in a real pickle."

"Oliver Harrington, though you're too proud to admit it, I know you're scared to death. You need to get over this silly fear," she said in a tone filled with care. "Every time there's a thunderstorm we go through this, and it hurts to see it."

Why articulate the obvious?

An ear-splitting crack of thunder rolled across the menacing sky. The house shook. Light flickered. Glass rattled.

"Ole ..."

All right, all right. He reluctantly pressed his back to the wall, eased around the doorjamb, gripped the railing, and forced himself to descend a step, his body growing increasingly rigid until he could no longer move. He coerced himself to settle in on the top step, rigid legs supple as a wrought iron bar. "Nothing's ever happened yet, has it?" he said through gritted teeth.

She lit a match. As fire flared, the stench of sulfur permeated the air. "You've got to get over this," she snapped. "You're too old to act like a child."

He couldn't see his furrowed brow, but he sure felt it. "Thanks for being so understanding," he muttered.

She rushed back up the stairs where she fell at his feet. "I'm sorry, Ole. I don't know what's gotten into me. I didn't mean to talk to you like that."

He drew her close and smoothed her hair. Could her harsh tone be grief finally breaking through? Seeing her remorse, he felt more relief than anger. "It's okay," he said.

She pulled back and looked up at him. "Forgive me?"

How could he not? Yet the truth in her grief-driven words still smarted. His fear embarrassed him, but what could he do about it? He'd tried everything. Avoiding it. Facing it head on. Ignoring it. Thinking it through. Nothing worked.

The aversion too far out of control to manage alone, too embarrassing to admit to anyone, what did it matter? He knew no one who understood this sort of affliction.

The light cut out, leaving them sitting at the top of the steps in the dim glow of the candle, and in that dim glow, Gretta remained at his feet. Thunder rumbled and the wild winds blew. After a short while she got up, descended the staircase, and at the base of the steps, she swiveled around, her eyes darting about the dark corners of the basement. "Maybe we should think about finding a different home," she said. "Would you like that? One that's built into a hillside with an entire basement wall exposed—a wall of real windows instead of scrawny ones like these. I'd like that better myself."

Reeling once again, he briefly squeezed his eyes closed to steady himself. He wanted to say 'but you're not claustrophobic,' but that would mean admitting it.

"I prefer the light," she continued. "It feels better. Maybe we can get a new start with our family then, too. Leave our painful memories behind."

He slid down a step, the closest he dared go without breaking into another cold sweat. "What about adopting? I can't put you through another pregnancy," he said, unable to conceal a break in his voice.

She shook her head. "I want your baby, Ole. I want our baby."

He hesitated. "And if you can't?"

She gave a basket near the shelving an absent kick, nudging it into place. "I don't want to think about that."

"We'll still have each other. To me, that means the world."

"Does to me, too, but I also need to be a mother. It's in my blood."

Another crack of thunder shook the cellar's foundation followed by the sound of steady rain.

Could the worst of the storm finally be over?

CHAPTER SIX

Sitting in a wingback chair in a stately residence overlooking Fountain Lake, Mabel Harding wasn't the broken woman Ole had anticipated. Before him sat a plate of warm rolls fresh out of the oven, the scent of cinnamon still swirling on the air. Sparkling crystal. Elegant china. Beautifully decorated home in roses and pinks and varying shades of robin's egg blue.

"That was quite the storm we had last night," she said. "Did you suffer any damage?"

Only to my ego. "A branch broke off our favorite oak. Missed the house by a foot. No damage other than that." He gestured toward her window. "Your yard appears intact."

"I was fortunate." She hesitated and then in a tone that bore a telltale remorseful quality, she changed the subject. "I can't imagine living overseas these days. Everyone's declaring war on everyone. The bloodshed is so dreadful, I feel selfish putting up a fight in my own tiny world."

"I understand," he said. "But don't feel selfish. It's better to put up a good fight before things spin out of control."

He lifted a crystal goblet to his lips, hesitated, then set the lemonade on a coffee table. Mrs. Harding's demeanor had returned to effervescent, which seemed unusual for a woman whose husband recently filed for divorce. Ole eyed her thoughtfully then nudged the conversation toward the crux of the problem. "Why would your husband want to break up your marriage?"

Her smile appeared displaced. "Your question certainly is direct."

"I don't mean to be rude," he said. "But if I'm going to represent you, I need to understand what caused your parting of paths."

"I believe you do at that." She let loose a sigh. "Seems he wasn't happy about losing his allowance now that he found himself a steady new lady friend."

"You don't seem to be—"

"What? Bothered? I'm not," she said as if she were merely tossing an emptied can of cold beans into the trash. "I fell out of love with him when we were on our honeymoon … completely out of love."

Stunned by the forthright response, Ole questioned her motives. Was she victim or perpetrator in their parting relationship? Deciding it best to probe, he said, "How long have you been married?"

"Seven years, going on eight."

"Was it something he said? Did?"

She fingered a thin strand of pearls and mindlessly tugged at the string. "I was terribly smitten when we courted. Thought we were a perfect match, really. We both came from money, or so I thought."

Or so I thought? Ole had a hunch where this was going, and he also sensed a broken spirit cowering beneath a false front. He waited her out as she collected her thoughts.

"He showered me with flowers and gifts, took me to the finest restaurants, and told me wonderful stories about places where he'd been." Her eyes danced and her voice took on a noticeable lilt as she recounted them. "Monte Carlo. Rome. Paris. Venice. London. Insisted we would travel the world after we married and when we returned home we'd raise a beautiful family together. Sounded wonderful. I planned an elegant wedding. Several hundred guests. Then we hopped a train to Niagara Falls for the perfect honeymoon."

With hard lines creasing her forehead, she appeared ten years her senior as she continued on. "But the day we arrived, we went to an upscale restaurant for a romantic lunch. As we got up to leave, he patted his pocket. Said he'd forgotten his wallet and asked if I'd pick up the tab … for the whole kit and caboodle. There was something about his innocent look that turned my stomach. It appeared contrived. After that, each time I opened my handbag and reached for my wallet, I felt violated. My feelings for him kept growing colder and colder, and I felt helpless to stop it. Then a month or so after our wedding, he took off on a five-day fishing expedition with a few of his friends. At least that's where he said he was going. Had the gall to ask me for spending money. Said he'd had a financial setback. Said he was waiting for his account to be replenished with a pending payment from a family trust."

"Were there any hints before you married that his character might be wanting?"

"None whatsoever. He was the perfect gentleman. Said he held out on getting married until he could find someone like me. But then he changed. Nothing about him felt right from our wedding day on. So I had him followed. He didn't go on a fishing expedition, Mr. Harrington. He took a train to Chicago … and gambled. The deposit to his account? It never did come. Since our honeymoon, he's assumed my money is our money. Or should I say his? When I complain about it, he threatens me."

"Physically?"

She shook her head. "He said there were ways of making my life difficult, ways to embarrass me. Turns out that was a lie, too. When I didn't roll over and play dead, he merely scooted off and found himself some other floozy who just happened to be financially well set, too."

"Have you confronted her about him?"

"Why would I?" she said, taking on a scornful look. "If that woman doesn't give a hoot that he's married, I'd say they deserve each other."

"She does know he's married then?"

"He told me she … you don't think he … not when we courted … that would be polyg…?" Mabel turned and stared out the window as realization appeared to settle in then turned back, her tone faltering. "He's intent on taking my money along with him, as much as he can get his grubby mitts on, that is. He has an attorney. Maybe you know the man. Nelson Prixton?"

Ole's stomach summersaulted at the mere mention of Nelson's name.

"I wasn't planning on getting legal counsel, but when Mr. Prixton asked for the bank statements from my deceased parents' estate, I drew the line. That isn't right, is it? I mean, how could they do such a thing?"

"That's what selfish people do," Ole said. "Greed is a vacuum that can never be filled, and it's my job to protect you from it. Tell me, did you make any large purchases while you were married?"

She shrugged then looked about the room. "This house, several plots of land, a few office buildings," she said indifferently. "He insisted it would be best if we invested our assets instead of letting them sit in the bank collecting a small amount of interest."

How cunning could that man be? "From what I've gleaned, you have no children, is that correct?"

With a mournful shake of her head, Mabel's indifferent façade splintered the moment she pinched her eyes closed. "It's a curse to be barren," she said.

"I know," he lamented.

CHAPTER SEVEN

fter promising to follow up with Mabel soon, Ole meant to hurry back to the office. Around the bend, however, an all-too-familiar Model T Speedster sat askew, half on the road, half off. Curious, he pulled up behind it, got out, and examined the abandoned automobile. Tires looked fine. He trudged to the front and lightly touched the hood. Still warm. He peered inside. A pair of binoculars lay haphazardly on the passenger seat. Why? After pondering the situation, he scanned the wooded area surrounding Mabel's property.

That swine. He's spying on Mabel.

A whiff of something pungent seared Ole's nostrils. Lowering on a knee, he checked the undercarriage and ran a finger through a telltale puddle beneath the Speedster. After a good sniff of the evaporating petro, he looked harder into the thicket, past several overgrown trees. Nelson couldn't possibly make a fast get away let alone a get away of any kind with a dried-up gasoline tank. He had to lurk around here somewhere.

"You can come out now, Nelson," Ole called out then listened into the quiet. He couldn't let an opportunity like this pass. After a measured moment, he returned to his car. Itching to catch the man red-handed, he nonchalantly sorted through his briefcase and waited him out.

Minutes later, still no Nelson.

Not finding anything more of interest to help pass the time, he closed his briefcase and glanced up at the man's car.

The binoculars.

Ole smirked, got out, retrieved them, brought them into focus, and called out again. "Looks like your gas line's got a nasty leak."

Nelson finally poked his head out from behind a thick-trunked oak, lifted a pointer finger to his lips, mouthed "shhh," and again disappeared from view.

Brilliant move, Nelson. Transparent, but brilliant.

A moment later he reappeared. Moist leaves squishing beneath his foot drops, he sidled up to Ole's Tin Lizzie smelling as if he'd taken a bath in a tub of cologne, a preferable fragrance to the gasoline. "Well, if it isn't Harrington, the great. Speedster goes on the fritz and you're the first to come along. How lucky can a man get?"

"Nice to see you, too, Prixton." After all this time, Nelson didn't look a day older. Not a gray strand on his thick shock of sable hair, perfect features, wearing the best clothes money could buy. And still as smug as ever. Ole glanced at the woodlot and with a quick bob of his head, he said, "What's going on out there?"

"Saw a gray fox. It was after something. I wanted to see what it was."

"And?"

Nelson lifted a brow. "Some loud mouth scared it off."

"Crank her up. I'll give you a lift."

Nelson crank started the car and then hopped in.

"Where to?" Ole said.

"The office. I need to call a mechanic."

As the Model T hummed alongside glistening waters, passing beneath patches of mottled shade in the late morning sun, Ole gave

Nelson a cursory glance. "I see you're doing your own investigative work these days," he said. "You might want to be more discreet. As I recall, trespassing is still against the law."

"Excuse me? Checking out a plot of land to build a new home on certainly isn't."

"While wearing your Sunday-go-to-meeting clothes?" Ole picked up the binoculars at his side and shoved them at Nelson. "What are these for? Hunting down invisible boundary lines?"

Nelson's eyes narrowed. "Why did you pay a visit on Mabel Harding?"

"I'm her attorney."

"Since when?"

"A few weeks back."

"That a fact? You'd better brace yourself then. She's going to wear rags by the time I get done with her."

Ole pressed the hand throttle and the tires spat gravel. As they rounded a sharp curve, Nelson buttressed himself against the door as if his head were about to fly off.

Ultimately it wasn't Mabel's assets Nelson was after, that Ole knew. It was her father's assets. The poor man had worked a lifetime to build financial security to leave her well taken care of, but now he and her mother were both deceased. Was nothing sacred? Ole ached to say as much, but he refused. That would not be professional.

Nelson fixed his gaze on the road ahead. "I'm surprised Boss turned the case over to you. I figured you to be a greenhorn when it comes to divorce law."

"Give me credit, Nelson. I do know the law." And I know there's far more to winning than exploiting technicalities. I know Harding conned Mabel into sinking a fortune into community investments. Unfortunately, now I have the daunting task of tracing separate assets.

Nelson sat quietly for a measured moment, and then in a tone fortified with condescension, he said, "Too bad she doesn't have any kids ... no heirs."

The cruelty those words implied stopped Ole. What was worse? Nelson's mocking look washed over him as if a nerve had gotten whacked. It was as if the man was screaming 'you took my Gretta away from me and now you're getting what you deserve—you'll never produce an heir either.' Adding further insult to injury, Nelson's look took on the prophetic feel Ole had been fighting, leaving him wanting as if he'd drawn a short straw. Grief dogged him. His frustration of yearning for a child so badly, yet something he feared he would never be able to have, crushed him.

He gazed at his clenched palm, willfully splayed it on a pant leg where he rubbed it up and down, and then pulled sharply to the side of the road. "Your ride ends here."

WHEN OLE ARRIVED HOME AT CLOSE of day, he drew Gretta into a warm embrace. "This morning," he said, "I found out what the inside of a troubled marriage looks like. It's something I'd never want to experience, never in a million years. We get one stab at a good one." He pulled back and smoothed a lock of hair away from her forehead. "Unfortunately for some, that can prove to be a pretty nasty roll of the dice ... what do you say? How about if we go off on a nice trip somewhere? Rent a cabin by a lake? Go to a resort? I could use a break." He flashed on the wonderful places Mabel Harding had mentioned. "And then one day after the war is over we can go somewhere exotic. Monte Carlo. Paris. Venice. Just you and me. Celebrate our relationship."

"That must have been some troubled marriage," Gretta said, her eyes exuding tenderness. "But, Ole, we don't need exotic. We have each other. As for me, other than our fight to have children, I couldn't be happier. Maybe some day in the future, some day after you retire, we can feel freer about getting away. But for now, I'd rather stay right here in Amber Leaf and look for a new home." She flashed a coy grin. "You know. One with a basement that cuts into the side of a hill and has lots of nice windows."

Not a good time to mention that. Visualizing a basement, miserable thoughts of claustrophobia reared up. Excusing himself, he pulled off his tie and headed for the bedroom. He didn't want Gretta to worry about him. Ever. She was right about his needing to get over this idiotic fear. He would overcome it. As for that house, they wouldn't be needing it. Not if he could help it.

Looping his tie over the tie rack, though, he wondered how he was going to pull that off.

In the middle of night, he awakened with a start. Undoubtedly a wild animal had gotten caught foraging through a trashcan out in the back alley somewhere. A can had hit the ground with a crash, the lid still rolling, crunching on gravel.

He rolled over. Where's …? He had the bed to himself? He got up and tiptoed to the living room where he stood in the doorway, saddened to find Gretta sitting in an armchair. Alone. Staring out the window. Moonlight glistening off tear-stained cheeks.

How many were the nights she'd been suffering in silence and he had not a clue? Standing in the quiet, he recalled the words of King Solomon, words that took on personal meaning. 'There are three things that are never satisfied, yea, four things that say not, It is enough: the grave; … the barren womb …'

What could he do? What could he say? Speaking words of comfort to his beloved bride felt hollow.

For to this day he felt hard pressed to find comfort, too.

CHAPTER EIGHT

O le pulled into the parking area of Village Church as the bell tolled a woeful five times. Sitting atop a hill with a steeple reaching high into the sky, the charming house of worship emanated life. From birth to confirmation to marriage to one's final resting place, it brought folks together in joy and in sorrow. But on a day such as today with no one around, it felt as hollow as a parched and lonely desert.

He peered into the pastor's office, returned to the sanctuary, then the vestibule. The man was nowhere in sight. He glanced at the door to the basement and hesitated. He stood for a long moment, wondering, then sauntered out and walked the perimeter of the church, swatting a mosquito here and there in the early evening air. No pastor outside either. When he strolled back in, however, a voice called from below. "Ole, is that you?"

With gaze focused on the basement door, he took a step back and frowned. "Yes, sir."

"Come on down … Ole?" Pastor Collver sounded as though he were in an echo chamber. "Are you there?"

"I'll wait for you in your office." Ole turned on his heel, but stopped mid-stride when the resonant voice called out again.

"I could use a little help down here. Trying to move this table. It's a beast."

Drat. Ole couldn't go down there, but he needed to help the pastor. He glanced at a nearby pew, tempted to kick it. Who wouldn't excuse a man for not helping if he limped on an injured foot?

Before he could conjure up a credible excuse for irrational behavior, Pastor Collver's footsteps tromped up the stairs. He peered around the doorjamb, white teeth flashing beneath a bushy moustache. "Didn't mean to impose. I can move that table any time. Come, let's go to my office."

Ole silently whooshed out a relieved sigh as he followed on the man's heels.

A not-so-long moment later, the pastor sat behind his desk and straightened a few papers, undoubtedly notes for Sunday morning's sermon, then nudged them to the side. "How's the missus?"

Ole plucked off his fedora and rested it on a knee.

"Ahh. So that's the reason for the visit."

"Been keeping an eye on her," Ole said. "She puts up a good front, but isn't sleeping. Gets up in the wee hours nights on end. Sits and stares out the living room window, quiet as a church mouse, tears streaming."

"I've been wondering why you haven't been in church the past few Sundays. So that's it?"

Ole welcomed the understanding inherent in the lifted brow. "That's my fault. Can't help being protective. It's too hard for her to look at all those kids, hearing them laugh, hearing them cry."

It's too hard for me, not that I would ever admit it.

After a thoughtful pause, the pastor's chair creaked as he leaned forward. "Weeping may tarry for a night," he said, "but joy comes in the morning. For now that may be of little consolation, but I can't think of a better way to wash away grief."

"That's true," Ole said. "I'm concerned she has too much time on her hands to think, though. You wouldn't happen to have a project she could work on … joining a committee for some good cause, maybe?"

The pastor brightened. "We can always use the help here … always," he said. "But I might have a better idea. I know we aren't in the war, at least not yet, but I'm sure the Red Cross could use a little help, too."

"I hadn't thought of that," Ole said.

"Would you mind if I gave this some thought? When I decide where her talents could best be used, I'll be happy to follow up with her. Think I should be able to do that in the next day or two."

Ole stopped at the door and offered genuine thanks. But as he turned to leave, Pastor Collver picked up his wife's picture from the corner of his desk and looked at it reflectively. "I took Selma on a camping trip once when we first got married," he said. "Snared a rabbit. Skewered it over an open fire." He set the picture aside, his thoughtful gaze continuing to burrow into it. "Asked her to keep an eye on it while I went to the buckboard to gather a few supplies. Ants got into our picnic basket, so it took longer than I thought it would. When I got back, she was standing there, paralyzed. The rabbit was smoldering on one side, raw on the other."

Ole walked his fingers around the rim of his hat, bothered by the strange change in topic. "Why are you telling me this?"

"The look on your face when I came up from the basement. Same look my wife has on occasion. You're struggling with claustrophobia, aren't you?"

Struggling with it? There was no struggle. The affliction owned him. "I'd better be on my way."

"Sure you can't spare a minute?"

Ole reluctantly returned to the chair. "What happened to your wife?"

"She was alone inside the house one winter's day. Seems a large ember popped from the hearth, landed on an old quilt. Before she smelled the smoke, the flames roared out of control. She was only ten, maybe eleven at the time. The next thing she knew, she was laying outside on the grass, coming to."

"Did the house …"

"Somehow they were able to save it, but it needed a lot of work. She's got a nasty scar on her shoulder, her arm. The event turned her whole world upside down."

"Did she ever learn how to live with it?"

"Live with it? Yes. Get past it?" He shrugged. "I'm concerned about you, Ole. Maybe it would do you good to get your mind on something else."

"Like?"

"What we're addressing. Overcoming claustrophobia."

I don't want to get mind on something else. I just want it to go away.

"Tell me, were you claustrophobic when you were a little shaver?"

"Me little?" Ole said. "Take a look at me. I was born big."

"You know what I mean."

Ole dutifully shuffled through old memories as if he were a card sharp and they were a deck of cards—huddling in that first tree house, erecting a tent out of a blanket so he could devour books beneath it by lantern light, basking in the root cellar to cool himself on hot a summer's day. "Not that I remember."

"You weren't born with it then," the pastor said. "My guess is that somewhere along the way something traumatic happened to you, too, and you buried the memory, didn't deal with it. Now you're reliving and reinforcing the fear whenever you approach a tight space. Like my wife, you've accepted a spirit of fear as if it were normal."

The pastor's words smarted. "You're telling me I did this to myself?"

"I don't know that I'd go that far. And I don't know that trauma in and of itself necessarily causes claustrophobia. But if we can accept fear, doesn't it follow that we can deny it? What we think about, good or bad, does tend to grow, doesn't it?"

Ole frowned as he chewed on those words.

"You have a rational mind, Ole. Give it the reins. Keep facing this off, but don't make it an idol. In time I'm sure you'll get better. Always remember, faith focuses on God … His strength, grace, and love. Fear focuses on the crisis … its threat, uncertainty, and concerns. Focus on faith. Be an overcomer."

Oh that it could be that easy.

CHAPTER NINE

Ole stabbed a fork into his last chunk of roast beef. "Thought I'd take a drive out to Deacon's farm soon as we finish supper," he said. "Care to come along?"

Gretta looked at him, appearing confused. "Why tonight? He isn't expecting you, is he?"

"Got an interesting case I'm working on. You know how he loves detective work. Need him to do a little sleuthing. We won't be gone long."

She got up. "Want a little whipped cream on your bread pudding?"

"That'd be great."

"If you're done with that, I'll take it." She reached for his dinner plate and headed to the sink. "What's this case about?"

"Divorce case."

"I didn't think that interested you."

"Doesn't."

"Then why take it on?"

"Boss thought I'd be best suited."

"Why?"

"I'm going up against Nelson Prixton."

She thought for a moment. "Ahhh, so that's it. Boss is right. Go get him, Ole," she said with strength in her tone. "About going to the farm, though, would you mind going without me? I had a chat with Pastor Collver today." She stopped midstride. "That's not exactly true. I should say he had a chat with me."

"About?"

"Wants my help with some committee work. Got some calls to make. He said if I'm not too overburdened, the Red Cross could use some help, too."

"And you said?"

"I couldn't say no."

Good.

Tens of minutes later, the Model T rocked and swayed over hardened ruts imbedded into well-traveled country roads. When Ole pulled onto the farm, Deacon scuttled off the porch and hurried to the car with a barn-sized grin.

Ole rolled down the window.

"Aren't you a sight for sore eyes?" Deacon said in that raspy voice of his.

Ole couldn't hold back a grin. Deacon's mere presence made the world a more pleasant place. Confident. Hard working. Thorough. Honest to a fault. Engaging. How would Ole have survived living in this new land without him? The holidays in and of themselves would have been excruciatingly lonely. But not with Deacon around. He had invited Ole in. Made him an integral part of his family. He exemplified the father Ole only wished he could have had during his formative years.

"Good to see you again, my boy." Deacon ducked down and peered inside. "Say, where's your bride?" he said, but then his voice turned concern-filled. "How's she holding up these days?"

"She's having a rough time of it."

"What about you?"

"I'm here on business."

"Ole? In time you'll both be fine. I can feel it in my bones. You feel it, too, don't you?"

And that Ole did.

"What is it that you want with me?" Deacon said excitedly. "Don't hold back. What kind of business?"

"You available for hire these days?"

Smile shadows formed on weathered cheeks as Deacon looked toward the fields. "Corn doesn't need any help growing. No more cows or chickens to attend to. My youngest boy is taking care of them now, so what are we waiting for? Let's go to the house."

"It might be better if we talked out here," Ole said. "Issues with confidentiality."

Lanky yet spry in his dwindling years, Deacon quickly rounded the automobile and hopped in. "You've got me chomping at the bit. What's the assignment this time?"

"Divorce case. I need you to do a little investigative work behind the scenes."

"Divorces in this neck of the woods are pretty rare. Who is it?"

"Does the name Mabel Harding mean anything to you?"

"Sure does. Comes from big money. Lost both parents some time back as I recall."

"That's right. And now her ne'er-do-well hubby is trying to get his claws on her deceased parents' assets."

Deacon glowered. "How could he do such a thing?"

"That's what snakes do," Ole said. "Harding comes from money, too, but the ne'er-do-well must have burned through it. Seems he has a weakness for gambling. I've got a hunch he also has a weakness for rich ladies."

"Getting a little stuffy in here," Deacon said as he rolled down the window. "This should be an easy case to win then, shouldn't it?"

Inhaling in the cool night air felt good, passing time with Deacon even better. "That's what I thought," Ole said. "But his attorney is holding all the aces."

"And who might that be?"

"Nelson."

Deacon's face lit up. "Prixon?"

"That's right. We're going up against our old nemesis."

Deacon let out a chuckle. "This should be fun. What's that scoundrel's angle this time?"

"I get the feeling he thinks she made her bed when she said 'I do,' and now it's time to pay up."

"On what legal grounds?"

Ole mindlessly thumped the steering wheel with an index finger. "Harding talked her into making a good number of investments after they got married."

Deacon thought a moment. "Any kids?"

"No." Ole disciplined himself not to identify with that question. "I'm afraid not having an heir rips away our safety net."

"Judge Lawson won't need to protect the financial future of children that don't exist, is that right?" He crossed an ankle over a knee. "What about Mabel's money? Why would Harding walk away from her when she's the one holding the bread?"

"She cut off his allowance."

"Smart woman. What do you want me to do?"

"Seems Harding's already in thick with his next victim."

"He's cheating then?" Deacon said, sounding more hopeful than curious.

"Flagrantly from what I understand. But he can't marry again until the divorce is final. Knowing how Nelson operates, they'll blame his cheating on Mabel, and they'll do it with a vengeance."

"But if he's the one cheating—"

Ole let out a dogged sigh. "That's another problem. Mabel

openly admitted to falling out of love … while they were still on their honeymoon."

Deacon gulped. "Did she say why?"

"Yeah. Can't say that I blame her. They were off at a fancy resort during their first married lunch together, and he feigned having forgotten his wallet. She got stuck picking up the tab for their hotel, travel, entertainment, and all their meals."

"On their honeymoon?"

"What's worse, she said that he gave her an unmistakable feeling that she owed him … and that wallet of his never did materialize."

Deacon shook his head, his tone emanating strong loathing. "I hate the louse, and I've never met him. Doesn't seem right, does it? A man living off a woman like that? Why doesn't the bum get a job?"

Ole shrugged. "He does seem a bit lacking in pride, doesn't he? My gut tells me that if he could prance so easily from Mabel to his newfound love-interest, he might have developed a pattern. This is where you come in. I want you to find out what that parasite was up to before he talked Mabel into marrying him. Take all the time you need. Find his woman. See if you can squeeze anything out of her and get any other information you can from whatever sources possible. Go to the courthouse, the jail, find out anything, everything, even if it's nothing more than what he eats for breakfast. Learn his patterns, his interests."

"Don't worry, Ole. I've got a feeling this assignment is going to be as easy as it'll be fun."

"Guess I'd better hit the road," Ole said as he gazed out into the twilight.

Deacon opened the door. "I'll get the crank." He swung a foot on the ground then hesitated. "Say, the wife canned some nice preserves today. Want to bring a few jars home to Gretta?"

"I think she has plenty, but thanks. And Deacon?"

"Yes sir?"

"Give my best to your missus… and when you do start your new assignment, be sure you keep your guard up, especially if you find anything suspect. Like anyone who lacks conscience, I'd bet the family farm Harding's courting danger."

CHAPTER TEN

Though the kitchen smelled wonderfully of fried chicken, as Ole drew Gretta into his arms and gave her a full-on hug, his eyes settled on the basement door. He took a step back. "Chicken?"

"And dumplings."

"Oh, good," he said more as an afterthought then absently made his way toward the door.

"What's my brave man up to now?"

Ole looked back in earnest, but refused to say what he was think-ing … just letting go of nonsense, my dear. Just letting go.

It took several prods around the corner to snap on the cellar light, but he managed. He then rested an elbow against the doorjamb and debated his next move.

"You got a letter from England today," Gretta said.

He stopped short. England? His dad? No. It would be a cold day in Hades … Must be from one of his old cronies. So many of his school chums gone, getting massacred out there on the Western Front. What a slaughter. No one needed to die like that, and for what? They were good men. Really good men. "I'm not sure I'm ready to read another one."

"Can't say as I blame you." She let out a relieved sigh. "I can't tell you how grateful I am that you aren't still living there."

Me, too. To think I could have been one of them.

After a measured moment, she said with a lilt in her voice, "Her name's Olivia. I've never heard you speak of her before."

He looked back. "Who?"

"The person you got the letter from."

"Oh." He slipped a foot out then pulled it back again. "I don't know anyone named Olivia."

Gretta bobbed her head toward a letter propped against Ole's not-yet-filled coffee cup. "Must be related to Deacon and Maude."

"Why do you say that?"

"Same last name. Why would she write to you?"

"Must be a shirtsleeve relative of Emily's," he said not giving it another thought and then returned to his assignment, staring down the stairs, trying to convince himself how easy this would be. Focus on faith, not fear, he encouraged himself.

"She has beautiful penmanship."

He lifted a foot a smidge again, but this time it wouldn't move forward. "No doubt she's probably planning to come to America to surprise them."

"All of the way from England, Ole?"

"I came from there." Far more interested in conquering the steps, he leaned forward and righted himself. "Don't worry. I'll get to it soon enough." For some strange reason, his knee refused to bend.

"Are you having a good time?" Gretta said.

Ole glanced back again and muttered, "I appear to be making an utter fool of myself." Overcoming inertia proved a challenge. Freezing repeatedly in the same spot proved a challenge. Not sure how to over-come his mindset proved a challenge. "Think I need to secure this top step better," he said disingenuously. "It's a little squeaky."

"If you dwell on how scared you are every time you try to go down

there, no wonder your fear is growing. You're giving it a stronghold."
Gretta raised her chin. "Next time you give it a try, concentrate instead
on how strong the structure is, how it's a shelter in the time of storm, or
concentrate on what's down there—the canned goods, root vegetables,
the storage of our treasures. Now go read your letter. I think you've had
enough fun for one day."

I'll be sure to remember that, Sherlock. He closed the door behind
him feeling somewhat better about himself for having tried, and then
took the chair at the head of the table. "This is curious," he said as he
sliced open the envelope. But then he began to read.

> *23 June*
>
> *Dear Sir,*
>
> *As you've undoubtedly noticed from the envelope, my name is
> Olivia. I am writing at the request of my grandmum, Amelia
> De Haven. I regret to tell you that she succumbed to consump-
> tion this week past. Her loss has been nothing less than devas-
> tating. She was my life, having raised me since I was an infant.*

"What is it, dear?" Gretta drew a serving bowl from the cupboard.
"Who is Olivia? And what does she want with you?"

Ole looked up. "Amelia died."

"Who's Amelia?"

"Emily's mother."

"Emily? ... Oh." Gretta said, understanding apparent in her tone.
"I'm sorry to hear that."

Me too. He returned to the letter.

> *On her deathbed, she implored me to find you, insisting that
> I would be in need of family. I'm not certain how to state this
> other than straight out. My mother's name was Emily, and
> according to Grandmum, you are my father.*

His heart fluttered unmercifully. Hand trembled. Breath caught. He looked up for a brief moment, long enough to allow confused thoughts to attempt to decipher confused feelings. But they couldn't. A daughter? Impossible. To have missed out on raising a child? To have had love squandered? Inconceivable. Amelia could never have done such a thing … but if she did? Why? Confounded beyond measure, he read on.

For reasons unbeknownst to me, Grandmum chose to keep this to herself all of these years. She has written a letter in a sealed envelope and asked that I present it to you personally. With the hope of not being presumptuous, I've begun saving and at some point after the war is over and passage on the high seas more amenable, I wish to venture to America to make your acquaintance.

After you've digested this most startling news, I do hope you will find it in your heart to correspond with me. I deeply desire an opportunity meet your acquaintance through written word as well as in person. Grandmum assured me you are a good, good man.

With kindest regards,

Olivia

He slapped the letter on the table. "What a cruel joke," he spat. "What a cruel, cruel joke."

"What is it, Ole?" Gretta hurried to the table and lovingly drew her arms about his shoulders, comforting him. "What could she possibly have written that's made you so upset?"

"This letter … it's extortion." He picked it up and brandished it through the air. "This young lady claims to be my daughter. Can you believe such a thing? She insists Amelia raised her since she was an infant."

"Your mother-in-law raised a daughter you didn't know you had and kept her from you? How could anyone be that conniving? It makes no sense."

As Gretta seized the letter and began reading, Ole's thoughts ran wild. "Who do you think could be behind this scheme and for heaven's sakes why?"

"I have no idea," she said, her attention locked on the handwritten words. "But Ole, what if this isn't a scheme? What if it's true?"

Please don't get my hopes up. He stared off. "I need to have a serious chat with Deacon—him or his sister Maude," he said. "If they don't know anything, I'll have to ask him to do more detective work."

And this time it's not possible for it to be more personal.

CHAPTER ELEVEN

Wagon wheels crunching on gravel? Ole set his book aside and peered out the parlor window. "It's Deacon," he said. Gretta looked up. "I wonder what he wants."

"It's probably about the Harding case. Long as he's here, I need to find out about that Olivia girl, too. See what he knows."

"That makes me nervous." She set her knitting aside. "There's a big part of me that wants to believe her. What if he doesn't know anything?"

"I doubt he does. But we need to meet this head on, Gretta," he said in a firm voice. "It has to be a hoax."

"It's so beautiful out there today," she said as if deliberately ignoring him. "I brought a pitcher of lemonade and some cookies out to the porch. Thought I'd surprise you. Why don't you men go ahead and help yourselves?"

Ole plucked up Olivia's letter, which was laying next to the book, and headed outside, the screen door smacking closed behind him. "Deacon, my man, when are you going to break down and buy yourself a good automobile?"

He hopped down from the wagon and hitched the reins. "When are going to break down and buy yourself a good horse?"

"I'm not."

"But you want me to buy a Model T, do you? I will one day. Thought I'd take my good ole time, though. Wouldn't want Old Horse here getting jealous." The horse snorted as he gave its mane a tender pat. "Would we now, boy?"

Ole warmed at Deacon's loyalty. "Thanks for stopping by," he said.

"Timing worked out great. Had to come to town anyway. Need to pick up a good watch dog before I head back out to the farm."

Ole led the way to the porch. "Having problems out there, are you?"

"Yeah. Some predator found my hen house."

"I thought you didn't have any animals."

"Well, maybe a hen or two," he said with a wink. "And a cow or two."

"One or two?"

"Fourteen."

"You said—"

"I said my son was taking care of them now. We think it might be a raccoon. Lost a hen last night. Don't want to lose any more."

"Deacon, Deacon." Ole shook his head and chuckled. "Let's grab a chair. You're going to need it."

"Why's that?"

"I'll tell you in a minute. Find out anything about Harding?"

"Not a thing."

What?

Frown lines deeply embedded Deacon's weather-wrinkled forehead. "Getting answers is going to take a little ... say, what's this?"

Ole followed Deacon's gaze to the tray, to the pitcher with glasses, napkins, and warm cookies laid out with care. "Gretta brought that out a few minutes ago. Your timing couldn't be better."

"How do you rate, Ole? First Em, then Gretta? Two of the loveliest young ladies a man ever laid eyes on."

"Got lucky, I guess."

"I don't think so. Water seeks its own level and your water runs ocean deep," he muttered.

Ole poured two lemonades. "Help yourself. Now what was this you were saying about Harding?"

"Getting answers is going to take a little more doing. On second thought, a lot more doing. I keep coming up dry."

"What about his work record?"

"Couldn't find one. Doesn't make sense for a man of his stature, does it?"

"How about the military? Has he served?"

"No active duty documentation whatsoever."

"School?"

"No school records either. No birth certificate. No record of anything."

Ole sat dumbfounded.

"Has Mrs. Harding mentioned anything to you about his family?" Deacon said. "Where he came from? Friends? How he spends his time?"

"Other than a quick briefing at the onset, not a word."

"Looks like we'd better check into aliases then."

"That bad, is it?" Ole carefully set down his glass. "If Mabel wants to protect her assets so badly, you'd think she'd want me to know anything and everything there is to know."

"Maybe we need to run a background check on her, too."

Ole considered Deacon's suggestion. "That might be wise. I did sense she might be holding something back. The fact that she didn't mention a word about Jack's family, I found strange. When I asked about heirs, she shut down completely."

"That is curious, especially with her being the one seeking you out for counsel."

Picking up a cookie, Ole eyed it before taking a bite. "Maybe it's time for me to have another chat with the woman. Push harder … and as for you, get back to me as soon as you find out anything. Meanwhile," with his free hand, he drew out Olivia's letter and passed it to Deacon, "I have something far more important. Any idea what this is all about?"

Deacon squinted at the return address on the envelope and scrunched up his face. He then stretched his arm until it appeared he could stretch it no further and squinted some more. "It's too blurry. What's it say?"

"It's from England … from someone named Olivia … Olivia De Haven."

Deacon's bewildered tone hiked an octave. "Who?"

CHAPTER TWELVE

D eacon rifled through a pocket for his spectacles then unfolded the letter. He slowly set his chair to rocking and read without making a sound, his lips moving in sync with his eyes. But then his bushy brows white with age knitted together. He thoughtfully pressed the letter on a knee and stared out toward the lake, muttering to himself. "Olivia ... Olivia De Haven."

"Ever heard the name before?" Ole said.

"Can't say as I have." He scratched his chin. "I'm trying to think now. I heard about Amelia's passing, so that much rings true. But I've never heard boo about anyone named Olivia."

"Think, Deacon, think," Ole said, ill-at-ease with the forcefulness of his own tone.

"I'm telling you, Ole ... I don't know a thing about her."

"What about Amelia? Is there anything you can tell me about her that I don't already know?"

"I doubt it. I was so young at the time. Let me think. She was Emily's mother and my oldest sister, twelve years my senior. Married herself a tradesman. As I recall, he was just passing through at the time they met. His family lived back in the old country. I don't how or why he ever ended up in the States. All I do know is that after marrying my sister, one day he gets word that his mother had taken ill. She was bed-ridden and needed him, so they packed up their belongings and moved to England. The woman was sick for a long time. Amelia and her hubby never did come back, not even for a visit.

"As for Emily, Amelia let me know right off when she found out she was expecting. Sent pictures of the girl from the time she was an infant all of the way up to your marriage. Then she pretty much stopped writing. Seemed strange. I never could figure out why. They didn't have any other kids.

"And about Olivia, you were married to Emily, Ole. You know as much as I do. Like I said, Amelia and I barely stayed in touch after Emily's passing, and Amelia never mentioned anything about having a granddaughter." Deacon frowned. "Doesn't smell right, does it?"

"Smells like extortion," Ole said. "But why me? And why now?" He reached for the letter, folded it, and slipped it back into the envelope.

"How is Gretta taking this?" Deacon said. "Or does she know?"

"She knows alright. She was the one who gave me the letter. Feels precisely the way I do … that it's contemptible, but she's holding onto hope anyway. Who could think to do such a thing? There is one sticky wicket, though, that I can't seem to get past."

Deacon eyed the cookies. "What's that?"

"Her name." Ole hesitated. "Olivia … I remember it like it was yesterday. When Em announced that we were going to have a baby, she said 'come next spring, we will swaddle a little Oliver or Olivia.' Our son was named Oliver. Since I was off to war, Amelia named him. The only other person who could have possibly known that if we had a daughter her name would have been Olivia was …"

"Amelia?" Deacon turned downcast. "And now with the war going on, that really complicates things."

"Why do you say that?" Ole said.

"It gives the girl strong motivation to clear out of England, wouldn't you say? Since the war began, the Allies alone have already lost millions of men. That's mind boggling … more than a million a year biting the dust. And with Germany showering London with bombs the way they have, why wouldn't the girl try to find a way to clear out of there?"

"But she has to cross the Atlantic. That's way too dangerous with the Germans sinking ships at will."

"You've got a point there," Deacon said.

"Would you mind checking with Maude? See if she knows something you don't?" But that still wasn't good enough. Ole needed to know more. "Deacon?"

"Yes, sir?"

"Do you think there could possibly be a chance that …?" He shook his head. "Forget it. I don't want to get my hopes up. Gretta and I already lost one too many kids. We don't need to lose any more."

CHAPTER THIRTEEN

Ole arrived at Mabel's home unannounced. Through a steady rat-a-tat-tat of light rain, he was about to knock, but hesitated. Voices emanated from what was undoubtedly her living room. He peered around the corner of the porch. Sure enough. Jack and Mabel stood nose-to-nose and toe-to-toe near the living room window. Shouting.

"Give me those papers right now," he said.

"Why? So you can steal me blind? You've already gotten all you're going to get from me."

"Give me those papers or I'm …"

How should Ole play this? If he knocked, he might miss vital information, yet eavesdropping lacked integrity. He couldn't leave, that was certain. If the shouting escalated, Mabel might be in danger. So he waited.

"Or you're what?" Mabel said. "Going to the police? Do that and you can kiss goodbye what little money you're not entitled to."

All grew eerily quiet. Ole wondered for a moment whether he'd been seen. He quickly rapped on the door. No answer. He rapped again, harder. The door flew open. Startled, he stepped back. Slick, smooth-talking Jack scowled at him. "How long you been standing here?" he demanded. "And what are you doing here anyway?"

"Who is it?" Mabel asked from behind the door.

Jack brushed past Ole. As he bounded toward his car, he glanced over his shoulder and said with an unmistakable sneer, "Your lawyer friend. Maybe he can talk some sense into that unreasonable head of yours."

When Ole turned back, Mabel appeared unsettled. "Mr. Harrington? How much of our conversation did you overhear?"

"From where I'm standing, it sounded more like an argument. Mind if I come in?"

Her fingers flew to her lips. "Oh no, my cookies are burning." She hurried to the oven, leaving the kitchen door wide open. "Come on in."

"This isn't a social call, I'm afraid." Ole positioned his umbrella near the entry and stepped inside. "What's this about Jack threatening to go to the police?"

"He's delusional. Thinks they care enough to interfere. In case you hadn't noticed, that man has an amazing ego."

Ole stepped up to the table. "Do you mind my asking why Jack was here?"

She slammed the cookie sheet on the table, recklessly scraped up the hot cookies with a spatula, and slapped them on parchment paper. "He wanted to get the deeds to the house, our properties, and all of our buildings."

"But that should come through Nelson and me," Ole said. "Any idea why he would demand them from you?"

She lifted her chin. "Probably because of what wasn't on them."

What wasn't ... "Which is?"

"His signature."

"Do you mean ..."

She frowned. "I may have been foolish enough to marry the louse without checking his past, but I certainly wasn't stupid enough to let him co-sign the deeds on all of our properties, too. Or should I say *my* properties."

Her explanation didn't add up. "How could Jack be that short-sighted? Why would he let you get by with that?"

"Excuse me?" she said. "Let *me* get by with that?"

"I didn't mean it to sound … it's just that—"

"I knew what you meant." She busied herself spooning more cookie dough on another cookie sheet then hesitated. "That is curious, though, isn't it? I've wondered about it, too, with every single signature. Became suspicious about his motives. Why didn't he ask questions? Why let me manage it all by myself? That's when I figured he might have had a legal reason, but I can't imagine what that could be. I'm sure he wants the documents now so he can sign them after the fact. Anything to assure a free ride."

"I see." Ole eyed the cookies then unthinkingly grabbed one.

"Help yourself," she said.

He took a bite and as he swallowed, he lifted a brow. Though lightly scorched at the edges, it tasted scrumptious. To let go of a woman like this—elegant, poised, bright, and talented in the kitchen—Jack had to be by far the most foolish man Ole had ever laid eyes on. "I don't under-stand why your husband would want to walk away from a perfectly good marriage and such a beautiful home. There must be more you're not telling me."

She let out an apathetic snicker. "I cut off his allowance, remember? I'm nothing more to him than a wallet. So tell me, Mr. Harrington, why the unexpected visit?"

"I hired a private detective," Ole said. "He's coming up against one too many roadblocks. I was hoping you might help us with Jack's history."

She hesitated. "What kind of roadblocks?"

"No record of a birth certificate, former employers, trail of any family or friends. No record of previous marriages."

Her cheeks turned as red as the apples printed on her apron. "Previous what?"

"Sorry. What can you tell me about Jack's history?"

She shook her head. "This is really embarrassing."

"Let me be the judge of that."

"All right, I will. I don't know what I was thinking when I agreed to marry him. My mother died about ten years ago. Then several years later I lost my father. Immediately on the heels of his passing, I met Jack on a train on my way back from Chicago." She stabbed the spoon into the cookie dough then wiped her hands on her apron as if trying to wipe away her shame. "Got married a month later. Still can't believe I could do anything that foolish. He said he'd just moved to Amber Leaf. Said he was estranged from his parents. That bothered me. When I asked him about it, he said they got abusive when he tried to wean them off alcohol. That made sense, so I bought it. As for friends, his best buddy was in the service, or so he said. He mentioned some other friends he wanted to introduce me to the next time we went to Chicago. What I was too embarrassed to tell you before is that all of the guests at our wedding were my friends and family. And we never did return to Chicago."

Willing himself not to react, Ole reached for another cookie.

"Make sure you take the ones that aren't scorched," she said. "And if you're wondering why I would have gone ahead and …"

"Does he have any important papers lying around we could take a look at? Anything at all that would give us a hint?"

"All of his important papers seem to be conveniently locked up in a safety deposit box at his bank."

"In Chicago?"

"Yes, sir."

"What about those alleged friends of his? He must have gotten calls from them over the years."

"Not a one."

"That is curious, isn't it? What about this new woman? I believe you called her the floozy. Do you know her name? Where she lives?"

"No." Mabel returned to the dough and dropped several more dollops onto the cookie sheet. "He merely told me about her, or should I say he bragged about her?"

"And she knows about you?"

"According to him, absolutely."

"You're not sure she exists then?"

"No, I'm not. Can you believe the mess I've gotten myself into?" Mabel gave her head a quick shake. "How could I have been that naïve?"

"Actually, all of this might well go in your favor."

She slid the cookie sheet into the oven. "What are you talking about? We don't have proof of anything."

"Can you find out his travel schedule? I have a friend who does a little detective work on the side. This could well be worth his taking a trip to Chicago. Having Jack followed might be our only hope. That is, if he has a murky past. We've got to find a way to stop this guy from robbing you blind."

CHAPTER FOURTEEN

While Gretta lay in the bedroom sleeping, Ole sat on the back stoop. A light breeze barely ruffled the leaves, and though only mid-August, an autumn-like chill filled the air. He listened intently to the sounds of the night. Wonderful sounds. A distant barking dog. Nocturnal creatures scampering through the thicket. The steps creaking beneath his shifting weight.

Yet at the moment, his thoughts transcended Amber Leaf. As he sat in the quiet, a string of welcome memories revisited him. Memories of England. Memories he had suppressed, but memories that lay lightly beneath the surface nonetheless. Memories of Emily. Of their lives together. There was a time when such recollections were too painful to engage, but he could easily face them now.

If she hadn't died, he would still be living in England. His son would have been a young man by now. Would they have gotten on well? Or would they be as estranged as was Ole and his father? He hoped not. Would his boy be a scholar? What vocation would he have chosen to pursue? How many other children would Ole and Emily have had? What would they look like? Would they have resembled her? Or would they have resembled him?

Would he still be an officer in the military? Leading the fight on the Western Front? Or would he have moved on to political life? It hurt his head to count the innumerable unanswerable questions.

In the end, what did it matter? With the exception of not having children, Ole couldn't be happier in these United States. He loved Gretta every bit as much as he had loved Em, yet in an entirely different way.

But this girl. The one who called herself Olivia. If her intent was extortion, why was it that after giving it much thought he couldn't bring himself to hate her? After talking to Deacon and learning that he knew nothing of her either, how was it that Ole didn't want to let go of hope? Was he merely that desperate?

He sauntered back into the house. Still too restless to call it a night, he meandered into the study and reluctantly drew her letter from a side desk drawer. He read it again, studying it. The artful penmanship. Smooth strokes. Thoughtful writing. Much the same as his once beloved Emily's.

Sitting beneath the light of the lantern, the clock ticked monotonously on the wall behind him. He reflected on Jack Harding. On his cunning. On how Mabel hadn't questioned the man more thoroughly while still in possession of her heart.

How was this Olivia unlike Jack?

Ole knew nothing of her past either. It would be foolish to take her bait, to be drawn into her conniving world. Yet her name continued to cry out, haunting, like Emily's voice from the grave. The feeling too powerful to shake, he drew out pad and pen. Like Deacon with Harding, there was homework that needed to be done.

15 August

My dearest young lady,

At long last, I wish to acknowledge receipt of your letter dated

23 June. I have spent countless hours reading and rereading it. Contemplating it. Do know that I offer my sincerest condolences at the loss of your beloved Amelia. I knew her well and found to her to be most kind and caring, though tragically burdened by loss, first that of her dearly departed husband,

Glancing up, Ole lifted a brow … ne'er-do-well though he may have been.

and then of my dearly departed Emily and our infant son.

He thought for a moment. What next? How much information should he share with a suspect stranger? It would be foolhardy to say too much. Why make it easier for her to carry out the blackmail? Yet it would also be a waste of time, saying nothing of effort, to say too little. Of course this was a wretched scam, but what if there was even a remote chance …? What questions might he ask, things she couldn't possibly know or research that would entrap her? Until he could conjure up something profound, he needed to settle for sincere. He shook his conflicted head and returned to writing.

I do, however, find myself feeling rather confused. I chatted recently with Deacon De Haven, who would be your great uncle. He did, in fact, have knowledge of your grandmother's passing. But he also stated that he had never heard mention of anyone who went by the name Olivia, which we both found most puzzling. And while I did father a son, I certainly never fathered a daughter.

Which leaves me in quite a state. Do know that there is nothing I could possibly desire more than to believe we are related in that way. To say it would be a dream come true is most assuredly an understatement.

He thoughtfully tapped his fountain pen on the desk. That's good.

That's good. State your desires. Allow yourself a hint of vulnerability. Sucker her in. At the moment, though, he felt like a chump, like Mabel who naively chose to believe Jack's misrepresentations when they courted, yet Ole didn't want to help himself. He couldn't. Not when an inexplicable feeling down deep inside compelled him to believe the unbelievable.

> *Until we can make sense of this most peculiar situation, do know that I look forward to receiving further correspondence. Perhaps you might be so kind as to provide more information so that together we might find wherein lies the confusion.*
>
> *Meanwhile, please be especially careful, remaining alert at all times to the dangers that so easily befall all of us while the world so tragically continues in a state of war.*
>
> *Do know that I very much look forward to hearing from you again.*
>
> *Until then, I remain,*
>
> *Yours most sincerely,*
>
> *Oliver M. Harrington*

As he addressed and sealed the envelope, he envisioned the accounts he'd read of the Germans dropping bombs on England, showering the British with savage gifts of destruction. He considered the ships being torpedoed on the high seas. He thought of the loss, the suffering, and the extreme lack of staples. And he worried about her safety.

What if this young woman truly was his child?

What if something happened to her?

What if he never did get an opportunity to learn the mystery behind this young woman who bore the lovely name Olivia?

CHAPTER FIFTEEN

"Will the wife mind if you come and go for a few days?" Ole said.

Deacon rammed a nail through a step railing and tried to wiggle it. Rock solid. "She always minds. Since the kids left home, she gets a little spooked when she's alone. I can always take her into town. Drop her off at my sister's place. They enjoy one another's company, so she'll like that. So where am I off to?"

"How does Chicago sound? Seems Harding has taken up residence at The Edgewater Beach Hotel. Brand spanking new place on the shores of Lake Michigan."

"You want me to go to Chicago?"

"That's right. How soon can you …"

Deacon brightened. "Tomorrow soon enough?"

"Perfect. After you finish your assignment, let me know what train you'll be on. I'll pick you up at the depot … and one other thing … never, and I mean never, let your guard down."

A handful of days later, Ole stood at the depot. Iron pounding iron, the wheels of the 10:10 clacked and screeched as it pulled up to the station. Deacon emerged first through billowing steam, his expression unreadable.

"I found out why they call Chicago the windy city," he said. "But I didn't mind. That was quite the trip. A shiny Packard awaiting me, chauffeuring me off like I was a man of means. And the hotel? They don't come any finer than that."

Ole led the way to his Model T. "Find out anything?"

"More than we wanted to know. Shortly after I arrived, I spotted Harding in the dining room." Deacon shifted his baggage from one arm to the other and kept talking and walking. "He was eating alone. I hurried through supper then made my way to the lobby. Tried to be discreet. Lounged behind a copy of the *Daily News*, taking a sneak peek at anyone and everyone who passed by. Got to hand it to the man. He's slippery. Must have found a back door. He never did materialize.

"Then early the next morning, I spot him on the Beach Walk. Picked up his trail and stayed on it the rest of the time I was there." Deacon paused. "He'll be going to his own funeral if he isn't careful."

"Going to his own what?"

"Familiar with the criminal element in Chicago, are you?"

"Somewhat, maybe."

Deacon blew out a breath. "There's a thug there. They call him the king of the bookmakers. Race horses, pool, billiards, roulette, faro."

Ole stopped walking. "Dangerous stuff."

"That's right," Deacon said. "He has brass, too. Payoffs all the way from beat cops up to the chief of police."

"How does that affect Jack?"

"Seems he's one of his agents. Makes me wonder if he isn't one of the mischievous boys who's been setting off cannon crackers."

Ole walked on. "You think he's capable of that, do you?"

"If he's desperate enough, absolutely. And if I didn't know any better, I'd say his greed and sense of adventure greatly surpass his skill."

"Plays high stakes, does he?"

"Nosebleed high and the man's compulsive."

"What about his love interest?"

"That's the other part of the problem."

As Ole set hand to crank, Deacon opened the door of the Model T and hopped in, wedging his luggage on his lap. "I'm not convinced she exists."

Ole's brow's fused together. "You mean to tell me …" A moment later he hopped in, too, and gripped the steering wheel. "Why would Jack tell Mabel about her then?"

"I've wondered about that, too. Do you think it could be all smoke and mirrors? That he might be trying to protect her?"

"Doesn't seem likely. I don't know what to make of it, Deacon. That certainly does throw a wrench into things, though."

CHAPTER SIXTEEN

Olivia dropped a handful of envelopes on the kitchen table and nudged them neatly into place.

"Hadn't you best look through them?" her friend Mary said, emerald eyes bright with a spirit of inquiry.

Olivia shrugged. "I find myself squirming every time the mail comes." She gazed at the letters, forlorn. "I get frightfully nervous. I wish to hear from him too badly."

Why did her friend's penetrating look have to be coupled with the rise of a furrowed brow? Did she not realize that added pressure?

"Very well, very well." Olivia slowly sorted through the letters, fearful she wouldn't receive one from this man who was allegedly her father yet more fearful that she would. She lifted the top post then set it face down followed by the second and the third. On the fourth, her hand trembled. Her heart pitter-pattered. She gazed at Mary, eyes widening as if they had a mind of their own. "This letter. He wrote. My father wrote to me."

Mary gasped. "Open it. Hurry."

Olivia drew in a ragged breath. This was a private moment. A pivotal moment. Having no inkling of the letter's contents, she turned away giving Mary her back. She then reached for a knife and carefully sliced open the envelope. Her lips quivered as her eyes glided along the parchment. The pounding in her chest a distraction, she read then stopped. Read more than stopped again. To her amazement, the writing, the straightforwardness and profound honesty though mere ink on paper warmed her as nothing else could. Her father's heart finally revealed, she lowered onto a chair. "He says there's nothing he could possibly desire more than to believe I'm his daughter. Said it would be a dream come true," she said, her voice barely above a whisper. "Can you believe it, Mary?" She stared off. "My father says I would be a dream come true."

Mary flew to her side and peered over her shoulder. "I wish to read it. Please, allow me to read it as well."

Olivia absently passed the treasured words to her friend.

"Oh, this is wonderful," Mary said as she quickly read. "This is absolutely wonderful. I'll wager he invites you to America." When she finished reading, she folded and returned the letter. "I'll watch your flat. Gather your mail while you're away. No, wait. What if he insists you move to Amber Leaf? We were planning to grow old together, remember? Rock on our rocking chairs when we're old and wrinkled and too sore and tired to walk. Oh, Olivia. I should be at an utter and complete loss without you."

"You could come visit. Move there, too." Olivia giggled gleefully. "Think on it, Mary. You and me in America. What a blessed thought."

"I wonder what your father is like," Mary mused. "I wonder what it's like there, too ... if you have brothers or sisters. Wait! Perhaps if you have a brother, we might one day marry, and you and I would be sisters forever."

Olivia let out another giggle. "I must pinch myself. Make certain I'm not dreaming. But we must discipline our hopes. Not allow them to get too high. I may not receive an invitation."

"It makes me wretched that you can't open your grandmum's letter."

A light knock interrupted their reverie. Still smiling, Olivia turned to Mary. "That must be Mrs. Fletcher. She mentioned she wanted to stop and drop off something she knew I would enjoy."

"From upstairs?"

Olivia hurried to the door and yanked it open to find the jolly woman standing with outstretched hand.

"Mrs. Fletcher. Come in, come in."

"My," Mrs. Fletcher said as she entered the flat and presented a small jar to Olivia. "Aren't you in a delightful mood."

"She heard from her father," Mary blurted from behind.

"Her …"

"That's right."

Mrs. Fletcher's eyes focused on the jar as if something were amiss. "We aren't much on sugar. With the shortages these days, I thought you might enjoy some extra."

"Oh, this is wonderfully generous. Thank you."

But then Mrs. Fletcher looked at Olivia skeptically. "What's this about your father?"

"His name is Oliver Harrington," she said. "He lives in America."

Mrs. Fletcher gulped. "Oliver …"

"Might you know of him then?"

Why the apprehensive look?

"Amelia never said … are you certain?"

"Of course, I'm certain. She told me so on her deathbed."

"But …" Mrs. Fletcher appeared to stop herself. "I'd best get back upstairs," she said too quickly. "I told my husband I would stop down for a brief moment. May you enjoy the sugar, dear."

Olivia closed the door behind her and leaned the full weight of her back against it. "Something is amiss." She locked eyes with Mary's. "That woman has known us since I was an infant yet it appears as if she didn't believe me. Why? Might you have sensed that as well?"

Mary nodded an awkward nod.

Something definitely appeared amiss.

CHAPTER SEVENTEEN

Ole pulled up at the side of the gravel road and looked out across the barren cornfield where cows grazed on what little was left of the cornstalks. Deacon walked amidst them, the completion of a serene pastoral image if Ole had ever seen one. He cranked down the window. "I thought your boy was taking care of the animals."

"I gave him the day off," Deacon said with a sheepish grin.

Ole had never fetched cows before an early evening milking. Looked like fun. Getting his shoes dirty? Who cares? Inhaling the clean country air? Why not? He got out of the car. "Need a little help?"

Deacon sidestepped a heifer, took off his cap, and slapped it against a pant leg emitting a small puff of dust. "Envying the exercise, are you?"

"A little, maybe," Ole said. "What do you say? Give a greenhorn a try?"

"Happy to get the company. I guess I don't need to remind you to…"

Ole chuckled. "Be on the lookout for cow pies?"

The earth hard and uneven beneath the soles of his shoes, he trudged to the far field where he nudged along a straggler. A word here.

Another word there. "Here Bossie," Deacon called out, "we don't have all day." Tails swishing, content, unhurried, the herd obediently plodded along.

"We're thinking of growing the herd some," Deacon said as they neared the barn.

"We as in you and your wife or we as in you and your boy?"

"Me and my boy. One day this will all be his. We figure we've got one too many empty stalls. Might as well make good use of them."

The cows plodded in with a rhythmic cadence. "Want me to pitch a little hay while you do the milking?" Ole said.

"Help yourself. You know where the pitchfork is." Deacon grabbed a milk pail and stool and cozied up to the first cow. "Got a letter from England yesterday," he said, the hint of a forbidding inflection in his tone.

"And?"

Deacon's gaze tethered to a hay bale as he leaned his forehead into the heifer's flank, milk pinging against the bottom of the pail. "I'm sorry to have to tell you tell you this, Ole, but we may have unearthed the mystery. Turns out Amelia did have a granddaughter." With what seemed a loud pause, Deacon looked away. "She was adopted."

How was it that three tiny words could pierce Ole's heart like a savage arrow? He stood paralyzed for a pained moment then stabbed the pitchfork into a bale and spread the hay evenly along the manger as if to thoroughly bury the thought.

"From what I gather," Deacon continued, "Amelia lost leave of her senses after Emily died. They say she disappeared for a few days and when she came back, she locked herself in her flat for a couple of months. Wouldn't let anyone in. When she did go out, she seemed distracted, always looking over her shoulder, and when she talked, she didn't make much in the way of sense. Then one day she waltzes up and down the street pushing a baby buggy and announces that she has a brand new granddaughter. Shows her off to the whole entire world.

According to one of the neighbors, she'd been working in an infirmary at the time. Got attached to a young homeless girl that produced a baby out of wedlock. The girl was sick and knew she was at death's door. Everyone assumed she'd asked Amelia to take care of her daughter after she was gone."

Ole set the pitchfork aside. "So Amelia adopted herself an orphan. Why did the girl have to misrepresent herself? How could she not know I would have been thrilled to accept her as my very own either way?"

OLE WRESTLED OFF HIS COAT AND hooked it on the coat tree reluctant to turn around, reluctant to face Gretta. With Olivia's adoption stripping away any misguided hope that she could possibly be his daughter by birthright, all of Ole's having-our-own-children eggs were now tucked snuggly into one flimsy basket. He willed himself to cast doubt aside. At this point, he had no choice but to blindly trust Gretta's ability to one day carry a child to fruition.

"What's wrong?" she said. "Did something happen out at the farm? Is Deacon okay?"

"Got news about Olivia."

"And?"

"She was adopted."

"No, Ole, no." Gretta slid onto a chair and knotted her hands.

"Why wouldn't she just tell us? Why hide it?"

Gretta sat in silence for a too-long moment as if letting the words sink in. "What now?"

He shrugged. "I don't know."

She stared off emptily. "A child of yours is as much as a child of mine … as if I'd given birth to her myself."

"It'll be okay," Ole murmured. "I've given this some thought. If she is adopted, she's still family, and she probably needs us even more."

Gretta ran a hand over her middle. The sadness in her eyes gave way to love, emitting more warmth and hope than ever. "One day we'll have two children," she said as if trying to convince herself, "one adopted, and this one will be our very own."

After three losses in a row, however, that desire remained a questionable reach.

CHAPTER EIGHTEEN

Ole reread the letter of appointment and couldn't stop grinning. He'd made it. Partner. Of the prestigious law firm of Addison & Crowley. Tonight he and Gretta would celebrate. In a big way. He thrummed his desk. He needed to make reservations. But where could they go?

Rushing footsteps invading his reverie, he looked up as Nelson waltzed in unannounced and dropped a folder on his desk with a whump. "I'm sure you thought this case was a slam dunk," he said. "But you would be well advised to never be too sure of anything."

Ole eyed the folder and then Nelson who trotted out appearing every bit as smug as if he'd just landed a knockout blow.

Though apprehensive to look inside, Ole picked up the file and leafed through its contents. Unfortunately, finding the problem proved easier than finding a shard of mirror glistening in an open field under the noonday sun. A short moment later, he cranked up his Model T and headed out to Mabel's.

"I don't like surprises," he said. "Never have, never will. If we're going to work together ..."

To his bewilderment, she turned and led the way into the living room with the fractured gait of an elderly person, which from what he'd noticed so far was most uncharacteristic of her. She then gingerly lowered onto a tufted wingback chair. Was this a ruse?

"Have a seat," she said, but not without casting an unmistakable frown. "Just what is it precisely that you're trying to say, Mr. Harrington?"

He unsnapped his briefcase, drew out Nelson's manila folder, and handed her a stack of documents. "Do these look familiar?"

She nonchalantly flipped through them, one document at a time, but then her brows lifted and her gaze turned accusing. "Where did you get these?"

"They were passed on to me less than an hour ago by none other than Nelson Prixton," he said. "It appears as if we've been one-upped."

Again the frown. "But I don't understand."

Neither did Ole. The woman radiated innocence.

"Everything looks in perfectly good order," she said. "How did Mr. Prixton get these? And what problem could you possibly have with them?"

Ole lifted his chin. "Perhaps you might want to take another look," he said, "but this time I suggest you carefully review the last page of each document."

She flipped to the last page of the first document, and her mouth instantly formed a perfect *O*. "What … but how'd …" She nudged to the edge of her chair, horror-stricken. "How did this happen?"

"I was hoping you could tell me," Ole said, closely scrutinizing her reaction.

"How could I possibly … how could he …" She drew the document close and studied the signature page for a drawn-out moment. "Wait just a minute. Did you take a look at the date on this signature?" She held it out for Ole to see. "He got it notarized and signed it after the fact and without my knowledge. But how could he …"

"You really weren't a party to this then?"

"Of course not."

Though Ole felt relieved, her convincing response did little to change a troublesome reality. "That's why he wanted to retrieve your copies. Yours had been signed and notarized without his signature."

"That's right," she said then leafed through the rest of the documents, her scowl deepening. "He did that to all of these."

"I'm sure he felt that if he could get the originals and sign them, he'd be assured access to half of your assets, and he'd be home free."

Mabel's fingers trembled as she passed the documents back to Ole. "What are we going to do now?"

"I'm not sure," he said. "So you're telling me you had no knowledge of this whatsoever?"

"Absolutely not. I already told you that." She got up. "Wait a minute," she repeated and then disappeared into a far room. Again, something about her gait didn't seem right. First silence. Then a click. A thud. "Oh no," she cried out, nearly tripping over her own feet as she returned. "I was hoping those might be forgeries, but they're not. He stole them. Every last single one of my documents. I kept them locked up in the safe."

"He knew the combination?" Ole said.

"No, but he did know where I kept the combination. What was I thinking?"

"Don't be too hard on yourself. You couldn't have known."

"But the back dating. Doesn't that prove I wasn't a party to this?"

"For all we know, you could have volunteered them to him."

She glanced again at the new set of documents, her eyes drained of life. "I'll bet that weasel snuck into the house while I was out. Maybe if we could prove that he broke in … breaking and entering is against the law, isn't it?"

Ole gave his head a regretful shake. "Not if you're still legally married."

She stood in the middle of the room, arms dangling, gaze cast toward the floor. "I'm sure he's happy with himself."

"His attorney certainly grinned like the proverbial Cheshire cat when he presented them to me."

"How can we stop them now?"

"I'm not sure, but I promise you, I will think of something."

"Mr. Harrington?" Mabel's expression grew troubled as she made her way back to her chair and again carefully took a seat. "You said you don't like surprises."

Her tone triggered alarm. "That's right."

"I'm afraid we're stuck in a rather precarious spot then. We have to win this divorce settlement," she said, "and time isn't on our side. It's more than my not wanting him to get half of my assets." She hesitated. "I don't want him to get any of them."

Judging by the tenor of Mabel's tone and the fragility of her gait, her health was waning, but that Ole didn't care to face. "I'm afraid you have lost me here," he said. "You don't want him to get *any* of them?"

She stared off as if tortured by her own thoughts then muttered as though talking more to herself than to Ole. "I can see it all now, him spending my father's hard earned money on his new bride and frittering away the rest on gambling. That's not right."

"No, but that's what we're trying to keep from happening."

She shook her head. "At the moment, time is the bigger enemy."

He slipped the documents back into his briefcase while keeping a resistant ear on her words.

"I put off going to the doctor as long as I could," she said. "Some things you get a feeling about."

Ole looked up. "You don't have to …"

"Oh, but I do. I just received word this morning. Mr. Harrington … I'm dying."

CHAPTER NINETEEN

Ole stood at the door of Nelson's bland one-room office finding it strikingly wanting with its scarred furnishings, beat up book bindings, dust-laden shelving, and unwashed windows, saying nothing about no desk at which to seat a stenographer.

For a man of his expanded ego and professional savoir faire, his lack of hospitality appeared especially wanting. Or was it? After all, Ole had shown up unannounced. Were he Nelson, he would have felt humiliated to have a client enter such an unprofessional environment, let alone a contemporary.

But this wasn't the same Nelson.

And at the moment, to Ole's surprise, he felt badly for him.

"What can I do for you?" Nelson said, sounding mildly irritated.

Ole drew up a chair. "Nothing. But there is something I want you to do for my client."

Nelson raised his chin and looked down the path of his perfect nose until his eyes met Ole's. "By client, I assume we're talking about Harding."

"Mabel, not Jack."

"You want me to do something for *her*?" He chuckled incredulously.

"Now why would I want to do that? We aren't kids playing in a sandbox anymore, we're professionals looking after our own affairs. Or is that beyond your grasp?"

"She's dying."

"What does that have to do with me?"

Though few things shocked Ole, Nelson's indifference did. He sat back for a moment, speechless.

Time to play hardball.

"More than you know," he said. "From the information I was given, I wondered why you'd bother to take on your client ... so I took it upon myself to do a little checking behind the scenes."

Nelson grimaced. "Being a bit presumptuous, aren't you?"

"I prefer to call it being thorough."

Nelson picked up a pencil and nervously tapped it against the ratty desktop. "And?"

"How much do you know about Harding?"

He tossed the pencil back on the desk and casually crossed his arms as if he felt a need to hug himself. "I find that question rather inappropriate."

Ole looked about the unkempt office before formulating words. From all outward appearances, Nelson could ill afford to do due diligence or turn down a case. Any case for that matter. If the man's resources were, in fact, problematic, he may have no choice other than to put up a good fight merely for want of staying afloat. "Perhaps if you knew more about him, you wouldn't choose to waste your precious time," Ole said, purposely excluding mention of the word money. Why state the obvious?

Nelson scowled. "Say, what is this? You don't think I'd be stupid enough to drop this case, do you? If that's why you're here, forget it."

"I care about my dying client, and I want this case dropped," Ole said.

"That's not going to happen."

"You are familiar with Harding's propensity toward gambling, I assume."

Nelson sat stone-faced, his eyes not quite meeting Ole's, as if to hide the fact that he might have been jarred by the suggestion. "Of course, I am," he said. "He's done quite well."

"Has he?"

"You can prove otherwise?"

"I assume you're familiar with the king of the bookmakers then?"

Nelson paled. "Who isn't?"

"I wasn't until I got educated."

Nelson leaned back again and stretched, doing an amateur job of faking boredom. "What could the king of bookmakers possibly have to do with Jack Harding?"

"You don't know then, do you?" Ole said. "Jack is one of his boys."

Nelson shot up straight. "That's a serious charge, Harrington. You'd better be able to prove it."

"I don't need to. Think about it," he said. "Where is Harding gainfully employed? Has he ever held down a job? If so, I'm hard-pressed to find out where or for how long. Why does he spend so much time in Chicago? And why would he choose to divorce Mabel? Because she refused to continue to be reduced to a meal ticket? Since she's keeping a roof over his head, even you have to admit that makes no sense." Ole paused as Nelson sat speechless.

"Let me give you another free one," Ole said. "Jack insists he has another love interest, yet we can't find her. Who is she? Or does the woman exist? Why would he fabricate her? What's his motivation? And what about the Chicago's thugs? It's not like his appetite for gambling isn't relentless, and I'm sure we've all heard horror stories about those who don't pay their gambling debts."

Nelson stared off absently as if Ole's words entered one ear and merely passed through the other.

"You can't win this case," Ole said. "You know it, I know it, and your client will never be able to pay you."

Nelson's brows snapped together. "I smell a rat. What amazing timing to claim your client is dying. Attorneys don't set up other attorneys to succeed. We're all out for blood."

"Seems that would depend on whether we're in it for the money or to help our client," Ole said. "As for me, not only is Mabel Harding terminally ill, she doesn't need the stress, and she's already paid far more to that scoundrel you're representing than he deserves. I don't want her to pay him one red cent more."

Nelson sat quietly for a long moment as if to digest the troubling information, but then his demeanor transformed into one of accusation. "Your altruistic nature wouldn't have anything to do with Mabel not being able to produce an heir, would it … I mean, as I recall, you are personally familiar with that sort of situation."

Though Ole's hand clenched into a fist, he let the slight pass.

"We will go to court, Harrington," Nelson said. "And mark my word, we will win."

How naïve had Ole been to think he could reason with Nelson? He stood and gave the office another cursory look. He had come hoping to compassionately pull the plug on an unjust case, to shield what little was left of Mabel's health, to save her time and money, and was tempted to say that by the look of things, Nelson could stand to save time and money, too. But then he would be playing dirty like Nelson. And he refused to abase himself.

So he left with a tip of his fedora, no response to the slight, and no word of good-bye.

CHAPTER TWENTY

Ole looked out across the winter wonderland laden with virgin snow where evergreen branches sagged from the powder's heavy weight. Icebound islands melded into the mainland. And a brilliant sun reflected off low rolling hills and winding roads. After several hours of pure bliss, though his knees ached from squatting, his fingers and toes numbed with cold, he could not have cared less. The fish in the ice hole were biting, Deacon offered spirited company, and their gunnysacks spilled with walleye and crappie.

Deacon drew his fishing line across a cut in the ice. "Sack gets any heavier, we'll be hard pressed to carry it," he said. After a long moment, he added, "Heard any more from Olivia?"

"Not yet. I get the feeling she's pacing herself. I know I am. Hey … got a bite." Losing the fish every bit as quickly, Ole drew out the line and slipped more bait unto the hook. "I've been thinking about what you said."

"About Olivia, you mean?"

"About her being adopted. I can't stop questioning it."

Deacon answered that thought with a turn and an absent gaze out over the frozen lake. "Why? Questioning it isn't going to change reality," he said. "Accepting it might do wonders for giving you peace, though."

"It's not the adoption that bothers me. We can have next of kin we don't want to have a thing to do with yet have lifelong friends that are closer than family."

"That's true," Deacon said, "but what gets in my craw is the deceit. Why didn't Amelia ever mention her? Why didn't Olivia tell you up front that she was your adopted daughter? Like I told you before, something doesn't smell right."

Ole stretched, readjusted his weight on the footstool, and then dropped the line back into the hole. "That's how I felt about it, too, but then I got to be thinking … maybe Olivia doesn't know she's adopted. I mean … character is consistent, right? If Amelia didn't tell you about the adoption, maybe she didn't tell Olivia either." He hesitated. "There's something else … I need to prove beyond a shadow of a doubt that she's not my daughter by blood. Then and only then will I be able to set this crazy hope of mine aside."

"I'm not meaning to be unkind here, Ole, but how could you of all people possibly not know you had a child?"

"We have twins in our family line. What if she was a twin?"

"That makes no sense. Why in the world would Amelia keep something like that from you? I can't imagine anyone being that cruel."

For tens of minutes all remained quiet, a muted quiet, sound absorbed by the thick white blanket until from behind, an automobile puttered around the bend, backfiring every hundred yards or so. Ole gazed up at a nearby tree one snowflake shy of buckling. "Avalanche," he muttered. And the snow came tumbling down. "What do you say? Catch one more and call it a day?"

The tailpipe backfired again. Ole glanced back at the road and bristled.

Nelson.

"Got a problem that won't go away, Deacon."

"How so?"

"That's Nelson Prixton."

Deacon chuckled. "Must love attention or he'd get that contraption fixed."

"I doubt he can afford it."

"He's fallen on hard times, has he?"

"Appears so. The bad part of it is, he isn't one who likes to suffer alone."

Deacon glanced back toward the roadster as it disappeared around a bend. "Trying your patience, is he?"

"Keeps asking for proof of Jack's association with the criminal element. How do we go about proving something like that?"

"Maybe we could get a picture of them together."

It was as if Ole could see the little wheels turning in Deacon's sharp mind. "What would that prove?"

"It would show an association, wouldn't it?"

"Not necessarily," Ole said.

"There's got to be more we can do."

"What about that supposed love interest of his? I figure you still haven't been able to dig up anything on her or you would have said something."

Deacon drew his empty fishing line from the water and set the rod aside. "There isn't a stone I've left unturned, and I still come up dry."

"I'd lay a bet she doesn't exist."

"But why would Harding make up a thing like that?"

"He's probably desperate. Maybe he figures having someone else in the picture would make Mabel want to grant him a divorce. That's one way to get a cash settlement to pay off his gambling debts."

"That would be motivation enough, I guess," Deacon said. "You know, there is one more thing we might want to give a try, that is if you've got the budget for it. I'm digging deep here, so bear with me.

Suppose I went back to Chicago and finagled my way into a game of some kind."

"*You* gambling?"

Deacon lowered his line back into the hole and thoughtfully swirled it around. "Yeah, me. I've learned enough to get by. Had to for my job … before I started working the farm, that is. How about if I cozy up to the boys? Pretend I want in behind the scenes? I've exhausted my sources here in Amber Leaf. We've gotten all the information we're going to get. That Harding's slippery. A trip back to Chicago might be our best bet. Maybe I can hoodwink the boys into spilling the beans on him."

"That's too dangerous."

"And therein lies the thrill. Besides, what other choice do we have? As for me, I'd love the challenge. You give me the go ahead and I'll head out first thing come Monday morning."

"Let's do it then, but be careful." Ole turned hopeful. "I've been looking for a way to gain the upper hand with Nelson again and keep it. That just might do the trick."

"Why's that?"

That man can crawl lower than a snake. "He's too sure of himself. Doesn't hesitate to seize opportunities to take me down."

Deacon's rod dipped. "Got a bite." He carefully reeled it in. "Drat! A bullhead." He drew it off the line and was about to throw it back in when Ole stopped him.

"Hey, what are you doing?"

"Throwing it back."

"Why?"

"Don't like bullheads."

"Give it to me then."

"You mean you like 'em?"

"Nope. Love 'em."

"He's all yours." Deacon slipped the fish into the gunnysack. "Other than being ruthlessly demanding, has Nelson been behaving?"

"Man's incapable of disciplining himself."

"Ho-oh," Deacon said. "What's he done now?"

"Passed around cigars at the last club meeting."

"That's a good thing, isn't it? Who wouldn't go for a free cigar?"

Me.

"He made a public announcement that our babies would be growing up together."

"Didn't he know about Gretta …"

"He knew. Made sure everyone else knew about it, too. After tossing me a cigar, he blurted out, 'Oh, that's right. Gretta lost your kid some time back. Don't worry about it, Harrington. She can always have another one. Oh, wait, what was I thinking? Maybe she can't.'"

Sickened by the memory, Ole picked up the footstool and gathered his fishing gear and gunnysack. "And then the louse had the gall to laugh."

"You let him get by with that?"

"Let's just say I had enough strong hands pulling me back to save his sorry hide."

CHAPTER TWENTY-ONE

The day long spent, Olivia started to draw down the shade, but stopped at the mid point. Not again. The clatter of a bicycle fender scraping its rear wheel filled the chilly night air. Then came the young teen's callous cry. "Go back to Hunland, Kraut. You ain't welcome here."

She peered through the window and looked down the street. Though the bicycle had disappeared from view, a familiar figure sat in the shadows of a lamppost in the small park across from her flat, feet drawn up and to the side as if to fend off another taunting assault. She gathered her cape, tossed it over her shoulders, and shivered as she hurried out into the crisp night.

"Fritz, are you well?"

"As well as could be expected. Perhaps I should have known better than to ... I assume you heard the unpleasant raucous?"

"It was impossible to miss."

"What that boy appears to have difficulty comprehending," her kind neighbor said, "is that we Germans are fleeing the same bombs, bombs being dropped by our very own people. But how can I blame him? Every nation has its informants. In his estimation, I could very well be one of them."

"If only he knew you."

"He? Or they? Things will get much worse before they get better, I fear," he said with a slight tremor. "I keep scratching my head trying to fathom how in this day and age a small number of my people could forever change the rules of war. I'm appalled by them."

"Why are you sitting in the shadows?" Warmth flooded her cheeks at the insensitivity of the query. She found it difficult to imagine how distressing it must be for a German to live in England during wartime with anti-German sentiment spiraling the way that it had been as of recent. "I meant not to ..."

He patted the bench. "Come. Sit with me a moment." His eyes took on an intense form of despair as he tightened his coat at the collar and looked up into the night sky. "Perfect Zeppelin weather," he said in a deep though gentle tone.

She drew her cape tighter as well and also gazed up at the star-studded heavens. "Too perfect. I'm terrified of them floating across the sky the way they do ... like giant silver cigars. Do you fear they shall return?"

"That is their plan, is it not? To bring the trenches to our back doors? I saw a child several weeks past watching in wonder while his mother stood at his side watching in horror. Baby killers those Zeppelins are. Murdering people without looking them in the eye." He drew a lungful of smoke from his pipe. The tobacco glowed, emitting an illusion of warmth as the scent of smoke permeated the cold air. He sat quiet for a moment, appearing deeply troubled. "We received a post from my spinster sister several days past," he said. "Seems several bombs landed rather near her flat."

"They do target buildings," Olivia said, unnerved at the thought. "Whatever happened? That is if you don't mind my asking."

He shook his head. "Said she was horrorstricken. Knew not what to do, where to run for safety. Does one head for open ground or for a hidden cellar? She had little time. They had no sirens. No warning. She saw men shimmying up gas lamps, turning them off. They cut off the power. Everywhere there was darkness. Walls collapsed. Windows smashed. Buildings caught fire. Screams tore into the night. When she finally returned to her flat to find what was left of it, she found broken glass scattered across the floor. Other than that, she was fortunate. Everything was intact from her china to the pictures on her walls. But the bombs left craters. Scars everywhere." He turned to her. "We're all at risk, Olivia. I fear our way of life shall never be the same." And then he looked at her intently. "I can only imagine how tremendously difficult this must be for you without your grandmum. How are you getting on?"

Olivia considered the suffering, the fear, and the hate. How inviting the thought of fleeing England, of fleeing danger. She tired of desiring to run. With the blockade, however, crossing the Atlantic seemed hopeless. And her father … in the end would he want her? Or might she be a burden? She had already mentioned her desire to go to America. Now it was up to him to make the invitation. But would he?

"I've been giving some thought to resigning my position at the tailor's and volunteering to become a munitionette," she said.

"You would consider that? Even after the Silvertown explosion? That's rather dangerous business—life threatening, and don't forget it's also a serious risk to your health. My cousin's skin turned so yellow from TNT, they call her canary girl."

Olivia gazed across the park at the blast-proof entrance above a tunnel-vaulted room—another constant reminder of the war's oppression. "Someone needs to have the courage to do it or we shall never win."

CHAPTER TWENTY-TWO

Still no word from Deacon. Ole smacked his desktop. The man had promised he'd be in touch no later than last night, yet not a peep from him. He wasn't the kind to lollygag or go sight seeing. What could have happened? Do something, Ole told himself. He's in dangerous territory. Telephone the hotel. Make sure he is well and accounted for.

Before Ole could make a move, however, footsteps padded across the outer office. Too swiftly. The stenographer rushed in, alarm-filled words spewing out. "Mr. De Haven just telephoned, sir."

"Why didn't you put him through?"

"I wanted to," she said, "but he said he didn't have time to wait. He asked me to tell you he's being followed."

"Followed?" The word shot out of Ole's mouth.

"Yes, sir. Said he planned to zigzag across the city until he loses the man."

Ole didn't care for the sound of that. If anything happened to Deacon .... "Any idea when he'll arrive? Did he say?"

"Tomorrow at the earliest. Said he'd call again as soon as he can nail down an arrival time."

"Sorry for being short," Ole said. "And thanks ... for letting me know."

In the wee hours of the morning Ole stared at the ceiling, sleep a long way off. What had he done? How foolish could he have been to endanger Deacon and to that degree? Ole had acted impulsively. Didn't think things through. He hadn't sent the man to Aspen to attend a Sunday school picnic, he had sent him to Chicago ... where the big boys play ... the dangerous big boys.

But they were stuck. How could he and Deacon have gotten vital information on Harding without another site visit?

So what? Deacon has a wife, grown kids, and grandkids.

The telephone rang and he jumped. From the living room the grandfather clock struck one.

Gretta rolled over. "Who'd be telephoning this time of night?" she said.

Ole half-walked, half-stumbled to the kitchen and plucked up the receiver. "Hello?"

"I have a long distance person-to-person telephone call for a Mr. Oliver Harrington."

"This is Harrington, and I do accept the charges."

"One moment please," the Operator said. "Go ahead, sir."

"Don't talk. Just listen," the hushed male voice said. "Meet me at the depot at eleven in the morning." A click. An abrupt dial tone.

Through a strain, Ole recognized that familiar scratchy tone.

Deacon.

The next day, nerves on end, he rounded corners on two wheels all of the way from the office to the depot. At a quarter to eleven he waited and paced. At eleven straight up, the train hissed to a stop, brakes screeching. Though it seemed to take forever, passengers finally unloaded. Unlike the last trip when Deacon was first to get off, this time Ole stood and watched as a horde pressed past him. Deacon managed to get off last and walked past Ole with lips moving and eyes fixed straight ahead. "Don't react," he muttered. "I'm still being followed. Go inside the depot. Wait five minutes. Then come back out to the lot. Don't look for me. I'll find you."

Ole kept his gaze fixed on the depot as if Deacon didn't exist. He not only did as instructed, he waited inside an extra few minutes looking around as if trying to find someone then promptly approached a ticket agent. "Sir, can you help me?" he said in a voice feigned with concern. "I'm looking for a young woman with long red hair. She didn't get off the train."

"I'm sorry," the agent said. "We have no way of knowing what happened."

Ole made a display of nervously running his hands through his hair and pacing. "I'll wait a few more minutes then," he said, "…just in case."

He settled in on a bench in the middle of the room and looked over the stragglers. A too-well-dressed man with a hardened look stood in the corner. He appeared to watch Ole suspiciously then nonchalantly lit a cigar. He stood for a long moment then approached the same ticket agent. "One-way to Chicago, please," he said.

That's him.

As the man turned his back to pay for the ticket, Ole slipped out and casually made his way through the parking lot where he found Deacon squatting beside the Model T.

Keeping his voice low and a sharp eye out while he cranked, Ole said, "Let's get out of here."

Meanwhile, Deacon crawled in. He hunkered down in the seat and stayed there until they cleared well out of sight.

"I'm sorry," Ole said.

"About what?"

"Putting you in such a dangerous spot."

"I feel guilty getting paid for it," Deacon said with a chuckle. "Haven't had this much fun since I can remember … did you see the thug?"

"Sure did. It wasn't your imagination. He was a suspicious looking character if I've ever seen one. Gave me the hairy eyeball. He couldn't have known we were together. I'm worried, though. He bought a one-way ticket back to Chicago. When he gets on the train, he'll see you aren't there."

"Why would I be? Think about it, Ole. He's the one heading back to Chicago, not me."

Ole slowed at a fork in the road and then headed out on country roads. "No offense, but under the circumstances, that's little consolation. Something doesn't add up. Why would he stop following you now? You'd think he'd want to follow you home. See where you live."

"My getting off in Amber Leaf may have been all he needed to know. Harding lived here, remember?"

Ole slowed again, this time over a patch of deep icy ruts, the car rocking to and fro. "Give me the lowdown on what happened," he said, "and don't spare any details."

Deacon grinned. "That was a close one."

He really did look as though he'd had the time of his life.

"Everything was going great," he said, "like clockwork. Then this barbarian who goes by the name of Knuckles decided I looked like a Fed. Decided they needed to do a background check. Now you're talking to a man here who was going under an assumed name. I knew enough to clear out, but wherever I went, they shadowed me. I could feel it." Deacon's grin dwindled as reality appeared to set in. "In the end, it was a bust."

Ole gave Deacon a sidelong glance. "My gut tells me we haven't seen the end of this yet."

Nowhere near close to the end.

CHAPTER TWENTY-THREE

"O le?" Gretta said as she ran a dishcloth across the counter. "Would you mind running over to the Anderson's for a minute? Bill made a trip out to the farm today. Said he'd bring us back an extra sack of potatoes. I would walk over myself ..."

"But you think a hundred pounds is a little too heavy for you to carry?" With a teasing grin, Ole kissed her lightly on the cheek. "Be right back."

Ole had never been inside the Andersons' home before, but he'd certainly heard enough about the place. Though simple in design, it was rumored to have been well constructed with a skylight above the staircase, boasted multiple clothes shoots, up-to-date appliances, and was complete with a parlor for the man of the house along with an office, a separate parlor for his wife, a flour closet, and a mudroom containing windowsills laden with pots of freshly-grown herbs, even in winter.

As Mrs. Anderson opened the door, she massaged her elbow, pain appearing to emanate through tired eyes. "Mr. Harrington, how nice to see you again."

"Is there anything I can do for you?" he said. "You don't look well."

An amused simper propped up plump cheeks. "Just the rheumatism.

Nothing to be concerned about. Comes and goes … you must be here for the potatoes. My husband has them. You'll find him down in the cellar, back side of the house … oh, and while you're at it, would you mind asking him to bring up some potatoes for us, too? I could use a few for tonight's supper."

Ole sidestepped an occasional puddle of melting snow as he bounded toward the back of the house. Though mildly disappointed not to have gotten an invitation to peek inside, in time he was certain he and Gretta would have ample opportunity to visit the Andersons, tour their home, and satisfy their curiosity.

As he rounded the side of the house, however, he stopped abruptly. The entry to the root cellar was far different from any he'd seen with a low-lying roof hovering well above a narrow descending ramp. Very narrow. Very descending. At the bottom of the dirt gradient, a single door opened into the cellar—a windowless wooden door.

As he contemplated the descent, the muscles of his stomach and legs tightened, holding him back. His breathing became shallow again, as if it had a mind of its own. He gave his head a vehement shake. You're being ridiculous, he told himself. This is your imagination. Take a deep breath. Don't let fear get the best of you.

He had definitely moved past that by now.

Or so he'd thought.

Willfully shoving trepidation to the side, after inhaling deeply, he marched forward, descending the ramp as if claustrophobia did not exist. But at the halfway point, his knees refused to cooperate. They turned rubbery. What was worse? He felt hard-pressed to control them. Just a few more steps to go, he told himself. He forced another foot forward, pushing hands against the sides of the cold and narrow cinder block as if that could hold back the invisible force vehemently trying to suck him in, an ugly force closing in on his world. The further down the decline he crept, the darker it grew, and the slower he seemed able to move. Just shy of the door, he froze completely.

Couldn't move.

Dizzy.

Knees trembling.

Too paralyzed to let go of the wall for fear he'd fall.

Too paralyzed to turn around or lower to the ground in an effort to escape his half-baked imaginings.

He could cry out for Bill, but what would the man think if he saw him, a grown man he barely knew in a state like this? Ole needed to get out of here on his own, but how?

He squeezed his eyes closed, sucked in a deep breath, and attempted a turn, but was unable to release a trembling hand from a wall, let alone two trembling hands. He felt as if he did he would get sucked in for sure. His feet couldn't be less movable if they'd been nailed to the ground. Think, Ole, think! With eyes squeezed closed, he forced an awkward step back. Though only inches on an unsteady and uncooperative foot, at least it was movement. He forced another step back, again pressing his hands tight to the wall, barely able to move them. It was as though he'd been lassoed and pulled against his will, the noose drawing tighter and tighter. No matter how hard he tried, he could not seem to break free. Then another step back and another until he backed up far enough to make a halting half turn. But then what? Pressing his back tight to the unforgiving wall, he was finally able to sidestep. Slowly. Slowly. Three-quarters of the way up the incline, he cleared the entry.

He stopped and waited until he could breathe freely again and comfortably regain composure. "Bill?" he cried.

No answer.

"Bill? Are you there?"

The door creaked open. "Harrington? Thought I heard someone calling. Come on down."

"Another time," Ole said. Please don't press the point. "I've got to get home. Your wife asked if you'd bring up some potatoes. Said she needs them for supper."

Bill took on a confused look. "Sure thing. You want to get your—"

"Another time."

Distraught at the setback, Ole turned on his heel and trudged home. To think he'd been doing so well. Making tremendous progress. But then to take a hit like that? What happened? What was going on?

Fear. He had focused on fear again. How could something so simple be so maddeningly difficult?

Sooner than he liked, he entered the kitchen.

"Where are the potatoes, dear?" Gretta said.

"The potatoes?"

"That is why you went next door, isn't it? Ole? What's the matter? What happened?"

He pulled a chair from the table, plopped down, and slumped.

Gretta appeared at his side and lightly, lovingly rubbed his shoulders.

"The potatoes were in their cellar. I couldn't do it, Gretta," he finally admitted. "I couldn't bring myself to go down there."

"Correction. You couldn't bring yourself to go down there … yet. You will."

"You don't understand. I froze. I couldn't … after as hard as I've been trying, my body went into a panic again."

"Kind of like a chicken getting its head chopped off," she said thoughtfully. "They hobble around for a while before their little bodies finally figure out it's over and then they drop. Your body will catch up to your thinking, too."

Ole let out a defeated sigh. What she said made sense. Though she loved him desperately, at present he did not deserve her accompanying respect. He needed to earn it—for her, for himself.

"These things just take time," she said.

Yes, but what if there's more to it than that?

Ole took note of his thinking.

What if there isn't?

CHAPTER TWENTY-FOUR

"Harding's dead," Nelson shouted as he charged into Ole's office again, this time red faced and spewing spittle, "and it's all your fault."

"Hold on there!" Ole hopped up and closed the door like he meant it. "I think you'd better have a seat."

"Why close the door?" Nelson said in a voice loud enough to rouse anyone within a hundred mile radius even if they lay comatose. "You don't want your fellow workers to know what a dirt bag you are … is that it?"

Ole flexed a clenching fist. "Calm down and take that chair … or leave."

Nelson appeared stunned by the command. Though he didn't let go of his scowl, he did take a chair.

"What's this about Harding being dead?" Ole said.

"You tell me." Nelson drew a pack of cigarettes from a shirt pocket and tapped one loose. "He's been in Chicago. But then again you already knew that. He and I have been talking at least every other day if not more. He gave me the telephone number at his—"

"Edgewater Beach Hotel?"

Nelson made a spectacle of lighting a cigarette and extinguishing the match. "That's right. I telephoned him first thing this morning … manager said, 'I'm sorry, sir, but I'm afraid Mr. Harding is deceased.'"

"When?" Ole said, concern mounting. "When did he die?"

"Sometime during the night. A maid found him in his room this morning. Said it looked like foul play." Nelson paused. "There's more. They found a note on him."

"What did it say?"

Nelson's jaw tightened as he drew out the words. "No debt goes unpaid."

"Any idea how big his gambling debt is?"

Or should I say was?

"None."

"Does his wife know yet?"

"I have no idea."

"She needs to know. She could be in real danger. But why would you think I'm involved? That makes no sense."

Nelson gave his nose a smug lift. "Harding told me he was sure he was being shadowed, and you admitted you were following him."

"You can't possibly think I had him killed."

"Even I know better than that. But I do believe you were the cause. Therein lies the difference."

"How could you possibly think such a thing?"

"You were perceived as being a threat and they reacted. That's what gangsters do," Nelson said with a condescending look. "Or didn't you know that?"

"Think about it, Nelson. Why would his killers think we were a threat? We were discreet and did absolutely nothing that would put Harding in jeopardy. He was the one who racked up a gambling debt if you will remember. That had nothing to do with me. We weren't trying to collect. We were trying to stop him from collecting."

Nelson blew out a lungful of spent smoke. "Did it ever dawn on you that they thought you were trying to muscle in on his limited capital?"

Ole remembered the depot, the look on that tough's face, the one who had followed Deacon from Chicago. Could Nelson be right? Could Ole and Deacon have caused enough angst that the thugs would make a hit? That made no sense, not if Harding couldn't pay up. "The crucial words would be limited and capital," Ole said. "And if they did sense we were on Harding's trail, why would they care? We're nobodies in Chicago. You know that. You just needed someone to blame, didn't you? You just needed to sound off."

Nelson sat stone faced, not a hint of emotion, not a hint of response.

"And about the divorce," Ole said. "I don't mean to hit you while you're down, but you would never have won the case. Harding wasn't bright. Those deeds you produced? He stole them from Mabel's safe, signed them after the fact, and then had them notarized a second time. In the end, the notarizations were nothing more than acknowledgements, proof that he was who he said he was. That would never fly in a court of law, and you know it. I'm sorry, Prixton. This must be awfully tough for you."

Nelson stood. "Don't be too sorry."

"Excuse me?"

"You'll get yours. And I'll be standing at the head of the line cheering when you do."

Ole watched the door close then picked up the telephone. "Operator, get me Mabel Harding."

In the early afternoon, he drove out to the De Haven farm. Deacon was latching the bolt on the barn door when he arrived.

As Deacon sidled up to the car, Ole turned and stared off toward the barren fields lightly dusted with snow as if reading the harvested remains of rows of corn like lines on the pages of a book. "I've got a monkey on my back," he said then shared the particulars about Nelson's visit. "There's one thing I can't seem to get past … the hateful look on that man's face."

"Nelson's?"

"No. The one from Chicago. You took a circuitous ride home, remember? And yet he managed to follow you all of the way here then bought a one-way ticket back." Ole paused. "I'm worried about Mabel being in danger."

Deacon plucked off his cap, nervously smoothed his hair back, then slipped it on again. "The note said *no debt goes unpaid?*"

"That's right. I called her this morning. She already knew about Jack. Said the telephone rang in the wee hours. A male voice said, 'Mrs. Harding? I'm afraid your husband won't be coming home.' She said she knew what that meant."

"So they knew about her and where she lives?"

"That's a given."

Deacon plucked a toothpick from a bib overall pocket and thoughtfully picked at a tooth as if that helped him think. "What are we going to do now, Ole?"

"We?"

Deacon's eyes filled with what appeared to be a strong case of remorse. "I feel partly responsible. No, that's not true. I feel completely responsible. It was my harebrained idea to go back to Chicago. Maybe if I'd been more careful."

"I doubt this has anything to do with you, me, or Mabel," Ole said. "People like that want the money, and they don't hesitate to play hardball to get it."

"But still, the woman might need protection."

Ole thought for a moment. "I wonder in this case if it wouldn't be wisest to be direct."

Deacon looked at Ole strangely, appearing confused.

"Mabel's dying, Deacon."

His eyes widened and his mouth fell open. "She's what?"

It hurt to repeat it. "I said she's dying. The wisest thing to do at this point might be to call off the dogs. She gets another phone call, maybe she should just ask how much Jack owed and pay it. Her assets will all be going to charity anyway."

"But how will she get the money to them?"

"Open bank draft."

"You may be on to something there."

And if I'm not?

CHAPTER TWENTY-FIVE

Ole moved his queen diagonally one square and winked at Gretta. "Check."

Before she could make a counter move, the telephone rang. He gave her shoulder a tender squeeze. "Be right back," he said then went to the kitchen where he picked up the receiver. "Harrington here."

"Mr. Harrington? Mr. Harrington?" Mabel sounded frantic. "They're coming. They're coming."

"Calm down. Take a deep breath. I'm here. Now tell me … who's coming?"

"I don't know. They. Just they."

"When?"

"Jack's not dead."

Ole leaned a shoulder against the wall for support. His eyes widened involuntarily and air solidified in his lungs. "Jack's not … that's not possible."

"That's what I thought, too," she said, "but I heard his voice. It was him. I know it was him. They said if I called the police, they'd kill him right there on the spot. I'm so terrified, I don't know what to do."

Ole glanced at the clock. Half past eight. "When will they be there, did they say?"

"In about an hour. What should I do?"

"I'm on my way."

"But they'll see your car."

"No, they won't."

He grabbed his coat and headed for the door. "Be back in a little while, Gretta."

I hope.

"What happened?" she said. "Where are you going?"

"It's Mabel. I'll tell you all about it when I get home."

If I get home.

He parked the Model T behind a dwindling snow bank a sizable stone's throw from Mabel's house, trudged down a back alley, and past her shed. After looking high and low for any sign of life and not seeing or hearing a thing, he scuttled up to the back door and gave it a light knock.

"Who's there?" Mabel said, her tone vibrating with panic.

"It's me. Oliver Harrington. Let me in."

Once inside, she quickly bolted the door behind him then led him through darkened rooms to a back office where they sat taking care not to turn on a light.

"What are you going to do?" she said. "What can you do?"

"Leave that to me. When they arrive, be honest. Tell them your attorney is here, and he thinks he can help. Assure them that I pose no threat. Be sure to tell them I'm not armed."

Though Ole couldn't see her face, he could hear the incredulity in her quivering voice. "You're not … but …"

"Mabel, we have to play this smart."

"How smart is it if you get killed?"

"We're not that important. Now go to the living room and wait 'til they come."

He stood alone in the blackened room, the clock ticking relentlessly to the beat of his pulse. Was he being foolhardy? Was he trusting his own instincts too much? First Olivia. Now some thugs from Chicago. At least Gretta knew where he was. If Mabel and he were snuffed out, it wouldn't take long to find them.

Then again …

Should he call the police? No. That was worst thing he could do. If the thugs got wind of it, Jack would be dead for sure.

Or is he dead anyway?

The determined clock ticked on. How Ole wished he could silence the thing. It was driving him nuts. He sat quietly, unmoving other than to wipe the relentless sweat oozing from his palms.

What was that? A faint rap at the door? He listened closer. There it was again. Then the light patter of Mabel's tentative foot drops. The front door squeaking open. No words. Just footsteps. Lots of tentative footsteps.

Mabel was talking. He listened harder. Couldn't make out her words. His heart pounded, fluttering all of the way up into his throat. Footsteps started in again, growing louder. Then the light snapped on and he flinched.

"Mr. Harrington? You can come out now."

He followed Mabel into the living room where two cold-blooded hoods sneered at him as if he were a stooge. The smaller of the two stood, feet spread, willfully exposing a pistol strapped at his side. "Kind of taking a chance here, aren't you?" he said.

"Not at all." Ole held up both hands, palms out. "I'm sure Mrs. Harding has informed you that I'm not armed."

"Like I said, kind of taking a chance, aren't you?"

"Just trying my best to save a man's life. Now why don't you tell us what you want, and we'll see what we can do to meet your demands."

"Oh, yeah? I smell a rat." The thug slowly drew out his pistol as if to make a point as he flaunted it. "What are you up to?"

Ole held his arms higher. "Like I said, I'm trying to save a man's life." He paused. "No, that's not true. Jack's a snake. I couldn't care less about him. What I am trying to do here is protect my client. You see, gentlemen," he looked tenderly at Mabel, "Mrs. Harding here has some serious health issues."

The larger of the thugs sneered as he cracked his knuckles.

So this is the man Deacon called Knuckles.

"And we would give a rip about that because?"

"Let's just say that her days are numbered. Jack isn't worth compromising her life any more than he already has. Tell us what you want, and we'll make this go away. It's as simple as that."

Shorty lifted his chin and scowled. "As simple as twenty grand?"

"As simple as twenty grand."

"And how do you plan to make that happen?"

With eyes fixed on the hoodlums, Mabel stepped in front of Ole. "I have ten thousand in cash. It's in my safe. Here in the back room. You can come with me if you'd like. I'll give you all of it along with a check for ten thousand more. You can make it out to whomever you wish, even if it's to cash. All we want is for you to free my husband and leave us alone. Is it a deal?"

Shorty gave his sidekick *the look*. "What do you say, Knuckles?"

Knuckles shrugged.

"Look," Ole said. "You'll only know we're being straight up if you follow her into the back room and see for yourselves. This isn't a trap. We're sitting ducks here. Like I said, Mabel is going through a pretty rough time, and all we want is to make this go away. I'll come in the room with you, hands up the entire time. Take the money. Take the check. And please … just leave. I give you my word we have not and will not involve the police."

Knuckles scowled. "Why do a fool thing like that?"

"I'll answer that," Mabel said. "I was a fool to marry Jack. I had no idea what a scoundrel he is. And I don't want people in Amber Leaf knowing about it. I guess you might say I have too much pride."

For a long moment, it was as though Ole could see the wheels turning in Shorty's snarky head. But then with a wave of his gun, he said, "Let's get on with it. We gotta' get outa' here."

CHAPTER TWENTY-SIX

Ole returned home a sobered man. He and Mabel? Still alive? Able to face another day?

But what about Jack?

Not that Ole cared.

"What happened?" Gretta said.

He jumped at the sound of her voice. Relax, Ole, relax, he told himself. It's all over with now. "You're still up?"

"Yes, I'm still up. You left in such a hurry, you had me worried sick."

A satisfied smile broke loose. "I think we saved Jack Harding's life."

"But I thought he was dead."

"Surprisingly no. Not yet anyway ... money talks," he added in answer to the question in her eyes.

Hours later after finally getting a night of fitful sleep, Ole awakened to the sound of the telephone ringing off the hook. It was Mabel. "Jack's here," she said in a relief-filled tone. "He showed up a few minutes ago. Unscathed. He appears to be a changed man."

Ole took note of the words 'changed man.' "He appreciates what you've done for him?"

"And then some."

"Are you considering taking him back? ... No, forget I asked."

"How do I say this delicately, Mr. Harrington? ... Have you been indulging in a liquid breakfast?"

Ole could almost hear her smile.

And how wonderful it felt to laugh once again.

AFTER SEVERAL DAYS OF EMOTIONAL UNWINDING, on Saturday evening Ole and Gretta accepted an invitation to supper at the Andersons' home.

As they prepared to leave for the evening, Gretta looked around their parlor as if something was amiss. "I don't know why I'm so curious about their place," she said. "It's not as if we don't have a nice enough home of our own."

Ole followed her gaze from wallpaper to hardwood, from the pictures on the walls to the settees to the piano. "You have done an amazing job of turning our house into a cozy home. But they have some nice extras like a sky window. Maybe we should think about building one over our staircase, too."

She ran a couple of fingers through the folds of her dress. "Does this look okay? Not too dowdy?"

"Why are you fretting? Dorothy Anderson can't hold a candle to you. You get too dressed up and you'll intimidate her."

Gretta laughed. "I know I'm being silly. It's just that they're such nice people, and I would love it if we could become closer friends. Spend Saturday evenings playing canasta with them. Who knows? Maybe even go on a trip together every now and then."

He held open the door. "We'd better get going." Guiding her along by the small of her back, they trudged up the road and around the bend. "It'll be good for you to have a new friend close by," he said. "Besides, the better you get to know them, the more you'll see they're average joes, just like the rest of us."

"Oliver Harrington, you of all people are anything but average."

He flashed on his last trek to the Anderson home—that nervous display of tomfoolery down that incline.

Want to bet?

What if Herb and Dorothy compared notes afterward? Ole wondered. They undoubtedly did. What kind of halfwit shows up at a neighbor's home only to instruct the hubby to bring his wife some potatoes for supper? And then to walk away not bothering to haul away his own sack? But what could Ole do about it now? The past is dead. Why not leave it at that? And if the Andersons asked questions, he needed to own up to the truth even if it was humiliating.

Cursedly humiliating.

At least that would be honorable.

When they arrived, the Andersons welcomed them as good-naturedly as Ole had hoped and more. Surprisingly though their house boasted a number of interesting amenities, it lacked a certain charm. Didn't feel homey. But what it lacked in warmth, Herb made up in hospitality. Well read, well traveled, ambitious, and an avid sportsman, conversation with him flowed easily as minutes cascaded into hours.

During supper, Ole found it difficult to take his eyes off of Gretta. For all of her fretting, not only did she light up the room with her poise, charisma, and good looks, her cooking left Dorothy's markedly wanting. He chewed on a hunk of roast beef for the better part of several minutes before finally choking it down. He didn't know if lumpy was the right word, but the potatoes were laden with uncooked chunks of something or other. And the word tart took on new meaning as he indulged his first forkful of lemon meringue pie, his salivary glands opening like a spigot.

After playing a serious game of rummy, Ole said, "Herb, I can't get that sky light of yours out of my mind. Our staircase is begging for one. Was it constructed when your house was built or did you put in afterward?"

"Afterward."

He perked up. "That a fact? Mind sharing the name of your contractor?"

"You're looking at him."

"No!"

"Why don't we take a trip down to the cellar. I'd like to show you my shop … do you mind, ladies?"

While Dorothy said, "Not at all," Gretta's eyes widened with concern.

"It's getting late," she said. "Maybe you could do that the next time we come."

Ole gave her a quit peck and an unsure grin. "Be back in a few minutes."

"But—"

This was something he needed to do. "Be right back," he insisted.

As Herb and he rounded the corner to the cellar under a moonlit sky, Ole let Herb take the lead. He made a point of focusing on what Herb was saying rather than on any anxiety about the journey. Pleased with himself that his confidence had grown, about halfway down the ramp, he remembered the last time he descended it. It had felt more like a gangplank.

"A what?" Herb said.

Ole hesitated. Had he actually blurted that word out loud? "Claustrophobia."

"Ohh," Herb said. Was that sympathy in his tone? "That can't be a distant past." He pushed open the door and snapped on a light. "Are you okay now?"

"Your walking in front of me, obstructing the view, seemed to help some. I guess having the courage to admit how witless I feel about it eases the fear, too." He looked around the dim quarters searching for windows, high and small though they were, while at the same time seizing the doorjamb with a death grip. To his surprise, it felt rock solid to the touch. "Breathing's still a little shallow, but nothing I can't handle."

Herb gave Ole a curious look. "How'd you make so much progress so fast? That's kind of tough, isn't it?"

"Some things a man needs to let go of and claustrophobia is one of them."

Herb shook his head. "Let go?"

Finding it odd that the man didn't seem to want to let the subject go, Ole said, "That's right. I'm still anxious, but it's getting easier."

"That's why I had to carry the potatoes over to your place for you?"

"Yes. Thanks, by the way."

Herb's chuckle appeared nervous. "Want to hear a good one?" he said. "Your wife ... when I carried that sack down to your basement, I think she may have thought I was going to have a heart attack because I was so out of shape. Nothing could have been further from the truth." He lifted a brow. "Your staircase? It's steep alright, but it's also open. You can see straight through the thing."

"I'm afraid I don't understand," Ole said.

"How do I spell this out? I didn't have any problems going down, but climbing back up, I was too embarrassed to tell your wife I felt like I was going to pass out."

"You mean to tell me ..."

"Crazy fear of heights."

When those words finally sank in, Ole and Herb burst into laughter. They would be friends. How could they not? They were bonded by ridiculous fear.

Fear that was in the process of dismantling.

"Been tortured since I was a kid," Herb said. "Crawled up on the roof of a shed one day thinking I was smart. A crow swept in low, squawking. Like it was aiming for me or something. Lost my balance. I got lucky. A bush stopped my fall. Got a few scrapes and bruises. I didn't get hurt bad, but the crazy thing is, I've been bothered by it ever since. Seems to get worse with time. How about you?"

"I'm not sure if this caused the fear, but one day I decided I wanted to play grownup. Snuck a cigarette out of my father's smoking jacket," Ole said, "that and a box of matches. I slunk out to the shed. After a couple of puffs, I heard the gardener tromping around outside the door. Whistling. Snipping. Banging.

"I hid behind an empty crate. Waited him out. The gardener never did come in. But when the latch dropped and I heard him walk away, I panicked. It was black as pitch. No windows. And it was hotter than blazes. I remember crouching down by the floor where it was cooler and kept my head down, scared to death I'd suffocate in the place. Couldn't keep from hyperventilating."

The memory was still so strong, Ole felt as if he was still back in that dark shed. Mysterious creatures lurking about. Assaulting creatures. He could still feel the rigid tail of that rat striking his back and hear that incessant scratching. Claws flitting across dusty floorboards. Wings flittering against the ceiling, thumping against it, wings wanting desperately to push through the rafters, to break free. He couldn't figure out what it was at the time. A trapped bird? A rabid bat maybe? He had been miserable in the stifling heat. Drenched in perspiration. Inhaling kerosene fumes in tight quarters.

Taking courage.

He remembered thinking that if he knew what was in there, he'd calm down. He felt around and found the matches.

Lit one.

Too close to an oilcloth.

"The shed caught fire."

"You mean to tell me ..."

Yes, I mean to tell you. "I crawled for the door, trying to yell, but no words would come out. The next thing I remember was hearing Englishman—"

"Englishman?"

"My dog. He barked and the door flew open. I looked up and there stood my father. He was frantic. Carried me into the house."

"And the shed?"

"Burned to the ground."

"Did he ever let you forget it?"

Ole shook his head. "Never."

"Do you smoke now?"

"A cigar every now and then ... but no cigarettes."

Never a cigarette.

CHAPTER TWENTY-SEVEN

M abel's eyes glistened. She seized Ole's hand and drew him into her kitchen. "Mr. Harrington," she said, "you are far and away the bravest man I've ever had the privilege of knowing. I can't thank you enough for all you've done."

His gaze swept toward the linoleum where he visualized the basement tunneled beneath them. Brave? Not yet, but I'm getting there. "No thanks necessary. Any word about Jack?"

"You mean the man whose life you saved? I still can't believe you singlehandedly took on those two killers. You didn't shy away, and you weren't even armed."

Keep the compliments coming, Mrs. Harding. Keep them coming.

"He called this morning," she said. "Admitted how he messed up. Asked again for another chance. Wants to come home. Gave me his word he'd change."

"And you said?"

"Not on your life."

"What about that other woman?"

"There never was another woman, or so he says. He made her up. Said that was the most convincing way he could think of to get me to grant him a quick divorce. He was in so deep, he needed to get at my money. He's wronged me from the day he married me."

"What about his alleged death?"

"Oh, that," she said. "Case of mistaken identity. Seems they had a meeting in Jack's room the night before. How do I say this delicately? Jack's friend was eliminated, but Jack got lucky. He only got kidnapped. They decided he was worth far more alive than dead."

"And Jack was spared because of you?"

She nodded. "The next morning a maid found the body in Jack's room and management merely assumed it was his."

"I wonder if he'll be able to stay clean now."

Mabel drew back. "If that doesn't give him the cure, nothing will."

"What about the thugs? Think they'll be back?"

"I doubt it. If it's money they're after, they'll probably collect from someone closer to within hit range."

How Ole wanted to believe that … for Mabel's sake. "Any idea what Jack will do for a livelihood now?"

"He used to dabble with painting," she said. "He'll probably take it up again."

Houses? Somehow that didn't seem to fit the man's image. "What kind of painting?"

"Portrait art. Landscapes. That sort of thing. Come with me." She turned and headed toward a door that appeared to lead down to her basement.

Ole's knees wobbled. Far and away the bravest man she'd ever had the privilege of knowing? No, but he wanted to be. He had done reasonably well going down into the Andersons' basement. And he had been doing lots of practicing. But why push it?

"Got something I want you to see." She drew open the door and snapped on a light, which illuminated a staircase that dropped off into the bowels of Hades. "Follow me."

Now what am I going to do? he wondered. He wasn't in the mood to take on another challenge. Not today. But … go ahead. Get it over with, he told himself. Inhale. Now let it out. Keep breathing. Feel your feet on solid ground. It's not like you haven't done this many times before. This structure is sound. The steps are sound. Focus on faith, not fear. Keep moving. As he neared the door, he concentrated harder.

Relax. Let go.

This as an adventure.

Some adventure.

No, this might be interesting.

Mabel descended the stairs appearing lost in a world free of care and surprisingly more spry, as if she'd gotten a second wind.

Ole lifted a hand to the railing. Let go of pride. Don't let that monster hold you back. "You'll have to forgive me, Mabel," he finally admitted. "In the past, basements have made me feel claustro … closed in."

"This one won't," she said.

He wasn't sure if it was his candidness or her confidence, but to his surprise, his feet picked up momentum, rhythmically hitting the steps one at a time. As they neared the bottom, he felt unexpectedly comfortable. When his shoe touched the floor, he looked up, amazed. The basement, the full length and width of the house, cut into a hill, the far wall lined with windows with a view looking out onto the lake.

An open basement.

He flashed on Gretta's request for a new home with a wall of windows in its basement. Maybe her idea wasn't so bad after all—a new home and a new beginning with no closed-in basement and no bad memories.

Mabel then led them on to Jack's artist's table in the center of the room. "This is where he always did his painting." She held up a drawing. "The man definitely has talent. I'm sure he'll do fine."

"What about the divorce?"

"He'll give it to me now. How could he not?" She then picked up a painting of a quaint villa. "And this is what I wanted you to see. Isn't it beautiful? It's in Monte Carlo," she said, sounding as if she were singing. "I've wanted to go there since I can remember, and now I'm planning my trip."

"But what about—"

She grinned full on. "Saw the doctor this morning. Seems I'm responding to treatment unusually well. Long story short, I'm not going to die, at least not yet ... not if I can help it."

CHAPTER TWENTY-EIGHT

MID JANUARY 1917

Ole drew his chair to the table. Sniffing the warm cinnamon rolls, his spirits soared. Another grand breakfast—two eggs over easy, four thick strips of bacon, and a steamy cup of black coffee. After a week of eating like royalty, he couldn't help wondering. What was happening to Gretta lately? Had she run out of oatmeal?

Though not a man to carry a brown bag, as he headed off to Addison & Crowley, she slipped him one then kissed her finger and lightly touched it to his cheek. At noon he closed himself in his office where he dined alone. A ham and cheese sandwich slathered with mustard … wrapped in pink linen? He needed to talk to Gretta about that. And a slice of blueberry pie.

At half past five, he lingered in the Model T, staring at the house. Which Gretta would greet him this evening? The one he'd married who'd given him more happiness than a man deserved? The one submerged in a sporadic world of grieving? Or this strange new creature filled with surprises—surprises he was rather beginning to enjoy?

To his amazement … none of them.

No Gretta to greet him at all.

No supper on the stove.

He found her in the living room, the epitome of contentment, knitting what appeared to be a blanket.

She looked up. "You're home already?"

That was an unusual thing to say. "It's half past five."

She glanced at the clock. "Oh yes, I guess it is." Getting up, she swept past him. "I'd better get supper on the stove."

"What? No hug? No kiss hello?"

"Why don't you go out for a walk? It'll be ready by the time you get back."

Taken aback by her nonchalant behavior, he followed her into the kitchen like a neglected puppy after its master. "I was hoping we could take a walk together after supper."

"I think I'd rather stay inside tonight if you don't mind."

He dutifully punched his arms through the sleeves of his coat, drew on gloves and a pair of overshoes then hesitated at the door, briefly studying her. A moment later, he strolled across the road and along the perimeter of the lake assimilating his thoughts in the quiet of night. It was one thing for him to withdraw from Gretta, which he found necessary to do during times of crisis, times when he needed to think, but for her to withdraw from him? What happened? That hurt.

Around the bend, a fallen log blocked the meandering path. He stopped, rested a foot on it, and gazed out over the frozen water. It was beautiful out here. God's world. So peaceful.

Behind him in snow-covered brush a twig snapped. Curious, he glanced back. A deer and its fawn were grazing on dry foliage. His eyes lingered on the fawn while his mind fought the parenthood it represented. For a brief moment it was as though Gretta's pleasant attitude helped him to not care as much. Yet it was one thing to make peace with tight spaces. That he was doing with all of his being. But to make peace with having no offspring? Now that was something quite different.

Though he found it difficult to take his eyes off the fawn, he looked up. Please don't require that of me. He then gazed out over the frozen lake and grieved.

But if You must, You are the potter, and I am the clay. And clay molds to the potter's wishes, not the other way around.

His stomach let loose a growl. He needed to get home. Find something to nibble on until supper was ready. After all, he hadn't eaten a bite since the lunch hour. That sandwich wrapped in …

His heart thumped.

No!

Gretta couldn't be with child. Not this soon. They couldn't risk losing another one. She needed more time. He needed more time.

Or had she reconsidered adopting? Now that was a possibility.

He hurried home, though by the time he reached the porch, his appetite had subsided. All through supper, Gretta remained quiet. He left her to her thoughts sensing it would be premature to draw her out.

Later after doing dishes, she finally broke silence. "Would you mind putting a few logs on the fire?" she said then returned to knitting … that small yellow blanket.

While stoking the fire, he kept a curious eye on her. He then eased onto the rocking chair and rocked slowly back and forth for a few thoughtful minutes. His curiosity pushing him over the edge, he stopped rocking. "You haven't been yourself this entire evening."

She hesitated. "I'm not sure what to say or how to say it."

"Spit it out," he said. "It's not like you to act like this. I'm beginning to worry."

She set her knitting aside and peered over her glasses. "What color napkin have I been wrapping your sandwiches in, or haven't you noticed?"

Ho-oh. "Pink."

"Didn't you find that rather effeminate?"

"Yes, but I didn't want to say anything." I still don't.

"And what kind of pie have I been slipping into your lunch bag lately?"

"Blue ... do you mean to tell me?"

She grinned a confident grin. "My abdomen is filling out, Ole."

"You mean?"

"It's different this time ... my symptoms." Though her brow furrowed, her eyes continued to sparkle. "No nausea. Do you think that could be a good sign?"

"I don't know." He wanted to take the plunge and be happy, but the news gave him pause. "You're sure about this? You aren't just putting on a little weight?"

Her smile grew broader if that was possible. "I'm sure. This time I plan to spend all of my time in bed if that's what it's going to take. We will have this child, Ole. I won't disappoint you again. That's a promise."

CHAPTER TWENTY-NINE

For the next number of days, Ole continued to make a habit of trekking down the basement steps then back up again. Tonight was no different. With every challenging step, he focused on thoughts of faith, relinquishing the fearful ones, fleeting though they were becoming. After several successful attempts, his confidence swelled. He could now make it to the basement floor, over to the canned goods, and back up the stairs again without incident.

So he went back down.

At the bottom of the stairs, he ventured toward the woodpile. In a far corner sat the baby carriage precisely where Gretta had placed it some months back. Something about it seemed magnetic, as if drawing him to it. Though feeling closed in, he needed to build endurance, so he tugged a handkerchief from a back pocket, knelt on a knee, and slowly wiped away an accumulation of dust.

As he did, memories niggled at him, memories that refused to release their grip, memories that drew him off again to a world far away. He recalled the letter he had received from his father informing him that he'd lost his wife and son in a carriage accident. He recalled the devastation that overwhelmed him at the time. To this day it still felt real and raw. He'd never thought it possible to feel such an all-encompassing emotional pain. But he had.

He wiped clean the spokes and recalled the last time he'd seen Amelia. Her recounting of Emily's demise. Of his son's demise. He recalled how he'd felt as he walked into her flat. Tortured by the sight of that baby carriage sitting in an alcove on the way through to her kitchen. Tortured by the memory of what sounded like a baby's brief whimper. Then retracing his steps back through Amelia's living room on his way out. Tortured by the memory of that baby carriage that had been there and then magically disappeared. Questioning himself. Fearing he may have gone mad.

He got up and after stuffing the handkerchief back in a pocket, he thoughtfully made his way back to the steps. But had he gone mad? Was he onto something after all? Could that cry have been Olivia's? Could he have been that close, in touching distance, to his one and only living child? How he would have loved to have seen her cooing in her crib. To have felt her warm and delicate in his arms. No. Amelia did not possesses the ability to be so cruel. She wouldn't have kept his little girl from him.

Or did she?

Was that the missing piece of the puzzle? Amelia having stolen Olivia from him? If so, she must have had an awfully good reason. But that's impossible. No reason could be that viable. Nothing made sense.

Put this behind you, Ole.

He scaled the last couple of steps. "Gretta, do we have any sketching paper?"

"I think so. In my sewing room. What do you want it for?"

"Thought I'd sketch a prototype."

"Of?"

"A rocking horse."

"For the baby?"

Ole grinned. "For our son when he's old enough to ride."

"You mean for our daughter. Don't tell me you're thinking of whittling one."

"Need something to do while you knit. Gets a little lonely for a man getting only a part of his bride's attention."

"You have all of my attention. Always." She handed him *The Amber Leaf Tribune.* "You haven't opened this yet today."

Oh, but I did. Read it from cover to cover at the office. As usual. "Anything worth reading?" he said.

"It's all about the war." Her tone took on an edge. "All those soldiers killed. What's this world coming to? Each of those men had a family. A wife. A girlfriend. Children. Parents. Brothers. Sisters. I can't get the horror out of my head," she said. "Millions of people already dead. I don't want to imagine the suffering. And whatever for?"

He lowered onto the sofa beside her. "Too bad war needs to be such a necessary evil." A wave of disappointment fluttering through him, he gave her a sidelong glance. "Don't trust the reporting."

"Why not?"

"Newspapers are charged with keeping up the morale. Truth gets out about how brutal battles are, what a soldier's chances of survival are out there on the front, who would bother to sign up?"

She looked at Ole as if stunned. "If we do get drawn in … or maybe I should say when … I don't know how much help I'll be to the Red Cross when our baby comes."

"Don't borrow problems from the future, dear." Those will come soon enough.

"But we need to prepare for it. If President Wilson declares war, they could start conscription, couldn't they? Didn't they do that during the Civil War?"

"That they did."

"What if you got called up?" Tears welled. "I'd be devastated. I could never sit back and do nothing, not with you out there risking your life, too."

"Enough of that talk," he said. "How are you feeling these days? You don't mention much about it."

"I'm doing fine," she said. "Can't believe I haven't gotten morning sickness yet."

He found her statement more troubling than curious. "What does the doctor say about that?"

Her cheeks flushed a soft shade of pink. "I haven't seen him."

"Do you mean to tell me …"

She grinned. "Relax. I have an appointment first thing come Monday morning."

"How could you not …"

After a slight hesitation, she drew his hand to her abdomen and held it there. "Feel my tummy. Pregnant is pregnant. I wanted to make sure before I bothered him."

"You're sure you're feeling fine?" Ole said.

"Never felt better."

"How about the kicking? Have you felt any of that yet?"

"Nope," she said nonchalantly, "but I'm sure I will any day now."

He fixed his eyes on nothing in particular.

How he wanted to believe her.

OLE PICKED UP A DECENT-SIZED BLOCK of wood and carving tools from the shed. Meanwhile, Gretta sorted through old patterns and a supply of unused fabric then smoothed out a swathe of fine wool. "What do you think of this material, Ole? Do you like it?"

He took a closer look. "What color is that?"

"Midnight blue. Thought I'd sew myself another maternity dress."

"I'm sure it will be fine."

"Fine?"

Wrong thing to say. He laughed. "I meant beautiful."

She eyed the beginnings of his project. "What's that for?"

"Thought I'd start whittling that rocking horse."

"Wanting to exercise your artistic bent, are you?"

I don't know that I have one. "All you do is carve off the parts of wood that don't belong there."

"Won't that be a little small for our toddler to rock on?"

"This is a prototype."

Was that a laugh Gretta held back? She disappeared into the sewing room while Ole finished tracing a pattern onto the block. He studied it from various angles. Good job! And then he chipped away, which was even more fun until he whittled too much off the nose. Nothing to worry about. I'll make a smaller prototype, he decided. But then he chipped too much off an ear. And a hoof. At the sound of Gretta's footsteps, he quickly slipped a cloth over his handiwork and cleaned up the table. After enjoying a cup of hot chocolate, she returned to the sewing room and he to his sculpture. Late in the evening, she snuck up from behind.

"You've changed your mind, I see," she said. "You're carving a dog instead. It's kind of cute."

"It isn't a dog. It's a horse. I'm just not done with it yet."

Ho-oh! Here comes that I-love-you-more-than-life-itself-but-you're-really-doing-a-dumb-thing kiss atop the head. "It's that bad?" he said.

She squeezed his shoulders. "Why don't we buy one instead? This is an awfully advanced project for someone who doesn't have the time to hone his skill. I know you have it in you, but I hate to see you get discouraged."

He stretched his neck to ensure Gretta's attention and with a distinct edge said, "I suppose you'll be coveting my honest assessment of the dress you're so painstakingly sewing, too."

She smirked and gave him another reassuring kiss. "That won't be necessary. It's looking not too bad. But you must remember I've been sewing since I was little."

By late Saturday morning, Ole had succeeded in whittling the prototype from a rocking horse to a dog to what ended up resembling a rodent. He plucked a new hunk of wood out of the woodpile and headed out to Deacon's.

Deacon eyed the wood curiously.

"I was hoping I could use your talents as a whittler," Ole said.

"What are you wanting to carve?"

"A rocking horse."

Deacon hesitated. "How big?"

"Big enough for a toddler to have a heyday."

"A toddler? I think I can help with that," he said as if needing though not wanting to draw Ole out. "Let's take a trip to the shed. I'm sure I can find a bigger block of wood for us to work with."

As they walked along, Ole gazed out at the open field. Only too soon the animals would be put out to pasture again after having been barn bound for the duration of winter, and the fields would once again emerge from a blanket of snow only to repeat sowing and reaping come spring—and in the summer Ole's own child would make entry into this remarkable cycle called life.

Deacon stopped dead in his tracks and Ole accidentally bumped into him. "Sorry. Guess I wasn't paying attention."

"Why a rocking horse?" Deacon said.

Ole walked on ahead, drew open the shed door, and gave Deacon the look.

"You're having another baby?"

"Due in July."

"Due in July," Deacon repeated, concern evident in a following lack of response, that disparaging lack of response that drains a soul of hope.

Why should the prospect of having a child be a dream shrouded with the dross of doubt?

CHAPTER THIRTY

O ver the noon hour, Ole stepped inside the jewelry store. "Is my watch ready?"

The affable man with bushy brows standing behind the counter beamed. "Yes, sir, it certainly is."

"I don't know what I was thinking when I wound it too tight. I guess I wasn't …" An elegant bronze music box topped with miniature baby booties caught Ole's eye. "Say, what's this?" He picked it up. "May I?"

"Help yourself," the clerk said.

Ole drew open the lid and his skin prickled as the most beautiful rendition of Brahm's Lullaby poured forth from the small box. "Oh my." He set it back on the counter. Gretta should be home from the doctor's office about now. What better timing than to present her with a perfect gift when he arrived home this evening. "How much … no. What does that matter?" He broke into a full-on grin. "I'll take it. Can it be gift wrapped?"

Within the hour he stepped into the office with the delicate package in hand, his heart bursting with joy. As he crossed the floor, however, a stenographer called out, wildly waving him down.

"Mr. Harrington? Mr. Harrington?" she said, "You've got an urgent telephone call."

"From?"

Her face drained of color. "The hospital, sir."

"The hosp—" Repeating a mere portion of the word, he dashed into his office, slamming the door behind him. He plucked up the receiver. "Harrington here. Yes?" He held the receiver out in disbelief then drew it close again and listened. "When? But that's not possible. She left for the doctor's office early this morning, not the hospital. Okay, okay. Yes, you definitely have my permission to operate. I'm on my way."

Ole slammed down the receiver then stared at the telephone, stunned. The call had to be a grievous joke, yet it couldn't be. No doctor would be that unkind. Heart thumping. Shallow breathing. Thoughts racing. Gretta was all right. She had to be all right. She was certainly fine when he left home this morning. A split moment later, he stormed out of the office. Tires fishtailed on ice as he tore out onto the open road. When a pedestrian at a crosswalk jumped back to clear out of the way of his speeding Model T, he forced himself to slow down, but not by much. A forever few minutes later he pulled up sharp in front of the hospital, got out, and plowed through the front door. "My wife's in surgery. Where do I go?"

The attendant at the desk indicated the direction with a pointer finger. "Down the hall and to the right."

The cramped room had no windows. But what did it matter? Though panic was panic, small places certainly didn't hold a candle to the ravages of surgery. At the moment there wasn't a hole too small. All that mattered was Gretta. Their child. But he didn't want to think about Gretta. He didn't want to think about their baby. Doing so meant facing the reason she was here. In a cold operating room. Under a colder knife.

After what seemed hours, he jumped when the doctor peered in. "I didn't mean to startle you, Mr. Harrington," he said.

Ole got up and joined him in the hallway. "How is she?"

"She's recovering now. We'll let you know the moment you can see her … I'm afraid she's gone through quite a lot. When she stopped by my office this morning," he muttered softly, "I was hard-pressed to find a pulse."

"Do you mean …"

"What I'm trying to say is that she never was with child."

"But …"

The doctor looked as sad as Ole felt. "Like I told you on the phone, Mr. Harrington," he said, "she had a tumor … the size of a grapefruit."

"A tumor," he repeated. His head spinning, he looked off, paralyzed with shock. It felt surreal saying that word. He had said it, hadn't he? Would he awaken to find this nothing more than a bad dream? No, not a bad dream. A nightmare. This was one time he preferred a nightmare to reality.

"I'm sure she'll be fine," the doctor said. "But it may take some time."

"Will she be able to … bear more children?"

The doctor gave his head a sad shake. "I'm afraid that won't be possible. I couldn't be more sorry."

Ole's knees beginning to buckle, the doctor said, "Nurse? We need a chair here. Quickly, please." The doctor grasped Ole's elbow until he could lower onto the folding chair. "Will you be okay, Mr. Harrington?"

"Yes," he said with his words, but could not bring himself to look the man in the eye.

Now if only he could face his beloved Gretta.

When they finally placed her in a ward, Ole paused at the door. There she lay. All tucked in white. Pale as the bedding spread across her weak and scarred body. He leaned over the bed and lightly ran his lips across her cheek. "Gretta?"

She slowly opened her eyes, which immediately pooled with tears. "Ole—"

"Are you okay?" he said, the ache in his throat palpable.

She stared off as if her very life had been stripped away. Gratefully, it hadn't. But the life of a precious, precious child that in the end hadn't existed?

The only sound for the longest while was that of a patient who moaned in the next bed. During Gretta's last miscarriage when a patient moaned, Ole had felt the need to get away. This time he only cared about his precious wife's grief, his own grief, and had no emotion to spare.

He sat in a stupor inhaling the antiseptic smell of alcohol. Staring at the austere environment. Feeling a cool breeze whenever a nurse passed by. Forcing the reason for Gretta's hospitalization as far from his psyche as possible. Listening to her whimpering. Allowing her all the time she needed to feel the hurt.

Somehow feeling pain seemed far better than feeling nothing at all.

CHAPTER THIRTY-ONE

Ole plucked the envelope off the table. "This came today?" he said, stunned at his own response, stunned at how quickly he could vacillate from anxiously anticipating another letter from Olivia to feeling violated by having received it.

Gretta stepped up from behind.

"I'm not sure I want to read it," he said, feeling disappointed to the bone. "She's a viper. Setting me up. Making me think she was my very own. Why couldn't she just tell me the truth? Why misrepresent herself? I wouldn't have cared that she was adopted. I just needed her to be honest."

"That's your grief talking, Ole. You will need her, adopted or not, when we get to the other side of this."

He turned to Gretta with a heart filled with concern. "What about your grief, Gretta? How can you be so strong?"

"I'm not. Trust me, every time you walk out that door I cry until I can't cry any more. I'm still working that out of my system … now go ahead," she said. "Open the letter. Find out what she has to say. I'll busy myself in the parlor while you read."

As she walked away, Ole pulled up a chair and sat for a moment, preparing himself, though for what he had no idea, then reluctantly sliced open the envelope.

31 January

Dearest Sir,

How wonderful to receive your kind letter. It was as though I could hear your voice as I read the words you so eloquently penned. I hope with all my heart that one day soon we will both find this dream we are living a striking reality.

I understand my Great Uncle Deacon has inquired of me. As you undoubtedly know, he corresponds rather infrequently with a former neighbor who lives a stone's throw from my flat. Unfortunately, that unwitting acquaintance subsequently passed on incorrect information about my having been adopted, which I feel compelled to correct.

Ole's eyes widened as he reread that last sentence. With a tremor in his voice, he shouted, "Gretta? I think you'd better come in here."

She rushed back into the kitchen.

"You may have been right. Take a look at this. Read along with me."

"What?"

Resting her hand on his shoulder, she leaned in. He reached up, cupped his hand on hers, and together they read.

My grandmother was never one given to telling tales. To her good credit, she frowned on that sort of thing. The only untruth I ever detected was about you. In revisiting that assumption, however, that is also suspect in that the deception was merely inferred. You see, by what was left unsaid, I merely assumed we'd lost you on the battlefield. But in thinking back, I don't recall my grandmother having stated that directly.

With the pain of losing my mother on the day of my birth and no father figure about, my grandmum would lose patience with those who callously inquired about my heritage as though it was their right. Then one day after having been asked about my parentage one too many times, she retorted in jest that I'd been adopted, and for some rather odd reason, that word seemed to stick. It was as though I'd been branded, and unintentionally so. I do hope you find this explanation plausible. I have found that nothing can be more freeing than the truth.

You asked for more information to help us sort through our confusion. Perhaps it would be helpful for you to know that I continue to live in the same flat that my grandmother called home for the better part of her life. A number of neighbors have gone on to their final resting places, however, Harry and Elizabeth still live in the door next and the Fletchers in the flat above. Other than having put on a little added weight and a few extra wrinkles here and there, they all pretty much remain unchanged. Harry still has that biting humor, but we love him just the same.

According to our neighbors, Grandmum said you had visited our flat a good number of times when my mother was still living and stopped by once after her demise. But then you undoubtedly determined where I live by my post address.

War news continues to be daunting. I wish for you that your country continues to stay out of the conflict. We've lost a dreadful number of our brave young men. As you know, we've also lost a number of civilians with bombs dropping on our homeland and ships getting sunk out on the high seas. I pray daily for a quick end to these unusually perilous times.

It is getting quite late and I am feeling most tired, actually, so

I shall close. I must tell you, however, that the mere privilege of corresponding with you fills my heart to overflowing.

I so look forward to hearing from you once again.

Yours most sincerely,

Olivia

Ole blew out a breath. As Gretta stood quiet and stunned, he folded the letter and gently tucked it back in its envelope. It penetrated him to the core. Not knowing what else to do, he got up and strolled into his study where he gently slipped the letter between the hallowed pages of the family Bible.

Then in the wee hours of morning, he awakened with a start, his mind racing uncontrollably as that old memory once again tortured him.

That afternoon long ago at Amelia De Haven's flat.

That crib in the alcove as he entered.

The start of a baby's cry.

Then nothing.

Remembering back, Amelia had excused herself when he first arrived, leaving the kitchen for a short window of time without explanation. Why? She then returned and prepared a pot of tea. Ole never thought to question it, to question her. Surely Amelia didn't have it in her to be so cold as to …

Pull yourself together, Ole. You're trying too hard again, hoping for the impossible.

CHAPTER THIRTY-TWO

Ole listened into the quiet to the familiar sounds at Addison & Crowley—the clock wearing down, desk doors grating closed, footsteps pattering out the door. In past weeks, along with those sounds had come a feeling of dread, which often grew stronger at the close of a Friday afternoon.

But not today.

He thought of Olivia's letter and his heart swelled.

When he arrived home, Gretta was frittering about the kitchen, humming.

"How do you do it?" he said. "After everything ... do I need to worry about you?"

She pecked him lightly on the cheek then busied herself at the stove, scooping a dollop of butter into a skillet and stirring as it hissed. "I'm okay, Ole."

Though she sounded as if she believed herself, he wasn't convinced. "Don't you need to grieve more? Get it all out of your system?"

"I know it may sound strange, "she said, "but I think in the end the tumor might have been a gift." She gave him a confident look. "And don't gape at me like that. I'm not holding onto false hope any more. I think I'm finally able to let go."

"But what about that child we needed to have?"

"Adoption isn't out of the question. I'm at peace with it now." She then spooned a bowl of sliced onions into the skillet and continued stirring, the aroma filling the kitchen the way her presence filled a room. "I think we should wait a while, though."

"See how things turn out with Olivia first?"

"Absolutely," she said.

Later that evening after Gretta crawled into bed, Ole padded back to his office and drew the music box from a lower desk drawer. Staring at it as if it were candy for the eyes, he ran a loving finger across the baby booties positioned on top. He hadn't been able to bring himself to return the box to the jeweler's. That would have admitted defeat. Neither did he have the heart to present it to Gretta. Doing so lacked compassion.

He thought of the possibility of Olivia being his daughter. Although it seemed a dream that surpassed imagining, avoiding that reality would do nothing to change it. Perhaps if he did take courage and sought hard for the truth, he would be free to accept his fate. He and Gretta could then move on with adopting yet another child.

As he lifted the lid on the music box, it was as though he felt the brush of angels' wings as Brahm's Lullaby filled the air once again with tinkling music. It hurt so good to hear it.

But was Olivia alive at this point? He mustn't wait too long. She could all too easily become a casualty of war. He squeezed the painful thought from his mind then once again drew out a sheet of parchment and in flickering lantern light laid pen to paper.

23 February

My dearest Olivia,

I am in receipt of your previous post. It continues to be a joy to hear from you. I trust this letter finds you happy and well and the dreadful war receding from your doorstep. When last I was in England, I had just returned from Sudan where I experienced the savagery of warfare, an understanding it would be preferable for no man to endure. Do know that my heart continues to go out to you during this most perilous time.

On a more pleasant note, here in Amber Leaf spring looms around the corner. We've had a rather white winter this year. Our home overlooks Fountain Lake, which continues to be frozen over. It's been awe-inspiring gazing out at the winter wonderland. But we also look forward to seeing blue waters once again, colorful blossoms, and trees thick with leaves. We are most fortunate that our great state of Minnesota is a haven for sportsmen offering fishing, hunting, boating, and a myriad of outdoor activities. Lest I leave you with the impression that we live in a blissful paradise, we do experience harsh weather fluctuations such as extreme hot and cold temperatures along with high humidity and powerful storms. But those do lend themselves to fascination in their own right.

And now the reason for this letter. As you can imagine, I continue to wrestle with the awkwardness of our situation. Though I've found comfort in your explanation of your alleged adoption, which did appear quite plausible, I am certain you understand how I might also feel a conflicting need to be prudent to a fault. Ours is not a situation I choose to view lightly.

As I am certain you also understand, being an attorney, I deal with facts. Perhaps truth might be a more fitting word. Though it might appear impolite, please understand my motivations as I respectfully request a photograph of yourself along with proof of your place and date of birth. I submit herewith for your satisfaction as well a most recent photograph of myself.

Perhaps any future correspondence you might forward to me directly c/o Addison & Crowley, Amber Leaf, Minnesota, USA. My bride retrieves our mail from the post office only periodically whereas at the office I receive it on a daily basis.

I very much look forward to receiving your next post.

Until then I remain, yours most sincerely,

Oliver M. Harrington

He reread the letter several times before folding it and stuffing it in an envelope. As he did, an inkling of relief seemed to fight a smidgeon of hope too stubborn to let go.

CHAPTER THIRTY-THREE

Boss straddled the chair with shoes propped on the corner of his desk. If he leaned back farther, he'd meet with the floor, which had happened in the past. Hands splayed across his middle, he busily twiddled his thumbs.

"You wanted to see me, sir?" Ole said as he pulled up a chair.

"That I did, Harrington. Seems some sorry soul has made it a habit of rifling through my daily paper." He lifted a brow as if for effect. "Makes a man feel rather violated."

"Sir?"

He looked down the bridge of his nose and eyed the tips of his shoes as if deciding whether or not they needed a shine. "Always seems to leave a page or two slightly off kilter when he nudges the thing back together."

"He, sir?"

"No." Boss carefully drew his legs down as if to avoid another mishap, flipped open a cigar box, pulled out a cheroot, sniffed the thing, and then slowly peeled off the cellophane. "You," he said. "You don't get the newspaper at home? Can't afford it? Hinting for a raise, are you?"

"We get it at home."

"Yet you read it here. Every day." Boss bit the tip off the cigar and absently discarded it. "Must be hiding something from your bride. Now what could that possibly be?"

"Sir?"

"Let go of the innocence, Harrington." Boss carefully balanced the cigar on the edge of his ashtray. "Hearing the sound of distant drums, are you? That haunting sound of bugles blowing?"

Why did those poignant words need to reach into Ole's heart like an invisible fist and squeeze the life out of it? "Not that I would admit to, sir."

"Stop with the sir stuff. That's not your style."

Ole finally broke a half smile.

"Leaders come a dime a dozen," Boss said. "Sure they take up the baton, but the majority do it for all the wrong reasons—ego, power, a base need to prove themselves even if it is at the expense of others.

"But then there are the true leaders. They're the one in a million. They have a gift, you see. They're purely motivated. Have nothing to prove. Thorough thinkers. Targeted thinkers. They consider all their options before advancing. They're not selfish. They go for the win-win."

"Why are you saying this?"

"It's pretty clear, wouldn't you say?" Boss's chair squeaked as he sat back again. "The way I have it figured, a man with your background must have a hard time reading the paper these days. All that unnecessary carnage. Gallipoli. The Battle of the Somme. War of attrition out on the Western Front. Germans advancing too far too fast trying to drive the Brits out of France."

"You don't need me for this conversation, do you?" Ole said.

"Not really." Boss plucked up the cigar and lightly tapped the tip against the ashtray as if tapping off nonexistent ashes. "You'd have to be blind not to read the signs of doom. They're heavy in the air. Any day now America is going to jump in with both feet. And we're going to need leaders. Real leaders. Men who will do anything and everything in their power to protect lives, not destroy them."

"What you're saying is …"

Boss sobered. "There are very few men I would consider following into the trenches. But good men like you … it would be an honor to follow."

Ole considered the weight of those words. They weren't a compliment. They were a responsibility. A yoke about his neck.

"Think about it." Boss took a deep drag from the cigar then slowly blew out a stream of gray smoke. "When the time comes," he said, "whatever you decide, just know that you will always have a position at Addison & Crowley even if I'm completely overstaffed."

Why did Boss always have to pride himself in staying one step ahead?

Ole stood. "Will that be all?"

"Yep … and Harrington?"

"Yes, sir?"

"Thanks for the nice little chat."

CHAPTER THIRTY-FOUR

The stenographer entered Ole's office peering over the top of a daunting stack of mail. "It's all opened and sorted," she said as she placed it in his inbox, "except for this." She plucked a large envelope from the top, her countenance unsure. "It looked personal so I ..."

"You did fine."

He glanced at the now familiar penmanship. Another letter from Olivia.

He glanced at the clock. Time for staff meeting.

"Will you be needing anything else, sir?" the stenographer said.

"No. That will be all."

He gathered his notes. The letter could wait.

No, it couldn't.

He stared at the not-so-thin envelope, fingered the edges of what must be several sheets of paper and something stiff. A photograph? He sliced it open. Though a picture tumbled out facedown, he couldn't bring himself to pick it up, to look at it. At the moment, what he would find seemed far too difficult to face. But he did smooth open the letter and began reading.

19 March

My dearest Sir,

To say I felt comforted when I received your last post would be an understatement, especially in light of the adoption rumor, which I regretfully fear may have further complicated an already complex situation.

Thank you ever so much for so quickly responding to my last post and for being so kind as to thoughtfully forward your photograph. I've framed it and positioned it in a place of honor on the mantel above the hearth. And as requested, I've enclosed a most recent photograph of myself as well, though without comment.

You expressed your concern about me during this time fraught with danger. That was most kind of you. I had not the faintest notion war could be so dreadful. As I'm sure you know, the Germans shower us with bombs at will, which I find a most unwise strategy on their part. The harder they bombard us, the greater our resolve. True, it is harrowing to have to flee for our lives, never knowing where the bombs might land or when. But when we consider our soldiers out on the battlefield facing worse horrors and against far worse odds, how dare we complain? However, the suffering, the fear, hardship, destruction, uncertainty, the insanity of it all is enough to bring us to our knees and make us want to stay there. Need I say more?

You are most fortunate to live in a far away land for the unfavorable news here continues to be relentless, every day offering yet another generous measure of grief. I am pleased to say, however, that I continue to fare well under most adverse circumstances. Surprisingly I find that the sun still shines, the robins continue to sing, and, though scarce at times, I do have food on the table. We can only hope that one day soon this awful war will be over and our lives will once again return to normal, though a more unpleasantly enlightened normal that will prove to be.

Thank you so much for sharing with me the imagery of the beautiful view from your home. It sounds magnificent. A white winter. Blue waters. Colorful blossoms. I do hope with all my being that one day in the not-too-distant future I will have the privilege of also seeing your home and surroundings. For now, though, that remains castle in the air far too wonderful to reach.

Please make no apologies about the awkwardness of our situation. I prefer that you be skeptical. It is critical that you believe in and fully accept who I am. To that end, you requested proof of my place and date of birth. The best I can produce at present is a duplicate copy of my certificate of birth, which hopefully offers that proof. However, you will notice on the certificate that my mother is listed as Emily de Haven, but my father is stated as unknown. I found that curious. But for now, that is all I am capable of offering.

I do hope I will have the pleasure of hearing from you again soon.

Until then I remain, yours most sincerely,

Olivia

Dumbstruck, Ole read the letter once again and scrutinized the birth certificate. Perspiration poured through trembling hands for the place and date of Olivia's birth mirrored that of his beloved son. He picked up the photograph, inhaled a slow though deep breath, then turned it over ... and gasped.

Emily?

My dear, dear Emily?

How was it possible for Olivia to bear such a remarkable resemblance to her?

He pressed his full weight to the back of his chair and squeezed his eyes closed, a lump in his throat making it next to impossible to swallow. If the picture of Olivia was somehow a fraud, that girl's ability to deceive exceeded amazing.

But what if it wasn't a fraud? What if she wasn't extorting? What if she indeed was who she claimed to be?

Yet how could that be possible?

The bombing. If only they could stop the bombing. What if … he plucked up the telephone receiver. "Operator, get me the Oliver Harrington residence, would you please? … Gretta?"

Ole jumped at a light knocking at his door.

"Mr. Harrington? You're late for the staff meeting."

Late for a silly staff meeting? Or late for a treasured daughter?

GRETTA HELD THE PHOTOGRAPH BENEATH THE lamp's light and studied it. "She's lovely, Ole. She's absolutely lovely." She flipped it over and back again as if wanting to see more. "There's a quality about her, isn't there? A certain softness. She has your same eyes."

"All of the rest of her features are the spitting image of Emily. Gretta?" He placed a hand on hers then gave it a light squeeze. "She was born on the same day, at the same hospital that I lost my son."

Gretta's eyes widened. "You don't think …"

"I don't know what to think."

"You need to send for her, Ole."

"I know," he said. "But the Germans are stepping up their submarine warfare again. For now, it's way too dangerous."

"But don't the restrictions come and go?" Gretta said. "Crossing the seas is dangerous, but having bombs fall like hailstones is dangerous, too."

Ole mindlessly rocked on his heels. "I've thought about that. Maybe we could book passage and keep her at the ready."

"Why don't you give it a try?" Gretta said. "What do we have to lose?"

"But what if she isn't ..."

Gretta blinked. "What if she is?"

CHAPTER THIRTY-FIVE

O le rested a foot on a log and propped a shoulder against the side of Deacon's barn. "Earlier this week I got another letter from Olivia," he said. "Like you, I'm skeptical ... but there's something you need to see."

"Sounds serious. I only wish we could trust her."

"That's what I want, too, but I've got to tell you. Her sincerity? It's beginning to win me over."

"Be careful, Ole," Deacon warned. "That's what a good con does. Sets you up to believe the impossible."

"I know, but it's more than that." He plucked the contents out of the envelope and handed it to him. "Take a look at this. She enclosed a picture along with a copy of her birth certificate. What do you think?"

Deacon eyeballed the photograph. "Why, she is the spitting image of Em." Appearing taken aback, he thought for a long moment then said, "But we all have people we resemble, don't we? How can you be sure this isn't a trick? Do you have any idea how many people have asked me if I'm related to Woodrow Wilson? They say I could be his brother."

"There's more. Take a look at this birth certificate." Ole unfolded it and passed it on as well. "That's the same place, same date my son was born."

Deacon looked it over carefully. "But it wouldn't be hard for her to get that information, would it?"

"I doubt it. But don't forget that she lives in Amelia's flat. Knows the same neighbors I knew when I was there. She's upfront. Doesn't appear to be trying to convince me as much as she's trying to fit the pieces together herself. If she was adopted, what are the chances Amelia would have been able to find, let alone adopt, a little girl who was a mirror image of her daughter? She certainly wouldn't be able to have seen that likeness when Olivia was an infant … would she?"

Deacon shook his head, his expression thoughtful. "What do you propose to do?"

"I want to send for her."

Deacon bounced on his heels. "I sure hope you're not heading into a trap. Extorters are out for money. They'll get it any way they can, and you just might be opening the door for her … wide."

Please be wrong. "I can't get past how I feel." Ole carefully tucked the picture and birth certificate back in the envelope. "Gretta and I have been aching to have a child. You know that. True, Olivia is pretty well grown now, but just think … we might have our own child after all."

"But what if …"

"I've got to have the courage to face this," Ole said. "How will we ever learn the truth if I don't?"

"What about Gretta? Is she up for it?"

"Yes."

Deacon shook his head and gave his neck a thoughtful rub. "I'd probably do the same thing if I were you. Sure hope it works out okay. That dear wife of yours doesn't need any more grief."

GRETTA RAN A FINGER ALONG OLE'S cheek. "You've barely spoken a word all night."

"Deep in thought, I guess." He hesitated. "I've gotten a little resistance from Deacon, but I think he's beginning to listen to reason."

"About?"

"Olivia."

"That doesn't surprise me. He's only been looking out for you, for us. It's probably good that he keeps us grounded in reality."

Ole gazed deep into her eyes. "Are you okay with my inviting her here? I mean, are you really okay with it?"

Gretta smiled her answer.

After she retired to bed, Ole strode to his office and again drew out pad and pen.

31 March

Our dearest Olivia,

Thank you so much for your most welcome post of 19 March. I must admit that when I saw your photograph, I did see Em, my dearly beloved wife and your beautiful and loving mother. She will always occupy a warm place in my heart. It is impossible for her not to do so. And as for the birth certificate, it does state the date and place of your birth, which coincidentally are precisely the same as that of our dearly departed son.

You also again made reference to the war. It appears as though it will not be long now before America dips in a toe if not a foot. As I'm sure you've been informed, the Kaiser has invited Mexico into alliance as a belligerent in an effort to keep our military occupied at our southern border, which as you can imagine has infuriated our citizenry.

I say that to say this, you also mentioned a desire to see, as you called it, the beautiful view from our home. Contrary to your stated belief, that is not a dream too wonderful to come to fruition. I am most happy to book your passage. However there are solemn dangers to consider. Journeying across the Atlantic is anything but safe these days. Germany can't seem to make up its mind, changing its restrictions on the high seas at whim. Though I find introducing you to that danger unconscionable, neither are you safe in England. Passenger ships are few and far between, but should be significantly safer than that of merchant ships.

That said, we would be thrilled if you would come visit our home. I invite you to board the first ship out of England the instant the Germans again lift restrictions. Should you choose to come, do let me know and I will be most happy to proceed with the arrangements immediately if not sooner.

Until then, I remain, yours most sincerely,

He reread the letter. He needed to set it aside, wait a few days to make certain this wasn't an act of impulse driven by need. After penning his signature, he folded it and slipped it inside the envelope, but did not seal it.

How humiliated would he be if this were indeed a hoax?

What right did he have to put Gretta through the heartbreak of foolish hope followed by the strong probability of another loss?

Yet, how crushed would he himself be if Olivia chose not to accept his invitation?

CHAPTER THIRTY-SIX

With dust particles shimmering on shafts of sunlight pouring through the tall slender windows of Village Church, Ole eyed several dapper boys in their late teens sitting in the front pew, and he feared for them. They appeared so young with the possibility of long and full lives ahead of them and yet so eager to do their patriotic duty.

If only they could maintain their innocence.

If only they wouldn't have to endure the heinous evil lurking on the road ahead.

If only they would not feel an obligation to one day join him in appreciating what only those familiar with the atrocities on a battlefield fully understood—the smell of fresh blood, the stench of death, anguished groans, screams. Staring into the enraged eyes of the enemy. Seeing the tip of that bayonet hurtling straight for him. The whistle of bullets whizzing past. Wondering each day if this would be his last.

He returned his attention to the chancel and listened with a keen ear as Reverend Collver leaned forward, his white grip cutting deep into the lectern. "It's happened, folks," he said, "hasn't it? What many of us feared has come upon us. After a decent stay of neutrality, President

Wilson decided we can't stand on the sidelines any longer. Our country is being threatened. Our people are being killed. So he's asked Congress to approve a war to end all wars, a war that will make the world safe for democracy. And Congress said yes."

As heads bobbed and light chatter permeated the room, Ole fixed his gaze on the hymnal shelved on the pew in front of him. Thinking. The President had no choice really. When the German Empire chose to scheme against America, it crossed that line of no return. Now it's gotten personal … real personal.

"I've searched the scriptures," Reverend Collver said, "and found a passage I'd like to share with you today. You'll find it in the book of Second Timothy, chapter one, verse seven. 'For God has not given us a spirit of fear, but of power and of love and of a sound mind.' First, let's consider the spirit of fear. We can't trust the Germans. They've incited fear. Willfully chosen to make us their enemy, so much so that we can no longer remain neutral."

No, we can't. Ole stared off, quivering once again at the horrors of the past, the horrors yet to come.

"Second," the pastor said, "let's consider the power of love. It seems incomprehensible to find love where unbridled hate exists, does it not? But it's there. Love of country. Love of family. Love of freedom. So much so that brave young men are willing to lay down their lives for it …"

To Ole's chagrin, the boys in the front row bumped shoulders and shared proud grins.

"… and our countrymen," the pastor continued, "are willing to open their wallets, to give to our cause until it hurts.

"Next, let's consider the power of a sound mind. Our secretary of state is convinced a German victory would mean the overthrow of freedom and democracy. I couldn't agree more. The Germans want to win the war by ending it their way, but we've already gotten a bitter taste of what that means, haven't we? Their atrocities against Belgium say it all.

What they've done there they wouldn't hesitate to do to us. Make no mistake. Our country is of a strong mind. Now we must fight the good fight."

After the closing prayer, Gretta turned to Ole with a look of sheer relief. "I can't tell you how grateful I am that your military service is a thing of the past."

He looked away. She couldn't be more wrong. That distant bugle call? It was growing increasingly louder, capturing his heart, capturing his soul.

Moments later as the car rumbled down the roads of Amber Leaf, Gretta turned to him again. "I don't understand the Germans. What are they thinking?"

Just then a young boy ran out in front of their motorcar, and Ole slammed on the brake. The boy appeared startled to see him and more startled when he glanced back at a larger boy gaining on him.

Ole rolled down the window. "Hey," he yelled, and the second boy backed off, but not without a menacing scowl.

"They aren't thinking," he said. "They're like that young tough over there ... the bullies on the playground ... and bullies don't think deep. They decided they've got the right to do whatever they want if it suits their cause. But it's more than that. Some men just love the fight." Driving on, Ole glanced at Gretta. "Remember what Pastor Collver said about those atrocities against Belgium? That the Germans slaughtered thousands of French and Belgian civilians? And with no warning whatsoever. Think about that, Gretta. Imagine the terror those poor people felt."

As Ole prattled on, within him that call to fight continued to grow stronger. He was on a tear and couldn't seem to stop himself. "Looting and burning towns. Occupying Belgium. And to add insult to injury, the Germans forced those poor people to work for them like slaves. Imagine if they'd done that here. To us. An enemy marching in, violating our people … taking what they wanted at whim, and then turning around and enslaving us? That's unconscionable."

Gretta mindlessly fidgeted with her handbag. "Is it true what they say? That they've been unloading poison gas in the trenches along the Western Front?"

"Have been for some time now." And their Navy is making a graveyard out of the Atlantic. Sinking the Lusitania. Sinking neutral ships. Attacking seaport towns in Britain.

As Gretta sat quietly, Ole pulled into the driveway. "This is serious business."

"Ole, do you think our government will start conscription?"

"They already have."

"What if you—"

"Eighteen to twenty-five year olds," he said.

But they need officers. Badly.

"Things are going to get worse now that we've joined the fight," he added.

Tell her, Ole. She has a right to know.

"What is it?" Gretta said. "Is something bothering you?"

He turned and looked her directly in the eye. "The more we talk about this, the more I'm getting the itch to volunteer."

Her eyes widened. "No, Ole," she said. "Please, don't."

CHAPTER THIRTY-SEVEN

Ole tucked another letter from Olivia in a pocket and proceeded out to the country. Having recently put in considerably hard and long hours at the office, this day was too perfect not to relax and hunt game. Within the hour, he sat on a buckboard and gazed up into a brilliant azure sky. Then he and Deacon hopped off and trudged through a grove, high grass swishing beneath their boots.

"How'd you get the afternoon off," Deacon said, "… or did they fire you?"

Shifting the rifle on his shoulder, Ole held back a grin. "Careful with your words there. It's the calm before another storm. Thought I'd take advantage of it while I can. Not getting much in the way of exercise is making me soft."

Deacon indicated the direction with a nod. "There's usually a good-sized herd over the next hill this time of day. Maybe we'll get lucky."

Ole plodded on. He had yet to see a deer, let alone a squirrel. Or a rabbit.

When they neared the top of the rise, Deacon sidled up behind the wide trunk of an oak. He pressed his back to the tree and peered past it. He turned back, placed a finger to pursed lips, and gently raised his rifle.

Ole eased around the other side of the trunk. Deacon had called it right. A buck stood proud as a sentry in the grove below. He appeared on the alert as if smelling the scent of a predator.

Deacon fired. The buck dropped. And Deacon grinned. "Looks like we'll chow down on venison for supper after all."

They trudged down to the grove and appraised their prey. Together Ole and Deacon field-dressed the buck where it fell, dragged it to Deacon's buckboard, and lobbed it on, Ole suppressing a grunt at the weight of the thing. "I've flung 'em lighter," he said. "You should get plenty of good meat out of this one."

When they returned to the farm and neared the barn, Deacon stopped short and curiously eyed the letter poking out of Ole's pocket. "Is that what I think it is?"

"Came in the morning's mail. Haven't had a chance to read it yet."

"I assume it's from Olivia."

"You assume right."

"Haven't had a chance … or didn't take the chance? There's a big difference." Deacon stood quietly for a thoughtful moment. "I don't know if you've noticed, but we've been talking about Olivia quite a lot lately. You'd better prepare yourself. Even if you are successful in convincing me, that's not going to change reality."

Thanks for the encouragement.

They lugged the deer from the buckboard to the barn, which again was no easy task. "I'll tell you what," Deacon said. "You go ahead and read the letter while I start skinning. If this Olivia person has anything convincing to say, you know where I'll be."

Lifting his chin, Ole watched for a moment as Deacon took to the knife and then he headed back out into the great outdoors.

A stump abutted the side of the barn. Perfect place to read. Ole plunked down and drew open the letter.

15 May

My dearest sir:

Thank you for your latest post. My heart leapt when I received it. I've read your words and pinched myself more times than one could count. I wished to reassure myself they were real and not a dream.

Before addressing the content of your letter, I believe it best to update you on the happenings here in England. The strawberries I planted in the planter box outside the front window of my flat are flourishing and delicious. We also have a community garden where we collectively raise tomatoes and potatoes and various other sorts of fruits and vegetables. Later in the season we will busy ourselves canning and hopefully will preserve enough to carry us through the long winter months ahead.

I've been in the employ of a small tailor shop immediately around the corner. While not particularly rewarding financially, it does provide me with an adequate living. I've spoken with the owner and am most pleased to tell you that I've received permission to take leave as soon as it's safe for passenger ships to leave port. I hope to be able to make passage within the next several months so that I will be able to return to England again well before winter sets in.

The thrill of such a long voyage and the hope of seeing your wonderful country, but mostly the hope of finally getting to make the acquaintance of the man my mother fell so deeply in love with warms my heart as nothing else has. I shall inform you immediately when I learn we are able to finalize passage.

Until then, I remain, yours very sincerely,

Olivia

Ole carefully refolded the letter and slipped it back into his pocket. *She's coming.*

This young lady who claims to be my daughter is still alive, and she is coming to America to finally meet the man she believes is her father.

And she can't wait to get here.

When he stepped inside the barn, Deacon said indifferently, "Well, what did she have to say?"

"She's coming."

He eyed Ole skeptically. "How could she not know she was an orphan?"

Ole lowered onto a hay bail. *You're going to make me admit this, aren't you? Well, here it goes.* "She doesn't believe she is."

Deacon continued to absently skin the deer. "You're sure you know what you're getting yourself into?"

"I'm not sure about anything." Ole leaned to the side and propped an elbow on a wooden rail. "I only know that a man has to do what a man has to do."

Stopping his knife in mid air, Deacon looked as if he was confused about where next to wield it.

CHAPTER THIRTY-EIGHT

Sitting at the desk in his home office, Ole set the *New York Times* to the side and slowly drew a rare cigar from an upper desk drawer. Removed the cellophane. Fingered it. Took a disinterested sniff. Tossed it back in the box and headed for the kitchen. "Gretta, I need to get out of the house for a while."

She wiped her hands on her apron and looked up at him with concern-filled eyes. She hadn't said much since he announced he was thinking about signing up. Often appeared dazed. Dropping things. A platter. A fork. Yet she didn't complain, which made his hurt for her more intense. But for as much as he loved her, he struggled harder with that higher calling and that unsettling need to answer it.

"This war stuff has me off kilter," he said. "Don't know what to do with myself. Thought maybe I'd go into town. Get a haircut. Involve myself in a little war talk with men who are caught up on the news. Maybe that'll help."

When he arrived at the barbershop, the two shaving chairs were both taken, the wall lined with anxious scraggly-haired customers. No place to sit. No one talking. The shop struck him as uncharacteristically quiet for an early Saturday morning, uncharacteristically quiet for a barbershop any morning of any day of the week for that matter.

"You wouldn't happen to have any more chairs, would you?" Ole said.

A barber slipped into a back room and hauled out a couple and unfolded them. "Have a seat. Be with you soon as we can."

Ole considered the quiet. Perhaps he was projecting, but by the look of things, no one wanted to break a reverent silence, yet everyone ached to talk.

The door flew open. The bell above it jangled. And Nelson hustled in at a fast clip before coming to an abrupt halt. He looked around. Though appearing respectful of the mood, he looked more frazzled than lost. One glance at Ole and his perfect face scrunched. The manner in which he plopped onto the chair next to him said more than words could ever say. Resentment. Disdain. When it came to poker faces, Ole couldn't imagine a worse player.

As the clock on the wall ticked away the minutes, the door flew open again. A young man who went by the name of Chris walked in, and the mood in the room changed.

One of the barbers finally broke the silence. "How old are you, son?"

Chris shifted from one foot to the other. "Twenty-one, sir."

"You celebrated hard on your last birthday, I take it?"

"No, sir. It's tomorrow. That's why I came in for a haircut." A row of straight white teeth became increasingly visible. "Got a big party planned."

Ole eyed the men along the wall lined up like ducks in a row as if he could read their minds. It was only too obvious that this boy so young and innocent would soon march off to war.

Nelson sat quiet, too, appearing to study Chris. But there was something somber about Nelson's look. If he and Ole had a respectful relationship, that look might concern Ole.

"You signed up yet, boy?" the barber said.

"No, sir. Planning to first thing come Monday morning, though." He drew his shoulders back. "Can't wait to show the Germans what we're made of," he said as if trying to convince himself. "They could use a good licking."

Then came a chorus of praise and the dam burst, the barbershop filling with war chatter.

Nelson turned to Ole. "I'm signing up, too," he announced.

"Why? Conscription is only for the twenty-one to thirty year olds."

"For now, it is. Give it time. That'll change."

"Why the interest?"

Nelson scowled. "Why not?"

Ole could understand a young boy being deceived by the allure of war, but Nelson was pushing forty. Hard. "You've never served in the military, I take it."

"And you have?"

"Sudan."

"So you had your fun then."

"Never fun." Ole kept his voice low and an eye on Chris so he wouldn't overhear. "Going off to war for the first time is like playing your first ballgame. It doesn't dawn on you that you won't be sitting in the bleachers until you're out on the field."

"I'm not afraid," Nelson said.

Or so you say, Ole thought. Not every man is meant to wear a uniform. The Ole's of this world, yes. The Nelson's of this world, a resounding no. Ole remembered being in the throes of war, the cries of brave young men marching out on the battlefield only to march no more. And the suffering? After the victorious had seen the horror in the enemy's eyes as he drew in his last breath—at their expense—they had the privilege of reliving it in a series of nightmares for years to come. And then there were the hospitals behind the scenes where soldiers experienced a whole new kind terror away from the public eye. Lost limbs.

Lost eyesight. And what about those tragic cases—the ones who'd lost their minds?

Nelson got a far-away look in his eye. "If you fought in Sudan, you were in the cavalry, Harrington. This war is different."

"War is war."

"I hear the soldiers on both sides already dug twenty-five thousand miles of trenches," Nelson said as if he hadn't heard Ole. "Reinforced them as they went along. If you lined them up from end to end, they say they'd circle the entire globe. Plenty of space to keep your head down. Sandbags on top to absorb the bullets."

And neither side can budge. "The more the soldiers dig in," Ole said, "the harder it is to fight. Germans got there first. Grabbed the high ground. When it floods, water pours through the low-lying trenches. It's miserable. Soldiers can't help but get trench foot."

"Well aren't you the optimistic one?" Nelson said with a sneer. "Ever heard of duckboard? They've built plenty. That should take care of that."

This guy wasn't about to listen to reason. "What about the gassing?"

He lifted his nose. "Ever hear of gas masks?"

Ole backed down when the weasel crossed a leg, exposing a hole the size of a walnut in the sole of a well shined shoe. And then he remembered his visit to Nelson's spartanly office. It was obvious that his business could have been doing better. If he had to guess, Nelson didn't want to go to war. He had to go. The man had fallen on hard times. Needed money. And Ole's dismantling of the Harding case certainly hadn't helped matters.

For a while there, Ole began to feel badly for Nelson until he said, "What about you, Harrington? You've got experience. They could use a few good officers … or have you turned yellow?"

CHAPTER THIRTY-NINE

O le slathered his face with a thick coat of shaving cream and ran a sharp blade across his cheek.

Or have you turned yellow?

He drew his razor through the water basin then made another pass, Nelson's taunting words popping up out of nowhere. Repeatedly. It made no sense for them to cut to the bone.

And yet they did.

Why?

What about that powerful draw that had been trifling with Ole for days? He hadn't turned his back on it. Even gave Gretta a heads up to prepare her for his departure.

And what about Boss's explicit words of praise? They both knew Ole would answer the call.

He stared hard into the conflicted eyes in the mirror. What's become of me? he wondered. What am I waiting for? Has age finally caught up with me?

In Sudan, during the heat of battle it wasn't possible to fight more valiantly. He'd been too focused on strategy at the time, too respectful of imminent danger to toy with apprehension, and he'd certainly earned enough medals for bravery. Those they don't divvy out like chocolate bars. But in Sudan, when he battled on horseback, fought on the open desert, and slept in flimsy tents, his issues with claustrophobia had never been an issue. That seemed to sneak up on him over time.

This war, though, the Great War, was different. This war meant sleeping piggyback nights on end below deck in close quarters, no portholes, on multi-tiered bunks, and that was just to get to Europe. It meant crawling around in trenches higher than his head or riding across the battlefield in the tight and unyielding cavity of an iron tank.

This war meant putting his personal demons to the test. Had he conquered them sufficiently to survive?

After chewing on his conflicting thoughts a while longer, he headed down to breakfast. He didn't need to announce his intentions to Gretta. She read his mood.

"You're signing up," she said.

"I am."

The sugar bowl she cradled crashed to the floor and shattered, shards of porcelain and fine white granules splayed at her feet. She hurried to the pantry and grabbed the broom and held on to it as if it were a lifeline. "No, Ole. Please."

"I have to go."

"Why? You're past the age of conscription eligibility."

"I want to go on my schedule, not the military's," he said. "Besides, they need officers, and they need them now. Nelson's already signed up."

"You told me he signed up out of ignorance and need."

"That's right, he did. But they need men with experience, too … men like me."

"What about your claustrophobia?" she said.

"I've gotten a lot better. Did fine in Anderson's cellar. You saw that." Come to think of it, I did fine at Mabel's, too—once we got downstairs.

He retrieved the dustpan from the pantry and angled it against the floor as Gretta continued sweeping.

"But this is different," she said, the alarm in her voice escalating. "What if that feeling of being sucked in overtakes you again? How are you going to handle that? What if you panic aboard ship? You'd never be able to look yourself in the mirror again. You sign up, there's no turning back."

He kept his gaze focused on the broom bristles, shifting the angle of the dustpan to meet them. Gretta wasn't worried about the claustrophobia. That he knew. It was a ruse, an excuse to talk him out of risking his life.

"What about Olivia?" she said. "She's taking the next available ship to America, isn't she?'

"I hope so."

"You're the reason she's coming, Ole, and you won't be here for her."

He seized the broom, placed it in the pantry, then returned, and lightly cupped her chin. "No, but she needs to get out of there. I've written. If she doesn't get my letter on time, you'll be here for her."

Gretta drew back. "She'll be devastated."

"She'll get past it. She was probably relieved to get the invitation. A free trip to America? Riding a train from the East Coast to the Midwest? What young girl wouldn't love that?"

"Don't be unkind."

"I'm not. What about us, Gretta? We're the ones who'll be devastated if we find out this is a fraud. But we need to face reality, discipline ourselves to keep a back door open … just in case." He gathered his brief case. "I hope she gets here soon. Daughter or not, the company will be good for you."

He pecked Gretta on the cheek and then stepped out under a gray September sky where he hesitated. Looking up, he wondered.

Am I doing the right thing?

CHAPTER FORTY

In the early afternoon, Ole signed up with the American Expeditionary Forces.

And they accepted him.

The next handful of days, it hurt to watch Gretta, to feel her steadfast love intermingled with pain and fear.

Too quickly they stood at the train depot. They didn't say their goodbyes—they held one another in a tight embrace and felt them, the rich making of a memory fulfilling enough to carry him through the entirety of the war.

But the military didn't care. They didn't hesitate to reduce Ole to a dog tag as intense days of training ensued. Before he realized what was happening, he found himself lying below deck, breathing in, breathing out, breathing in, breathing out, grateful claustrophobia had slackened its tight grip, relieved the malady was now manageable.

"Wanna cigarette?" a young man in a bunk across the aisle said.

"No thanks."

The kid stuck out a hand. "Buddy Schmidt."

"Ole Harrington."

"Where you from?"

"Amber Leaf."

"Minnesota?"

"Yes, and you?"

"Iowa. Spencer, Iowa.

In the faint light, the boy appeared to bear straight white teeth and the eyes of a timid doe. He looked no more than sixteen, seventeen at the most. "How old are you, son?"

"Son?" He lit up. "Hey, I'm older than you think. Be twenty-two next week."

"You don't look it."

"Wait 'til you see me on deck in broad daylight. Got a few wrinkles already."

Ole shifted on his bunk. "What do you do down in Spencer?"

"Work my dad's farm." Buddy flexed a bulging muscle and beamed. "Been lifting hay bales since I was a kid."

"Got a girl down there, do you?"

Though Ole couldn't see in the darkness, Buddy appeared to blush. "Not me, sir. One caught my eye, though, but I can't seem to get up the gumption to court her."

Ole suppressed a grin. "A little on the shy side, are you?"

"Not that I feel comfortable admitting," he said.

"The war will take care of that."

"You ever fought before?"

"Sudan."

Buddy inhaled another drag. "I thought you sounded British. You didn't happen to be an officer back then, did you?"

"That, I was."

"What are you doing down here with us then?"

"Mistake in the ranks. Ship is officer heavy and one bunk short."

"How long you been in the States?"

This kid really needed to talk. "Sixteen, seventeen years now, I guess."

"Like it there?"

"Very much."

Buddy looked around uncomfortably then lowered his voice. "Say, you worried about us taking a hit from one of those torpedoes?"

"No," Ole said.

"Really?" Buddy's voice took on a hopeful tone. "How come?"

"I doubt a U-boat is going to want to mess with a fleet. That would be suicide. Besides, our ship is on the inside. Odds are against it."

Buddy lifted a cigarette to his lips, drew in a long drag, held it, then blew it out, his feigned confidence betrayed by a slight tremor in his hand. "Ever been to France?"

"This is my first time. How about you?"

"First time, too. Sure hope Major General 'Black Jack' Pershing knows what he's getting us into." Buddy hesitated. "Say, I saw you before. When we were in training. You handle yourself pretty well."

You definitely didn't see me in training. "Those were quite the workouts, weren't they?"

"Were you scared when you fought in Sudan?" Buddy's tone sounded as if he needed encouragement.

"If you aren't scared, you're a fool. A word of advice?"

"Yes, sir?"

"When you head into battle, assume you're already dead. It helps quell the fear."

He gulped. "But—"

"You either march out strong or you get dragged along, whining and looking like a coward. It's either power or fear. The choice is up to you."

"I get it, sir. Thanks."

OLE SPENT THE MAJORITY OF THE next afternoon on deck playing cards. About an hour into the game, Buddy stopped by to say hello.

"I need a smoke," he said after a short while and wandered off. "Enjoy your game."

The boy was right. During light of day, his youthful face did bear a few wrinkles from what appeared to be hours of squinting under a hot sun.

Ole looked over every now and then. The poor kid lingered near the port side rail, leaning his back against it, a tremble still present in his hand every now and then. The waters relatively smooth, after a while Buddy hiked up onto the railing and dangled a foot over the side. He looked off into the blue appearing absorbed by something that had caught his attention. He looked back at Ole as if needing his approval. "Porpoises," he said with a childlike grin. "Whole school of 'em."

As Buddy reached into a pocket for another cigarette, he didn't appear to notice a large swell rising starboard side. Without warning, the ship rolled.

Hard.

And Buddy slid into frigid waters.

Head first.

Clipping the rail on his way down.

Ole vaulted up and took a running leap. "Man overboard," he yelled. After a quick dive, he righted himself then dog pedaled as if Buddy's life depended on it. And it did. To Ole's immediate left, Buddy barely remained visible as he plunged lower into the sea. Ole dove deeper, grabbing him from behind, then quickly yanked him up. Though Buddy choked and fought, Ole maintained a tight grip.

A lifebuoy hurled over the side of the ship. Ole reached for it. It was as though it dangled, teasing him, as it swayed back and forth barely out of reach. Then with a strong lunge, Ole seized it. He slipped one arm through the doughnut while holding a tenacious grip on Buddy with the other. Slowly they rose to the deck. Hands reached and grabbed until Ole and Buddy made it safely on board. Ole stood bent over fighting for breath while another soldier resuscitated a limp Buddy on the slippery deck.

A respectful hour later, Ole headed down to sickbay where he knocked before entering. Buddy was sitting on a cot, lucid yet forlorn. He looked up. "You saved my life."

Ole shrugged.

"I'm sorry, sir," Buddy said. "I don't know what I was thinking. Guess I wasn't."

Ole crossed the small chamber and gave him an assuring pat on the shoulder. "You didn't see the swell."

"But still. It was stupid to sit on the railing. It's not like they didn't warn us. I don't know how to thank you—"

"No need to say more," Ole said. "But another word of advice?"

"I'm listening."

"Never waste an accident."

"What do you mean?"

"You learned one of the most valuable lessons you could possibly learn, and we're not even out on the front yet." Ole paused. "We soldiers watch out for one another. You'll never gain a better friend than a war buddy."

Buddy's lips curled upward and his brightened eyes. "I'll be keeping an eye on you, too, sir," he said. "You can hang your Stetson on that one."

CHAPTER FORTY-ONE

From the aft, roiling water marked a dwindling trail across the high seas. To Olivia's relief, the ocean liner had journeyed safely past the blockade. She inhaled a deep whiff of salty sea air and twirled around. Hugging herself, she looked up and grinned. "Grandmum, I'm on my way to America. I'm about to meet my father and stepmother for the very first time ever. I wish with all my heart they will like me."

On the second day out to sea, she staggered to the main deck. The wind had howled for the greater part of the morning, the water choppy, immense swells pitching the ship relentlessly from one side to the other and back again.

"You look as gray as the paint on the ship," a soothing voice said from behind.

She turned and gazed into mischievous eyes. The dapper young man with a handlebar moustache looked as though he could be the lead singer in a barbershop quartet. "Don't worry," he said. "Soon as you get your sea legs, you'll be fine."

Sea legs. What a blessed thought. "How might I accomplish that?"

"How do I put this delicately?" he said then plucked at his suspenders and snickered, a blush flushing his cheeks. "You'll need to lose your lunch, I'm afraid."

She followed his gaze toward a smattering of pathetic-looking passengers straddling the railing. Void of color. Moaning. "I see," she said, though the cure appeared anything but pleasant.

"I'm Jeremy Lang and you are?"

"Oliv … excuse …"

She sprinted to the railing and, falling in line with the other retching travelers, draped herself over it for the better part of five minutes. Too seasick to be embarrassed and feeling amazingly better, she returned to Jeremy's side. "It appears you'd make an excellent doctor," she said. "Your cure worked wonders. As I was saying, my name is Olivia."

"Nice name. Where are you headed, Olivia?"

"To the States."

"The States," he said, raising a teasing brow. "That nails it rather precisely, wouldn't you say? Mountains? Desert? Great Lakes? The Plains? North? South? East? West?"

First too ill and then too vague, she offered a dignified nod. "To a small town in southern Minnesota. A place called Amber Leaf."

"Nice name for a town." He looked around. "Would you mind joining me on that bench over there? I'd like to get to know you better if you wouldn't mind." He guided her by the small of the back. "Family there?"

"My father and stepmother. And you?"

"I'm on my way back to Harvard," he said, though he appeared strangely unhappy about it. "Another year to go."

"You are studying?"

"Law."

"Because?"

"I'm hoping to one day become a Senator."

"Allow me to hazard a guess," she said. "Your father is heavily involved in politics. He wished his son to follow in his footsteps. And though your desires remain elsewhere, you feel you have little choice."

He gulped. "How'd you know that?"

"By the expression on your face when you announced you were returning to Harvard, you looked as if you'd rather go to the dentist to get a tooth extracted. And you are from?"

"Born and raised in Nantucket."

"Oh my! I've always thought New England sounded like such a wonderful place," she said. "Idyllic really."

"How long will you be in Minnesota?"

"I'm uncertain. It depends on …" The sudden though unanticipated significance of her journey took her pleasantly by surprise.

"Yes?"

"I'm meeting my father … for the first time." A beautiful rush of gooseflesh flowed through her at the mere mention of those words. "It's a rather long and complicated story."

"I'm sure your get-together will go well." He paused, a twinkle glistening in his striking eyes. "I'd like to spend a little time in the library before this evening's dinner. Would you care to join me? These trips can be dreadfully long and lonely without anyone interesting to talk to."

She studied this proper young gentleman for a long moment, taking pleasure in his candor. "I should be very glad to do so."

The ensuing hours slipped past quickly, the increasingly rolling seas vying for their attention. They enjoyed a late evening meal, but not without occasionally blotting misplaced sauces of varying kinds from their cheeks, often with an embarrassed snicker. After dining, using one arm for support along harrowing passageways, Jeremy offered his other arm as they took a wobbly stroll toward her cabin.

With a handful of short hours behind them and but a few precious days before them, she dreaded this wonderful evening drawing to a close.

"Perhaps we could meet up for breakfast at first light?" he said, sounding hopeful.

"0800 hours in the café on deck?"

He grinned. "0800 hours, it is."

As he disappeared down the ship's long passageway, she doubted whether life could possibly be more wonderful.

The sea calmed and during the next several days, she and Jeremy spent every waking hour together. Though the food smelled and looked divine, her appetite abated. They strolled the deck, engaged in meaningful conversation, primarily about the war—how it started, where it was heading, what could be done. Each day they made the time to linger in the library reading together with warmth radiating from the mere touching of shoulders. Each night they spent hours on deck gazing up at the moon and stars while sharing their dreams.

The last night of their voyage, a fierce storm raged. Giant swells. Bolts of lightning. Muddled thunder through violent winds. And the rain. The blessed rain that masked threatening tears as she said a final goodnight to Jeremy. He walked away appearing as sad as she felt.

Inside her stateroom, the ship listed mercilessly. She took a few staggering steps to her suitcase and searched through her things. She drew out her grandmum's letter, the cherished letter addressed to her father, and hugged it to her heart. This wonderful piece of parchment would explain everything and make right the past.

Or would it? Would her father share its contents with her? If only she might steal a hurried glimpse, but that would be unseemly. She slipped the envelope back in the suitcase. This document was far too valuable to displace.

As she nestled in for a pleasant night's sleep, the ship continued to list unrelentingly. She found it difficult to sleep, but finally succumbed. Then in the middle of the night, she awakened with a start when her head met with the headboard during a nasty pitch. Anything not secured came crashing down.

When she awoke at daybreak, she gazed through the porthole. Though the winds had ceased and the seas calmed, conflicting feelings of remorse and excitement taunted her—remorse for having to say a final goodbye to her newfound friend, excitement about the opportunity of saying hello to a father she had never enjoyed the privilege of knowing. She quickly tidied up the stateroom, picking up a few things that had scattered across the floor during the storm. She stopped abruptly when she reached her luggage. She must not have secured it properly. It had jostled open during the night's mayhem as well.

Late morning, she and Jeremy stood on deck and gazed at New York Harbor, the sun shining bright in a robin-egg blue sky. As the Statue of Liberty towered into view, he drew her close and whispered, "I wish we could stop time."

"I do as well," she said, and meant it.

More quickly than she wished, they arrived at Ellis Island. "Will you have family waiting for you?"

"My father, and you?"

"After we pass through customs, I'll be off to Grand Central to fetch a train." She gazed up at him, hopeful. "We will correspond, will we not?"

He gave her a crushing hug and held her for the longest while, then drew back. "I wouldn't have it any other way. When do you plan to return to England?"

"I'm uncertain. A few weeks? A month perhaps? It's open ended."

He folded a note into her hand. "This is my address and telephone number. Keep me apprised of your visit. Let me know when you'll be heading back to New York. I'll meet you at Grand Central. That's a promise."

He lifted her chin and swept her lips lightly with a tender kiss. Then drawing her tightly in his arms again, he held on as if for dear life, and in his embrace she felt intense warmth and caring.

But then he drew back and that look returned, that look he'd been unable to hide when he'd said he was returning to Harvard to complete his final year.

Please let this not be a sign of things to come.

CHAPTER FORTY-TWO

Standing in the middle of Grand Central Terminal, Olivia gazed up at the towering walls of the greatest station in the world and took a dizzying look around. From the galaxies painted on the ceiling to the marbled halls, to the museums, the boutiques, and restaurants, she'd never imagined such a sight. After getting her fill of wonder, she dashed to the telephone room. "Operator, I should like to make a long-distance call to Mr. Oliver M. Harrington in Amber Leaf, Minnesota, please."

"That will be …"

Unwanted warmth invaded her cheeks. "He asked that I telephone him collect."

"Yes, ma'am."

Her stomach fluttered as she listened nervously to a jangle far up the line. "I'm sorry," the Operator said after a half dozen rings, "but there's no answer. You might want to try again later."

Try again later? Of course. The ride to the Upper Midwest would be long and tiring, and there would be a number of depots scattered along the way, a number of opportunities to make another call.

She half walked, half floated to the shortest ticket line, her timing superb. Only a half hour wait before journeying on her first leg of the trip, changing trains in Chicago. She fell in line with a group of harried passengers, descended a long ramp, and boarded the train. Before it rumbled down the tracks, she plunked her suitcase in the sleeper car, continued on to the lounge, found an overstuffed chair, and settled in. Several chairs over, she sensed a rugged looking man who appeared to be several years her senior riveting an intense gaze on her. Do not make eye contact, she told herself. And keep your ring finger free from sight. Let him assume you're married. She plucked up a copy of the *New York Times* and pretended to read.

Her efforts proved ill conceived for a puff of air fluttered the corners of her newspaper as he plopped onto the closest chair. "Little lady traveling alone?" he said.

She ignored him.

"It's going to be a long ride, miss. Plenty of time to get to know each other." He leaned in closer. "Paper's upside down."

She shot up in an effort to relocate herself to another chair. However, he stretched out a leg, blocking her. "Where you going?"

Setting her jaw, she said, "If you'll excuse me, please," then pushed past and found another chair across the lounge.

A short moment later, he got up, scurried across the aisle, and plopped onto another chair adjacent to hers. "So you're going to Amber Leaf, are you?"

She winced. "May I ask how you knew that?"

"I was in line behind you at Grand Central." He sprawled back in the chair, crossing his feet at the ankles. "Who's in Amber Leaf?"

Again, she ignored the question.

"You sure are a stuck up little thing, aren't you? Got a husband?" He reached over, grabbed her ring finger, and held it up. "Nope."

How might she get this determined young man to leave her alone? She flashed on Jeremy. Though he didn't yet qualify as a suitor, maybe if this brute was led to believe she did, in fact, have a love interest, he would back away. "I'm in a relationship." She warmed at the comforting sound of those words.

"Oh, yeah? Where is he?"

"Harvard."

"That a fact? You'll never see him again."

"Why on earth would you say such a thing?"

He lifted his nose. "Guy like that has a big ego. It's wartime. After he graduates, he'll want to impress all the pretty young ladies with a shiny new uniform. Those snobs are all like that. So he'll join up and the war will make hamburger out of him. Guy's a sucker."

Might this have been the cause of Jeremy's forlorn look when they disembarked the ship? Please, no. "Why are you not in service?" she said then chided herself for further engaging an unwanted conversation.

"They don't take 4-Fs."

"You certainly look healthy. Why would they not accept you?"

He cut loose a wicked laugh. "Guess they think we ex-cons are more trouble than we're worth."

His taunting laughter sent a chill down Olivia's spine. She got up and with pleasant demeanor said, "If you'll excuse me, I think I'd best go freshen up."

"Take your time." Surprisingly, he stood as if he were a consummate gentleman. "Meet me in the dining car at five. Like I said, I'd like to get to know you better."

I wish to keep my distance, but thank you just the same.

She returned to the sleeper car and rifled through her suitcase, looking for something more comfortable to wear since this would be one of the longer legs of the trip. As she sorted through her garments, however, she sensed something amiss. Her quickening heart quickly gave way to panic. *Grandmum's letter. Where is it? It must be here.*

She tore through the suitcase again, this time feverishly pulling out each item one at a time and stretching them out on the berth. The letter ... gone. But that was impossible. *Think back,* she told herself. *In* the middle of the night aboard ship. That storm. When it pitched hard, and she'd hit her head, a number of items had crashed to the floor. She heard it. But she checked the floor. The letter wasn't there. She drew a hand to her lips. What if it fell into the wastebasket, and she hadn't seen it? Or had it fallen beneath the bedding? She desperately examined yet again the now bare insides of her suitcase, an exercise in futility though it may be. How could her father and stepmother possibly believe she was who she said she was without proper proof? And what was it that her grandmum had said in that letter anyway? Olivia had no idea what had happened between her and her father. Why would her grandmum do to that her?

She continued her stay in the sleeper car taking time to thoroughly think things through. She would wait until six o'clock before dining. Somehow facing that domineering misfit seemed less menacing now. But what might she do about the letter? Proof gone forever? Perhaps if she telephoned the ship. She poked through her coin purse and counted her currency. Running dreadfully low. But what did that matter? She must disembark at the next stop to make contact with the ship.

In the late afternoon, the train arrived at a station in Ithaca. She hopped off. Soldiers, soldiers everywhere. To her amazement, trains heading west appeared sparsely populated while trains heading east filled to the brim. Excited soldiers. Naïve soldiers. Lonely soldiers about to learn the realities of war.

She quickly telephoned the shipping line. "I'm sorry, ma'am," the voice said, "but you may want to try again tomorrow. Horace is the young man you need to speak with, but I'm afraid he's gone for the day."

Wait until tomorrow? Wait too long, and it will be too late.

She boarded the train a second time. At six o'clock straight up, she proceeded to the dining car where she sat alone and ordered a light supper. After it arrived and she'd taken her first bite, wet breath hit the back of her neck and a deep voice muttered in her ear. "You're late. I said five o'clock."

A conductor happened by and caught her eye. "Everything okay, miss?"

Things could be much better. "I'm fine."

The conductor studied the man suspiciously.

"What's the matter, conductor?" Brute said, letting out another wicked laugh. "Looking for an excuse to exercise your authority?"

Red bled into the conductor's cheeks. He walked on, disappearing into the next car.

Olivia didn't bother to get Brute's name, neither did he bother to stop pestering her. He wasn't a healthy sort with which to spend time. His looks. His cunning. His smothering presence.

His having spent time in prison.

What might he have done that was wretched enough to warrant incarceration? Ignore the thought, she told herself. Some things are best not to know.

By the time the train rolled into the next stop, she no longer wished to concern herself with the man and wasn't about to put the conductor into a compromising situation on her behalf. "If you'll excuse me," she said, "I wish to get off to make an important telephone call."

"Hurry back," Brute said with another wily grin. "I'll save your seat."

She whisked past the sleeper car, quickly grabbed her bag, and hauled it off with her. Only too happy to wait for the next train, she half ran, half walked up to the next available ticket agent. "When might the next train leave for Chicago?"

"That's it right there," he said with a quick glance toward the platform. The train she had just fled? "Next one won't leave until tomorrow."

Drat!

She quickly made a telephone call to her father. No answer. First she was unable to reach Horace, now she was unable to reach him. Discouraged, she hurried out onto the platform, suitcase at her side, and gazed up at the train. To her chagrin, through the lounge window Brute caught her eye, glanced down at her suitcase and then glared at her. Her intuition warned her to keep a close eye on him. He wasn't the sort of man with which one wished to trifle. She watched, concerned, as he filed through the compartment as if a man on a mission. He appeared anything but happy. This was not good.

She quickly ducked behind a group of distracted servicemen caught up in what seemed to be a serious chat about happenings out on the front and then poked her nose past a loose elbow where she watched a pair of shoes ease off the train. They met with the ground, first one, then the other, and stood stationary for a moment, moving only slightly as Brute undoubtedly looked over the crowd.

"All aboard," the conductor cried. The whistle blew and the train started moving. Crouching low, she took a quick leap and hopped on board. Immediately inside the lounge car, she peered out the window only to catch Brute's enraged response. He slammed his cap on the ground and stomped a foot. He released what appeared to be inappropriate though explicit verbiage, though that she was unable to hear. Nor did she wish to.

She placed her bag in the sleeping car and returned to the lounge.

"That was a brilliant move, miss," the conductor said.

"Pardon me?"

"I watched you through the window. You played that young man just right," he said. "Saved me a contentious scene."

"I'm afraid I don't understand."

"I had a chat with the Pullman conductor. If that bum didn't back off, we planned to stop the train out in the middle of nowhere and throw him off. I'm sure a long walk to the next town might have done him wonders. By the way," he placed a tray on her lap holding a sandwich, a cookie, and a cup of coffee, "this is for you."

"I didn't order—"

"It's on us."

What a kind man. She ate and drank with small bites and sips and stared out the window, thinking. Time moved too quickly. Time moved too slowly.

After a night of sporadic sleep, early the next morning the train stopped in a small town with a ten-minute layover. Time for but one call. If she didn't reach this Horace fellow in New York, she would find herself in immense difficulty.

To her amazement, her call reached lost and found. The man named Horace answered. Though he knew nothing of the letter, he promised to make every attempt to find it.

Relieved, Olivia left a forwarding address in care of Oliver M. Harrington in Amber Leaf, Minnesota and then hurried back to the train, hopping on as the conductor made the final call.

One telephone call down, one to go. May the next connection go even better.

CHAPTER FORTY-THREE

By early evening, the train chugged into the Chicago station. Olivia anticipated the fifteen-minute layover—fifteen minutes to connect with her father or wait for the next train. Steam hissing, she tore off for the depot and headed straight for the telephone. "Operator, I'd like to place a collect call to the home of Oliver M. Harrington in Amber Leaf, Minnesota, please."

Collect call? No matter how many times she muttered those imposing words, they still made her squirm.

She listened intently. One ring. Please answer. Two rings. Please, please answer. Three rings.

A lady with a pleasant voice finally responded. "Hello?"

Olivia was beside herself. Too nervous to stand still, she shifted her weight from foot to foot, experiencing an occasional buckling of her knees.

"I have a long distance collect call for a Mr. Oliver M. Harrington, please," the operator said.

"This is Mrs. Harrington. I'm afraid my husband isn't here, but I'd be more than happy to accept the charges."

"Go ahead, miss."

A too-brief moment later, Olivia hung up the receiver, seized her bag, and plodded toward her waiting train. Had it been a pleasurable exchange, she would have twirled around and made a mad dash. But that was not the case. Her father had marched off to war and hadn't advised her? Tomorrow she would arrive in Amber Leaf. Be alone with her stepmother. No hope of finally meeting her father. At least not during this trip. Though the woman had sounded warm and kind, would she be accepting of Olivia? Consider her a part of their family? Would they have enough in common to get on well?

"All aboard," the conductor cried.

Olivia took one last look around the Chicago Depot. Nervous about what awaited her, she felt tempted to stay put. This would be her final boarding. No turning back.

A too short moment later, she plunked her baggage in the Pullman. A middle-aged couple sat across from her. The husband appeared rather pleasant, much like the picture she'd received of her father with the exception of his well-kept though bushy moustache. And his wife emanated the same warmth in her voice that Olivia had heard over the telephone wires a few short minutes ago.

The whistle blew. She jumped. And the train chugged down the tracks.

"You're traveling alone, miss?" the man said.

"Yes, sir."

"I overheard you speaking with the conductor. That accent. Are you, by chance, from England?"

"Yes, sir," she repeated.

His eyes swelled tender with concern. "Are you affected badly by the war in your part of the world?"

"I live in London, so yes, it has been dreadful."

"I can only imagine. Our son will be twenty-one next week. As soon as he turns, he insists he's going to sign up." The man shook his head. "He has no idea what he's getting himself into."

Not wanting to confirm the worst, Olivia peered out the window at the never-ending forest. "I don't know that I've ever seen so many trees."

"There's a lot of wonderful wildlife out there, too."

"Where are you headed, dear?" the man's wife said.

"Amber Leaf."

The woman perked up. "What a wonderful coincidence. That's where we're from. Do you have family there?"

Olivia balked. Would she violate her father by answering for him? Was he private about that sort of thing? What might she say that wouldn't reveal too much? The woman sat waiting and they appeared too kind not to be polite. "My father and stepmother."

The woman's eyes sparkled. "We must know them then. What's your father's name."

Olivia drew back.

"Miss?"

Her husband grasped his wife's hand, appearing to silence her. He sat quiet for a short while then said, "We never did introduce ourselves. I'm Reverend Collver and this is my wife Louise. I'm the pastor at Village Church in Amber Leaf. I'm not meaning to involve myself in your private affairs, but I sense there might be a problem with your parents. Is there any way I might be of help?"

"You're a clergyman?" Surely it would be appropriate to speak with a man of the cloth about such matters. "I've never met my father before," she said, feeling relief that she could talk about it. "He didn't know about me, that I'm his daughter, that is. I fear it's a rather long story. There's some sort of mystery behind it. I feel as if I need to protect him."

"I understand," the pastor said. "Perhaps if you shared his name that might shed some light on it."

"It's Oliver Harrington."

"Oli—" The pastor choked. His jaw dropped. He gazed at his wife as if something were terribly amiss.

"Please tell me he is the good person my grandmum told me he was," Olivia said.

"I can assure you there could not be a better person alive. It's just that of all of the people in the world, I can't imagine Oliver Harrington having a child he didn't know about. It doesn't fit his character. Besides, miss, since he's in—"

When the reverend's wife immediately and not so subtly squeezed his thigh, the reverend awkwardly cleared his throat. "This appears to be a rather sensitive matter after all. Maybe it would be more appropriate if his wife filled you in."

"I believe she already has. I understand that at the moment he's journeying the high seas." Olivia wasn't certain where to fix her gaze. Feeling increasingly ill at ease, she slowly stood. "It was a pleasure meeting you. Now if you'll excuse me, I believe I'll be off to the dining car for a cup of tea."

Could it be her imagination, or did the pastor and his wife appear relieved at her departure?

The hours passed by quickly. She wiped perspiring palms on her skirt then wiped them again and again. They refused to stay dry.

At half past ten in the morning, the train chugged to a stop in Amber Leaf. In a few short moments, at least a part of the fantasy will have become a reality.

Please, please like me.

Too apprehensive to take the lead, she held back at the end of the Pullman and waited for Pastor Collver and his wife to vacate the train. Why make this more awkward than need be? She pulled back again and again for passersby until she was last to get off. People milling about here, there, and everywhere. But no one looking for her? She bounced to her toes to see if she might find a middle-aged woman with a kind voice, but that appeared not to be. As the crowd dwindled, she stood dazed. Had her stepmother changed her mind?

The Collvers were nowhere in sight either.

Too uncertain to make another telephone call.

Much too early to turn back.

If only Jeremy were here.

She plunked her suitcase on the ground, sat on it, and stared off.

What was a stranded soul to do?

CHAPTER FORTY-FOUR

The crowd thinned until no one was left and still Olivia sat waiting. The door to the depot stood a gaping hole. Inside, not a soul around with the exception of a ticket agent who milled about mumbling to himself. Olivia trudged back outside and peered up and down railroad tracks dropping off at the ends of the earth. She then gazed up at the autumn trees and chirping birds surrounding her, which seemed to mock to her trepidation.

This is Amber Leaf.

Her father off to war.

No stepmother to greet her ... and after that warm telephone call.

What had the minister said? This appears to have been a rather delicate matter after all? Why would he say such a thing?

She stood. Take courage, she told herself. Make that telephone call just the same. You'll never know what's happening until you do.

As she made her way toward the depot again, however, a Model T sped around the corner and pulled up sharply into the parking area. An attractive middle-aged driver bounded out, appearing harried. The woman sprinted toward her. "Excuse me, miss, but are you Olivia by chance?"

"Yes ma'am."

The woman let out a relieved sigh, drew her into her arms, and held her tight. "Welcome to Amber Leaf." She released Olivia then took a full step back and looked her up and down. "My, my, aren't you lovely? Your picture didn't do you justice. I'm Gretta, by the way, and I'm awfully sorry I'm late." She glanced back at the car. "I took a short-cut. A thunderstorm blew through last night. I had to double back and take the long way around. Who could have known that half way here a fallen tree was completely blocking the road."

"I feared you'd changed your mind about coming."

"Oh, my dear girl. Never!"

What a blessed word. "It's marvelous to finally meet you." Olivia gave a dejected look toward the road. "I was so looking forward to finally meeting my ... your husband. To where was he deployed, do you know?"

A sad look washed over the dear woman's lovely face. "He's on his way to France."

Olivia gulped.

"He got the crazy notion," she said, "that he needed to do his duty for God and country."

"I'm not meaning to be unkind, it's just that he isn't a young man any more, and hadn't he already served in Sudan?"

Gretta reached for Olivia's bag. "Let me help you with that."

"I have it, thank you," she insisted. "It's not particularly heavy."

Gretta led the way to the shiny automobile then opened Olivia's door. "About your father not being a young man any more ... what is it, dear?"

Feeling a need to weep, Olivia stood dumbstruck. "Thank you for calling him my father."

"You have no idea how much you already mean to him, or should I say to us?" Gretta said reassuringly and continued on. "As I was saying, your father is a little on the old side and you're right, he did serve in Sudan."

"Why would he want to venture off to war again then?"

As Olivia slipped her bag into the back seat, Gretta hand cranked the car then hopped in. "They have a desperate need for officers, and he felt a responsibility to meet that need."

A short moment later, they were off. "He's had a few struggles in the past with claustrophobia," Gretta said.

"I'm so sorry to hear that. I do hope he handles the voyage well."

"Your father isn't one to be held back by what he considers nonsense. If he has a problem, he deals with it … by the way, around here he's known as Big Ole. I'll tell you all about him when we get home. Meanwhile, let me give you a cook's tour of our town. I think you'll learn to love Amber Leaf. We sure do."

As they rode along, trees everywhere were dressed in the stunning colors of red, orange, and gold. Beautiful shimmering lakes. Lovely parks. Charming uptown. The scent of autumn filling the air.

"That's where your father works," Gretta said as they drove past the law office of Addison and Crowley.

What a hallowed moment. Seeing this building, the door her father entered each weekday morning, was to step deeper into another part of his world, and it felt amazingly like home.

But when the steeple at Village Church emerged into view, alarm bells sounded. How could Olivia tell Gretta she had already shared a family secret with the pastor? A stranger at that? It would not be good to have her stepmother thinking she might be prone to gossip. What might her father think if he knew?

And with him being in Europe, how long should she stay? Would she ever get an opportunity to meet him now? Why not tell her he was off to war? She would never have come had she known.

"By the way," Gretta said, "your father lived for your letters. The first one jarred him. He wasn't sure what to think or what your motives might have been. But over time, he became convinced that somehow you are his flesh and blood, and so did I. He can't wait to read Amelia's letter."

Olivia flinched.

"We can't imagine what she could have written that will make sense of this whole thing." Gretta hesitated. "You seem distressed. Is everything okay, Olivia?"

No.

Everything is not okay.

CHAPTER FORTY-FIVE

Though all Army bases looked similar, this base in France possessed a different kind of feel—it gave Ole the shivers. Nondescript. Cold. Utilitarian. Evoking little if any emotion.

And of all of the units to unwittingly volunteer for and get assigned ... a tank unit. But then why not? They suffered the greatest need for officers.

Here his mettle would be tested. Here he would prove he really had it in him to manage his worst fear with no margin for miscalculation.

After looking over the base in every direction, he lit out for the rows of Renault FT light tanks. Climbing onto the first one he came across, he ran a thumb along its turret. Felt like any other cold hunk of metal. He opened the driver's hatch and peered inside. Change-speed and steering levers. Clutch and brake pedals. He glanced over his shoulder, then drew open the emergency door. With both portals open, the machine appeared far less confining than he'd imagined, so he leaned in to steal a better look.

"Hey," Buddy cried from behind.

Ole jumped, hitting his head on the turret. He fingered the smarting injury and muttered, "Wonder if this qualifies for a medal of honor of some sort?"

Buddy fixed his gaze on the tank. "Amazing piece of work if I've ever seen one. What do you say? How about if we hop in?"

"After you."

Buddy burrowed into the driver's seat. "It's a little tight in here."

"Forget how tight the thing is." Ole crawled through the emergency door and stared out at the terrain. "Concentrate on how you're going to drive a devil like this. You've got a job to do. The smoother the ride, the better your gunner's aim."

Buddy worked the clutch and brake and manipulated the levers. "Relax, sir. I doubt we'll get bumped around too bad puttering along at a whopping four miles an hour. And don't worry about me. Push comes to shove, I could row a porcelain tub across Lake Okoboji and keep the thing afloat." He looked up and around, his gaze focusing on the gun. "Hope we don't get busted eardrums when you gunners start firing those things."

Ole took a long practice aim, maneuvering the gun from side to side. "When we get into battle, busted eardrums are going to be the least of our worries." After a thoughtful pause and another practice aim, he muttered, "We doughboys have just arrived."

Buddy sat quietly, appearing steeped in concern. "I like the open feel now," the young soldier said, "but it's going to be a lot different when we close the thing up and plow through barbed wire out there in No Man's Land." His unsure voice softened. "Sure hope this thing doesn't turn into a coffin."

Thanks for the vivid thought.

Later that evening. Buddy joined him in the mess hall. Through a mouth filled with mashed potatoes and gravy, he eked out, "That's our CO over there."

"Major Patton?" Ole glanced over his shoulder.

"Next table there to the right."

The major certainly exuded presence. The soldiers sitting on either side of him appeared to lap up his every word. Either that or they feared him. That wasn't about to happen to Ole.

Though Buddy scooped up another fork of mashed potatoes and gulped it down as if he hadn't eaten in a week, the look in his eyes brought Ole back to the ship, to the bunk, to the first night they'd met. The innocence. The trembling. The desire to be a somebody. Buddy chased down the potatoes with a swig of water and said, "You know what I don't understand, sir? Maybe I'm a little old fashioned, but I've been noticing a lot of the boys cussing, getting drunk, taking advantage of the ladies. Instead of preparing to meet their Maker, they're living recklessly. Why would they want to do a thing like that?"

"I've wondered about that myself." A raucous outburst erupted at a table in the furthermost corner. "Could be fear, I guess, or maybe the foolishness of youth believing they're invincible."

Buddy stroked the stem of his mug. "Are you a believer, sir?"

Having walked in the young soldier's shoes, Ole understood the need crying out beneath the question. "Why are you asking?"

He shrugged.

"I am," Ole said. "How about you?"

"I don't know. Sort of, I guess."

As another boisterous outbreak ensued, Ole recalled life in Sudan. His arrival. Having been scared to death, too. He knew at the time that he had to overcome the fear if he wanted to make it and even then there were no guarantees. So he dropped to his knees and rattled the windows of heaven. It took a while, but to his amazement, God came through. Ole had gotten that peace he'd always heard about, but never really understood … that peace that passes all understanding.

Buddy perked up. "But I'm a good person."

"Out on the battlefield it doesn't matter how good you are," Ole said, "what matters is how committed you are. There's a big difference."

After getting a stomach full of what could have been a far worse meal, Ole and Buddy headed for the barracks. Outside the mess hall, a half dozen or so Red Cross nurses happened by. A cluster of rookie soldiers standing around on the boardwalk whistled and jeered like love-starved adolescents.

"They aren't being respectful," Buddy said. "That isn't right."

Veering off in the same direction, Ole and Buddy stepped in line behind the nurses. Several buildings up, another cluster of soldiers gathered in waning light, but these soldiers appeared battle weary. As the nurses passed by, they merely gazed at them with appreciative though despairing eyes, not a peep from a one of them.

Buddy gave Ole a thoughtful look. "That's going to be us in a few months, isn't it, sir?" he said.

A young nurse turned a warm gaze on Buddy. Clearly she'd overhead his revelation.

Stealing a good look at her, though, Ole stopped in his tracks.

"What's the matter?" Buddy said.

That nurse. She's the spitting image of my Olivia. Ole looked at Buddy. "Nothing."

No … everything.

CHAPTER FORTY-SIX

The mail arrived mid-afternoon. Ole embarrassed himself as he crowded in like all of the other impatient soldiers, waiting for his name to be called as if he were in his teens again out there on the football field waiting to see if he'd made that special team. But he didn't get a letter.

He got a bundle of letters.

And a package.

Since leaving Amber Leaf, Gretta had written every day if not several times a day. And she tucked each letter into a separate envelope before posting them individually. He sidestepped the crowd and huddled beneath a tall oak devoid of leaves. Leaning his back against its wide trunk, he began reading with the letter marked one.

29 September

My dearest Ole,

Your train left several hours ago and already it seems as if a lifetime has passed. I can only hope that I don't go mad merely waiting for your letters. Do know that I am living for them.

As soon as I finish this note, I thought I'd bake a batch of oatmeal raisin cookies for you. They always were your favorite. I will package them and promise to bring them to the post office first thing in the morning.

And speaking of the post office, I stopped by on my way home from the train depot. Guess what! Olivia sent me my very own letter. Hearing from her was such a joy. She said she sent a letter to you at the office as well, but wanted to write me so that we would have an opportunity to get to know one another personally via mail before she does arrive.

Your Olivia is on her way to Amber Leaf, Ole. You missed her. Just think … by the time you read this letter, she will already be here. It appears as if she hadn't received word from you yet when she left. Her letter and yours must have crossed in the mail. I have to admit that I can't wait to finally meet her. I've been keeping a close eye on the daily papers. There haven't been any passenger ship incidents that I've been able to see. She must have made it past the German blockade by now and hopefully is out of danger. I'll prepare the guest bedroom the minute I finish baking your cookies. But you, Oliver Harrington, are and will always remain my number one priority.

By the way, when I cleaned your office, I found a half-lit cigar in the ashtray. I sniffed it and got gooseflesh thinking of you. Should you come home and find the house smelling of cigar smoke, be kind to me. I found the scent so intoxicating that I placed it on the nightstand beside our bed. I plan to take a whiff the first thing every morning and the last thing every night while thinking tender thoughts of you. In the event that I decide to take up the powerful vice, be forewarned. If you chastise me,

I will proclaim complete innocence. After all, I will have been tempted by none other than you.

One more thing before I get on with my day. About Olivia's arrival, as I recall, she said she was bringing that letter along with her, that letter that Amelia had written. Would you like me to forward it on to you or keep it until your return?

Please take care in all that you do. I miss you horribly and so look forward to hearing from you.

Your loving wife,

Gretta

Ole carefully folded the letter, placed it back in its envelope, and looked up.

Olivia is in America now.

With my beloved bride.

Should Gretta send me Amelia's letter?

Yes. Absolutely.

No.

Amelia had requested that Olivia present it to him personally. Why?

He continued reading and thoroughly enjoying each of Gretta's letters, visions of her choking on cigar smoke bringing an occasional grin. He then tore open the package she'd sent and chomped on an oatmeal raisin cookie. It may not have been fresh out of the oven, but it wasn't half bad.

A half hour later he stopped by the barracks, picked up a law book that he'd managed to bring along, and sauntered back to the mess hall. Still time to read before supper. He found a bench in a corner where he doubted he'd be interrupted. After an hour or so of reading, the hall filled with hungry soldiers. He left the book on the table long enough to take a quick stroll through the chow line. When he returned, he found an officer leafing through his book. The man looked up. "Harrington?" he said.

Though Ole took note of the vocal inflection, the now familiar voice proved no cause for concern. He lowered his tray onto the table while looking into a captain's curious eyes. "Yes, sir?"

"This belongs to you?" The captain tapped the book title several times with a pointer finger. "An advanced book on law?"

Ole seized it. "Always been interested in law, sir."

"That a fact? Missing the court room drama, are you?"

Ole shrugged.

"I've been looking for you, meaning to have a word," the officer said. "Actually it's at the request of Major George S. Patton. Please. Have a seat. I would join you, but I've already eaten."

At the request of Major Patton? Ole poked at the tray, but had little interest in lifting his fork.

The captain continued to eye him curiously then chuckled. "Patton and I watched you doing calisthenics. Appears you no longer have the gift, my good man. A grizzly could have done them better."

Those words stopped Ole. He chose to view aging and the laws of nature a blessing rather than to fall victim to it. So he raised his chin, his tone steadfast. "Given the gift of time … my good man … you, too, will one day learn about the amazing transition that dignifies the aging process. Brawn has a will of its own, you see. It transfers from here …" he said pointing a finger to a bicep, "… to here." He tapped his forehead. "And it sharpens as it grows."

Was that a gulp?

The captain stood taller. "That's quite an impressive record you have."

"I assume that means you've done a background check on me."

"You assume right. In the end, mettle trumps brawn any and every day of the week. Tomorrow morning at 0900 hours we're holding a strategy meeting. Under normal circumstances, I would say be there."

"Sir?"

"It will be an honor to have you there, sir."

Then came the respectful salute.

CHAPTER FORTY-SEVEN

nticipation thickened the air. Officers sitting around a table in tight quarters remained riveted on Major Patton's briefing. The Second Battle of the Marne. Ole's soon-to-be first battle on the Western Front. What a thought. He was playing ball with the big boys again. Allied troops. Twenty-four French divisions. Eight U.S. divisions. Three hundred and fifty Renault FT tanks making their debut on the battlefield.

And he would be riding along inside.

He stared off, forcing himself to concentrate on the back and forth banter that followed.

"Do the Allies have a complete picture of the German offensive?"

"They know the German plan down to the minute, sir."

"But do the German's know our plan?"

"We set them up." A hint of pride penetrated that voice. "Planted a false strategy we made sure they'd find. We can only hope they buy it. We want to place their men in all the wrong places so we can catch them unawares."

That's good, Ole mused. Aim for the exposed parts of the German lines. Drive a dagger into their flank. Force their retreat.

After the meeting, he headed back to the barracks to spend time on his knees. A man who had an ounce of wisdom knew he needed all the help he could get—regardless of age, regardless of ability … regardless of brawn.

As he walked along, however, he passed that young nurse again, the one who bore an amazing resemblance to what might possibly be his flesh-and-blood daughter. Remarkable how he'd been concerned about losing Olivia to German bombs before he would get a chance to meet her. But now with a strange twist of fate, she was safely in America, and he was the one who could easily lose his life to a merciless barrage of shells before having an opportunity to make her acquaintance. Or was it a twist of fate? He chose to volunteer. Service was not foisted on him.

But that was different, he told himself. It was the Ole's of this world who chose to protect the Grettas and the Olivias from would-be dictators.

The nurse stopped at Ole's side. "I see you're readying for battle, sir."

"Yes, ma'am."

"You have no idea how relieved we are that you Americans are finally here," she said. "Fresh troops are great for morale. You can feel it in the air." Glancing over her shoulder, she said in a thoughtful tone, "I've seen a lot of young soldiers willing to charge to their deaths, but none with finer spirits than these men." She then turned back and looked up at Ole again, her cheeks growing a warm shade of pink. "I'm sorry. That was a terribly insensitive thing to say."

"Nonsense," he said. "We appreciate the thought."

"It's time to turn this war around." Determination emanated through sincere eyes, through the strength of her voice. "Time to bring the German army to its knees. Good luck to you, sir."

He nodded then straightened his cap and ventured on.

THE DAY OF RECKONING HAD ARRIVED. Anxious about the unknown that awaited him, Ole hopped onto the back of the Renault RT and off they charged. This battle contained a far different feel from any he'd been in, and he'd been in more than he cared to remember. For this war introduced the thunder of roaring engines. Clattering pistons. A growing absence of snorting mounts. The pungent smell of horse droppings giving way to that of noxious exhaust fumes. They painstakingly navigated across barren terrain pocked by mortar blasts and open trenches. Mowed down fields of barbed wire as if mowing down fields laden with cobwebs. And unlike in Sudan where Ole had led his men into battle looking up the wrong end of the sharp blades of shiny bayonets, these armored tanks were assigned the task of bombarding the Germans ahead of them while shielding their own soldiers from a barrage of enemy fire—courageous soldiers who charged on foot from behind.

For as long as time would allow, Ole balanced on the back of the Renault with one eye on the field ahead and the other on the open hatch of the light tank, anticipating the final plunge into that cavernous dungeon. Buddy was right about one thing—the Renault lumbered along relentlessly at a whopping four miles per hour.

When they finally plowed into No Man's Land, the Germans opened fire.

And Ole took the plunge.

Whining engine. Grinding track. Jostling about like a drunk on skates. Thin rays of sunlight pressing through small slits of armor. Bullets ricocheting off iron. Chips of paint exploding throughout the tight chamber. Mounting heat. Aching fists vibrating on a machine gun firing shells as fast he could load them. The light tank rocked wildly as incoming shells exploded haphazardly all about them.

And then there was the noise.

When the heat of battle ended, the tanks in retreat, he flung open the emergency door. A smoke-filled breeze hit his face. The enemy cowered at his back. It was then that a harsh though refreshing reality at long last hit him, and he emptied his lungs with a whoosh.

Who would have thought the day would come when Oliver M. Harrington would welcome hunkering down in a tight space?

But it did.

All that worrying?

Useless.

He'd handled it well.

Gretta would be proud.

He sure was.

And relieved.

Though the German advance to the west broke through the French Sixth Army, gained nine miles, and succeeded in crossing the Marne River, it had now been stopped by the French Ninth Army with the welcome help of American, British, and Italian troops. Maybe now the momentum of the war would change. With any luck at all, this could be a first step in a series of Allied victories that would finally end this hellish fighting.

If only he could see it through to the end ... rather than meeting with his own demise. After all, he mused, he was only one of millions who had already gone on to meet their Maker, premature though those meetings might have been. Why should he be any different?

But he wasn't ready for his life to end. He had a loving wife to care for, a beautiful daughter to meet—his daughter, adopted though she might easily be.

CHAPTER FORTY-EIGHT

tepping out under a brilliant autumn sky, Ole tucked Gretta's picture in the pocket nearest his heart then gave it a light pat. Better ask her to send another photograph, he mused. This one's fraying pretty badly around the edges.

He walked on. Someone shadowed him. He sensed it.

"Where you headed, sir?"

He glanced over his shoulder.

Buddy.

"Thought I'd check out the tank. Count the dents. That was quite a shelling we took yesterday ... and yes, you're welcome to tag along."

Buddy jammed determined fists into his pockets as he fell into step. "I still can't believe how I lucked out ... for when we go out into battle again, I mean. Getting to drive your tank."

"You might want to rethink that," Ole said, stopping short. "This is dangerous duty, soldier."

"I know. But for as scared as I was, I couldn't believe how exciting it was, too. I don't know that I've ever felt so alive."

"That all depends on what you call exciting." He turned and walked on. Didn't the boy understand it was near suicide to have to take the lead? "Colonel Patton doesn't believe in having his officers lead from behind."

"Sir?"

"We lead from the front."

"Got to respect a man who leads by example."

"I doubt he's doing it to set an example," Ole said as Buddy continued to march in step. A good officer needed control … to read the enemy, to calm chaos. With order comes success. Ole didn't know about Patton, but that's what he was banking on.

This time Buddy stopped abruptly. Appeared troubled. "Out on the battlefield, sir, aren't we easy target practice for the Krauts? I mean awfully easy?"

The boy understood after all. "Patton's no dummy. Smoke shells do a decent job of camouflaging armor."

Again they walked on, the tanks looming into view.

"Is it true what the boys are saying about him?" Buddy said. "That he crawled out into No Man's Land after dark just to check the terrain?"

"It's true, son."

"That man sure has guts."

"He is a brilliant strategist, no question there."

Ole hopped onto the tank and peered inside. "What in the world?" He pulled out several belts and dangled them high. "Any idea what these are all about? Or who put them here?"

Buddy puffed out his chest and grinned. "Fan belts on these tanks aren't the best. Decided to be prepared."

"I see," Ole said. "You're pretty sure of yourself, aren't you?"

"Try to be." A flash of sunlight glinted off his white teeth. "I noticed you've been busy gearing up for the next round, too, sir. You've got enough extra shells stuffed in here to take out a garrison all by yourself. But aren't you afraid they're going to weight us down?"

Ole lifted his chin. "I would blast their antitank guns all of the way back to Germany if I could, even if I had to do it all by myself. The

Krauts bombed Hades out of my homeland. I have family there, so as you can imagine, that didn't make me happy."

"Do we ever get past being scared, sir?" Buddy turned shamefaced. "That was a dumb question. Forget I asked."

"It's not the dumb questions we need to concern ourselves with, it's the dumb decisions that destroy us. And about being scared, I think excited might be a more accurate word. Colonel Patton is chomping at the bit to win this thing. His enthusiasm rubs off. As for me, the only thing that keeps me awake at night is the thought of taking on unnecessary casualties."

"No need to worry about that. You're in good hands." Buddy hopped into the driver's seat and played around with the levers. "We get into any trouble, I know a little about medicine. Not a lot, but I know the basics."

"You've had medical training," Ole said, hopeful.

"My uncle's a veterinarian. I used to stand over his shoulder. Learned a few procedures. When it comes to wounds, he says flesh is flesh."

"I'll bear that in mind, soldier." Ole looked over the shell-pocked tank. "I'll definitely bear that in mind."

After several more days of intense preparation, the engines finally roared again. Tracks squealed. And Ole couldn't stop worrying. What a harebrained time for useless second thoughts. Of all of the soldiers, why did Buddy have to get assigned to drive his tank? Wasn't it enough to have to watch out for his other men without adding the boy into the mix? Watching out for Buddy was on par with watching out for a son, his son, the boy he'd never gotten a chance to know. Oliver Junior would be seventeen now, the same age as Olivia. Being haunted by that loss was added pressure Ole didn't need.

Get your mind on the battle, he told himself. You'll have plenty of time to worry after it's over.

Peering through a wall of thick smoke, he rode on the back of the tank standing at the ready, concentrating, taking aim, waiting for smoke to dissipate enough to see his intended targets and make hash out them, to fire shells as fast as he could load them. "This is it, Buddy," he yelled and they hopped inside. Gunfire exploded from every imaginable direction, the sound deafening. Bullets ricocheting off the tank. Chips of paint exploding like confetti throughout the small chamber.

Halfway into No Man's Land with no possibility of turning around and amidst a continuing barrage of heavy enemy fire, Buddy yelled out, "Broken fan belt."

"What are you doing?"

He threw open the door.

"You can't go out there," Ole bellowed. "You'll get killed."

"What's the difference? We'll get killed in here, too. We're sitting ducks." He held up a fan belt. "This tank isn't going to fix itself."

Sweat dripping from his brow, pulse throbbing, Ole yelled, "Hurry up then!" and stepped up the shelling, surprised at how speedy and accurate his aim when the tank no longer moved.

Several rounds later, Buddy hopped back in. "Got a problem, sir."

"Machine gun fire ricocheting all over this thing and you think we've got a problem?"

"I can't be in both places at once. We need a crank start and you can't crank and fire at the same time."

Ole peered through a gap. The smoke shield thicker than a heavy fog again, he cracked open the emergency door, pushed through, looked up into the smoke-filled sky and then cranked like there was no tomorrow. The engine fired up and he hopped back in, a barrage of bullets whistling past. How he and Buddy missed getting hit other than by divine intervention far surpassed Ole's comprehension. He grabbed the machine gun and aimed. "Let's get going," he shouted.

Fighting to the point of exhaustion, the battle a resounding success, they returned to camp. Tomorrow they would be back. More fighting. More casualties. But also having gained ground. For now, though, that was enough. Momentum was on their side.

If only they could hold onto it.

CHAPTER FORTY-NINE

unlight streamed through the windows, the sheers dancing on the cool early morning breeze. Olivia drew the sheet over her shoulders and snuggled in. Amber Leaf continued to exceed her fondest imaginings. Gretta. Her father's marvelous home. The view of the lake. The charming town. Last evening's divine supper. Yet what about the letter? Her conscience?

Attend to that she told herself, and soon.

She rolled to her side and fluffed the pillow. To get up or not to get up? She lay in the quiet for the longest while thinking, planning, listening until faint sounds emanated from the kitchen below, welcome sounds of clanking pots and pans. And her feet hit the floor.

As Olivia rounded the door to the kitchen, Gretta plunked a heavy skillet on the stove. "Good morning, dear. How'd you sleep?"

"Wonderfully, thank you."

"Like bacon and eggs?"

"Love them." Olivia sniffed the air. "Is it my imagination or do I smell cinnamon rolls?"

"They'll be out of the oven in a minute."

"I'm feeling rather spoiled. I don't recall having eaten this well."

"It's time for us to make up for that then, wouldn't you say?"

Olivia melted at the generosity and warmth in Gretta's kind eyes.

After breakfast Gretta led her into the parlor where an armload of albums sat on the coffee table. "Thought you'd enjoy seeing some photographs of your father when he was a boy," she said.

To see more of her father's wonderful world? Curiously grateful for the opportunity, Olivia opened the first album and stared at the images scattered across the page. Images of her father as an infant. Images of him as a child in a buggy. Images of him as a young boy standing near the entry of what appeared to be … a mansion? Surely this could not be his home. Her alleged grandparents' home? She looked up. "Is this …?"

"I've only seen pictures," Gretta said. "Your father never says much about it."

Olivia dizzied at the grandeur. "Why?"

"They never got along well. Had a parting of ways before Ole came to America and then another one when he chose to marry me instead of going back to England. I'm sure he'll tell you all about it one day."

Eager to learn more about her heritage, or what she hoped to be her heritage, Olivia leafed through the rest of the pages, studying them, not wanting to take her eyes off of them as she imagined the quality of his life. Who was this amazing man, and how could she be so fortunate as to possibly be his daughter?

She set an album aside and picked up another, keenly aware how strangely at home she felt in this wonderful place. Exploring her father's life through pictures. Getting to know Gretta. She would never have thought it possible to lose so much when she lost her grandmum and yet gain far more with that very same loss.

Mid-morning, Gretta bounded into the room carrying in a tray of coffee and sugar cookies also fresh out of the oven. "You seem to be enjoying yourself," she said.

"These photographs, they're wonderful." She looked up. "He appears so confident and happy."

"I've never known a more honorable man." Gretta lowered onto an ottoman next to Olivia, her timbre appearing mischievous. "I wish we could open that letter from your grandmother. I wrote to Ole about it. Asked him if he would mind, but he insists we wait until he can read it in your presence ... What is it, child?"

Olivia gulped down a chunk of half-chewed cookie and placed the rest on a small plate. "I've been wanting to tell you, but haven't been able bring myself to do so. The letter? It's gone."

Gretta's jaw dropped. "But I thought ..."

"I had it with me, honest I did, but somehow managed to lose it when I was aboard ship." As she reluctantly poured out her heart, Gretta appeared strangely amused.

"Why are you smiling?" Olivia said. "Are you not bothered by what I just shared?"

"I'm sorry you lost the letter, dear, but you are definitely your father's child. He has a blistering conscience, too."

"I called the ship," Olivia continued. "They promised to look for it and will send it here if they find it. I won't have peace until it comes. But I must tell you about Pastor Collver as well."

Gretta drew back, lines of surprise cutting into her smooth forehead. "How could you possibly know him?"

Olivia closed an album and drew it to her chest, as if that could shield her. "I met him and his wife on the train."

"And?"

"I accidentally told them who my father is."

"Why would that be a problem, dear?"

Taken aback, Olivia said, "Your husband wouldn't mind them knowing?"

"You mean your father," she corrected, "why would he?"

"It's just that ... if only you could have seen the look on their faces."

Gretta chuckled. "There's nothing I'd have loved more than to see it."

"I don't understand," Olivia said. "If I were you, I wouldn't trust me, not in the slightest. I announce I'm his daughter out of the blue with no word of explanation and yet you take me in."

Gretta reached over and squeezed Olivia's hand. "One day the pieces of the puzzle will all fit together. Don't worry. No matter how this unfolds, just know that you are *our* daughter," she said with an air of sincerity, "and neither of us want to let you go."

May it always be as you say.

CHAPTER FIFTY

All week long Ole listened to young soldiers gloating about Friday evening when they would go into town and live it up eating exotic French food and drinking fine wine. The least-thought-out bragged about getting plastered, not taking into consideration the hangovers that promised to follow, hangovers he himself endured night after night in lonely rundown pubs in England after having lost his beloved Emily. But those days were long gone. Let the boys have their fun. He was happy to hole up on a quiet base on a quieter Friday night where nothing would go wrong.

He was busying himself outside the officers quarters shining his shoes when Buddy strode up with a schoolboy grin. "I don't know that it's possible to get those any shinier, sir," he said.

Ole set the cloth aside, slipped on a shoe, and tied it. "I take 'straighten up soldier, spit shine your shoes' literally."

"What do you say?" The kid leaned an elbow against the makeshift building. "It's Friday night. Been a grueling week. Don't you think we've earned a ride into town?"

How was it that an enlisted kid nearly half Ole's age would feel comfortable seeking the company of an officer? Ole must be doing something right. Could it be that they had inadvertently bonded like father and son? "You can get your mitts on a truck?"

"No sir, but I've met a soldier who can. He's driving in on official military business. Offered to give us a lift. Come on. We don't have anything better to do around this place."

Jostling around in a truck in early twilight, Ole took in the countryside of Langres. One day he would bring Gretta here. Show her where he'd been stationed during the war, tell her about his adventures. And they'd go to Paris to see the Eiffel Tower, the Louvre, and ride the metro. But that wouldn't happen until one day in the far distant future. For now, he was more than happy to settle for some excellent French cuisine even if it was with the boys.

The driver dropped them off at a charming French restaurant on a bustling street in the middle of town square with a promise to pick them up at half past ten. As they entered, a small string ensemble entertained from a tight corner. The bar was packed with eager young soldiers. Linen tablecloths and napkins. Floral centerpieces on each table with candles aglow. Classy menus detailing the evening's presentations—printed entirely in French.

"Can't read the menu either?" Buddy said. "What are we going to do, sir?"

"Do you like roast beef?"

Buddy lit up. "It's my favorite."

"Good. Then we'll order boeuf de rôti."

"How do you know to do that?"

Ole suppressed a grin. "With time, you learn to pay attention."

Minutes later, the lobster bisque did not disappoint. But when the waiter placed the steamy plate of beef before Ole, though Gretta would have found the artistic presentation exemplary, he found himself disappointed by the portion size. One taste of the rich sauce, however, and he re-evaluated his summation. This was one amazing meal too rich to eat too much. He sensed he would relive the taste again and again over a lifetime. If awarded a lifetime to live, that is.

"Trouble brewing," Buddy said.

"What?"

"Up at the bar there, that attractive little hussy with the mole painted on her cheek? She's been playing those two poor suckers against each other since we stepped into this place."

Ole glanced over his shoulder. One of the soldiers already wobbled from too much of some sort of liquid that appeared far stronger than wine. More hungry than curious, though, he returned to his meal. The potatoes au gratin rich with butter and aged cheese, and the French beans glazed with a buttery white sauce and garnished with delicate bits of bacon, proved mouth watering. Oh, that fine food tasted so good. Though the raucous at the bar escalated, Ole remained far too engrossed in pleasing his palate to care until an ear-shattering crash begged his attention.

One teetering young soldier waved the jagged edges of a broken bottle in the face of his terrified adversary, and all because of one not-so-kind lady's inappropriate affections. What were these boys thinking? As the music stopped, gasps rippled throughout the bistro. Ole hopped up and tore through the converging crowd. He seized the wrist of the stabbing hand and applied pressure until what was left of the broken bottle burst on the floor. "You might want to get out of here while you still can," Ole said to the recipient of the assault.

The pale young soldier quickly sobered and scrambled for the door, tripping and nearly falling all the way. As the other let loose a few expletives, Ole patted his shoulder. "Go back to the barracks, son. You could use a little time to cool off."

A few moments later, the waiter appeared at their table. "Thank you for saving the evening, sir. Your meals are on the house."

"It wasn't the house's fault," Ole said. "If anything, I should pay you. I jolly rather enjoyed the exchange."

"Spoken like a true gentleman, sir."

After the waiter disappeared, Buddy turned to Ole. "You handled that fight like a pro. How did you know what to do? And where did you get your confidence from?"

"Age and experience. Never discount them, soldier. In the end, they're blessings."

At half past ten, Buddy said, "The truck should be here any minute now. Guess we'd better get outside."

After Ole picked up the check, they headed out into the night. He glanced at his watch. A half hour had passed and they still stood outside the bistro. Waiting. And pacing. And waiting some more. "We'd better find another ride."

"Let's give him a few more minutes," Buddy said. "I don't know what could be keeping him."

Feeling sated with one of the best meals Ole had ever enjoyed and happy with himself for having put a quick end to a barroom brawl, he eyed the charming shops across the street. It was then that a truck barreled around the corner.

"Here he comes now," Buddy said.

As the driver pulled abruptly to the curb as if making up for lost time and they hopped in, Ole got a whiff of something that caused him concern. Was it his imagination, or did the driver have his fill of spirits tonight, too? Before he had time to reconsider and hop out, the driver stomped on the accelerator, and the truck tore off with a start.

Causing Ole further concern was speed. The way the driver raced along the deserted streets of Langres, one would think they were merrily tooling along barren sand dunes. Ole gripped the seat as they rounded the next corner on two wheels. If he said anything, he might tempt the inebriated driver into proving he could push it faster.

Buddy looked at Ole, his eyes a plea.

But what could Ole do? Think, Ole, think.

From the right side on the road up ahead a horse and carriage entered the approaching intersection.

No time to stop.

A rearing horse.

The squeal of brakes.

A crash.

The nauseating sensation of somersaulting in midair.

A sickening thud.

CHAPTER FIFTY-ONE

Gretta tucked a last piece of old-fashioned fudge in the tin. "Your father is going to love this. The only thing he enjoys more than my cookies is my fudge. Man has an unbelievable sweet tooth." She wrapped the tin in brown paper, tied it with twine, and then with a far off look, she said, "I wonder what he's doing now, what he's going through."

Olivia wondered as well. It didn't seem right somehow, him risking his life while she and Gretta enjoyed theirs so. Spending time with her stepmother was as wonderful as spending time with her grandmum had been. Feeling accepted and wanted. Chatting about things that mattered. But would it last? Could it last?

"I'm not certain how long I should stay," Olivia said. "I'm concerned I won't get a chance to meet him now. And if the letter never comes, then what?"

"How long would you like to stay?"

"I was thinking perhaps another week, possibly two. Might that be too long?"

"Not long enough. This is your home," Gretta said as she lifted a finger. "Listen. I think I hear someone coming."

A light rapping rattled the back door. Gretta scuttled to the porch. From the kitchen Olivia heard a young man say, "Cablegram, ma'am," and an overwhelming feeling of dread made an unwelcome visit.

Then came the sound of foot drops. Gretta returning to the kitchen. Trembling hands. Eyes filled with sheer terror.

"What is it?" Olivia said.

"This." Gretta handed her an envelope and lowered onto a chair, fat teardrops forming. "Will you read it for me? I can't bear it. I just can't."

With trepidation, Olivia reached for the envelope, reluctantly sliced it open, and read the words she feared reading. "He's been wounded."

"No, please no," Gretta said, tears now streaming down her cheeks.

Olivia drew the cablegram closer. "He's in hospital in France. They're transferring him to the States as soon as he's well enough to travel."

"Does it say what happened? How bad he is?"

She shook her head as she returned the wire to Gretta. "I'm afraid that's all it says."

Olivia's gaze pivoted from the wire to the wrapped package on the table, devastated that a gift of love prepared from the cupboards of home a few short minutes ago could symbolize pure joy one moment and incontrovertible grief the next.

CHAPTER FIFTY-TWO

Ole forced his eyes open. *Why are they so heavy? Why is everything so fuzzy? My head? It's pounding. Everything hurts. Where is everyone? Why the eerie quiet?* He rolled to the side.

Not a good idea.

An explosion of pain rippled down his leg. He reached for his thigh, running a hand along it then attempted to lift his leg again. The deadweight of a hundred pound sack of potatoes couldn't feel heavier. Swollen. Barely moveable. Energy spent, he rolled back and gazed at the ceiling. *Why is it moving? Swirling like a whirlpool?* He forced his eyes to open wider. There. The spinning slowed.

Something felt tight against his face. He ran a finger along it and winced at a shot of pain. *Bandages? What happened?*

An apparition in white moved past. *Was that a swishing noise?* "Excuse me?" he said. "Miss?"

She stopped midstride and approached his bedside.

"Gretta? Olivia?"

"You need to lay still, sir."

"Where am I?"

"In hospital. You were in a pretty nasty accident. Lost lots of blood. We're lucky the doctors didn't lose you."

"Accident?" He gazed at a wall of windows lining the sterile room. "That's right. I remember now. Something happened. That …" He flinched at another stabbing pain. "… truck?"

"Shhh," the nurse said. "Save your strength."

Able to only comfortably move his eyes, he continued to look around. "Where's Buddy? Is he …"

"He saved your life."

"Buddy did?" A flutter tore through Ole. "Is he all right?"

"Couldn't be better. A fractured arm. Bandaged leg. Few scrapes and bruises. Other than that, he's fine. He's at your side every chance he can get. Asked me to get word to him the minute you came to. He'll be back again before you know it."

Ole eyed his gauze-covered arm. "How bad?"

"You needed quite a few stitches, but it's not broken."

"The cast. My leg. Will I … walk again?" Fearing the worst, he pinched his eyes closed as he awaited the answer.

"I'm sure you'll be fine."

He let out a relieved sigh. "And the driver?"

She turned toward a bed across the ward.

"That's him over there?" Ole said.

"Yes sir."

"He's lucky I'm too bound up to get my hands on him. He was drunk. By the time I realized it, it was too late." Ole attempted to shake his head, but another stabbing pain prevented it. "There was no stopping him. My wife …"

"I'm sure she knows by now. They'll be moving you back to the States as soon as you're strong enough."

"You mean I'm getting kicked out of the war?"

Raising a confused brow, she lightly patted his shoulder. "Get some rest now. The doctor should be along soon."

The next time Ole opened his eyes, a stranger sat on a chair next to his bed quietly studying him. "You don't look like a doctor," Ole said.

"I'm not. I'm a chaplain."

"Hence the collar?"

The man nodded. "I like the quiet in here," he said, looking about the ward. "It's restful."

"Enjoy it while you can."

"Sir?"

"See the soldier in that bed across the room there?"

The chaplain turned. "What about him?"

"This place isn't going to be quiet when I can walk again. He's the guy who put me here."

"How did he manage that?"

"Driving drunk."

"Oh, so you're the one."

"Heard about it?"

"I get a heads up before doing rounds. Under the circumstances, I'd probably want to wallop him, too."

"But you're a chaplain."

"I'm also human. I have to force myself to don a chaplain's armor every now and then when I get in a fix … you know … the Word of God."

Ole chewed on that for a moment. "Which one?"

"Which Word? In everything give thanks for this is the will of God in Christ Jesus concerning you."

"I'm not thankful, Chaplain. Don't forget, I'm the one writhing in pain here."

"I understand," he said. "Incidentally, I hear you're not all that happy about going home."

"They sure gossip around this place."

"Having problems there, are you? Anything you'd care to talk about?"

Ole stared off. Home. The word hit him in a strange sort of way. He had expected to return to the States with his head held high having exhibited remarkable courage in the throes of battle. Having conquered the enemy. "There's a part of me that would rather face a German tank with nothing more than a bow and arrow than to face home about now and another part of me that can't wait to get there." He glanced at the cast on his leg. "How can I face my wife with something as dumb as this? What will she think?"

"Oh, so that's it. You certainly are a man of pride, aren't you?"

Ole ignored the question.

The chaplain's expression turned thoughtful. "Do you think it might be possible that the accident that landed you here could be by divine design? Did it ever dawn on you that maybe God wants you to go home … for all of the right reasons?"

"And if you're wrong?"

"I could very well be."

Ole glanced at the bed across the ward. "What about him?"

"From what I've heard, he had good reason for getting drunk, just not a good reason for driving that way."

"And that reason would be?"

"I don't know this for fact, but according to the rumor mill, he got a Dear John from his girl the same day his best buddy got killed."

Ole's jaw tightened. "That didn't give him the right to play Russian roulette with my life."

"A word of advice?"

"Sir?"

"If you want peace about this, you'll need to take full responsibility for your own participation."

"How could you even begin to think I'm in any way responsible?" Ole said, incredulous.

"Who decided to go into town on a Friday night knowing there would be lots of young soldiers whooping it up?"

"What does that have to do with anything?"

"I've got a better one. Who jumped into a truck with a drunk driver?"

"I didn't know he was drunk."

"There were no signs?"

"Well, maybe he did pull up to the curb a little too fast."

"You didn't smell alcohol?"

"Sure I did. Just too late."

"I rest my case."

"You make me feel as if this was my fault. I thought chaplains cared about people."

"We do. Very much. The most loving thing I can do for you at the moment, kind sir, is to keep you from turning bitter."

The chaplain stood. "I best return to my rounds." He leaned forward and whispered a heartfelt prayer in Ole's ear. As he turned to leave, however, he hesitated at the foot of the bed. "At some point, you're going to have to let that soldier off the hook."

"Don't want to."

"And the sooner the better," the chaplain said. "You can't undo the accident, but you're too smart not to let go of the bondage."

"Says you."

"Are you a man of God?"

"On a good day ... very much so."

"Another word of advice? It's not good enough to just believe or talk our religion. We have to live it or it's not going to work for us."

Ole started to smile, but it hurt too much. "You're certainly a good manipulator."

"I prefer to see myself as a good encourager," the chaplain said. "Perhaps you'd do far better to love that young soldier than to hate him. In the throes of war, he may have saved you from a far worse plight. You are on the Western Front, you know ... just something to consider."

CHAPTER FIFTY-THREE

Buddy entered the ward and headed straight for Ole, scowling at Driver before pulling up a chair at Ole's bedside. "I'm glad to see you're back amongst the living," he said. "You gave us a real scare."

Ole rearranged his blanket, a nervous habit he was picking up while passing time. "I hear you've been keeping vigil." A pain-filled knot formed in his throat. How does one thank a man for saving his life?

"Didn't have anything better to do," Buddy said. "They gotten you out of bed yet?"

"They're animals. No respect whatsoever for the wounded. Forced me to get up and walk before my first cup of broth. Didn't matter how much pain I was in, how much I moaned … what happened? Last thing I remember was seeing a horse and buggy crossing the road ahead of us, then lights out."

"Yeah." Buddy flashed another look of contempt toward the far bed. "Harebrained show off. That guy shouldn't have been behind the wheel let alone driving that fast."

"We had no way to stop him."

"You remember him slamming on the brakes when that horse and buggy trotted out into the crossroads?"

"Yeah," Ole said, cringing at the memory. "But that's all I remember."

"That buggy had the right of way. When soldier boy lost control, the truck skidded sideways and overturned. The door flew open and out you went. I made a soft landing on top of you."

"Glad I was good for something. What was this about you saving my life then?"

"Oh that," Buddy said indifferently. "The way you were laying there, I was sure you'd broken your leg. But when I saw how wet the road was, my gut told me I was looking at blood, not mud. I checked it out and sure enough. Got lucky I found it in time. Did a tourniquet thing."

Ole lay quietly and allowed those words to sink in. That was a too-close brush with death. "Thanks," he muttered and then continued in reverent silence long enough to communicate profound appreciation for his treasured friend's amazing deed. "How are things out on the front?"

"I wouldn't know. They shifted the bulk of our forces to a new line north and northwest of Verdun."

"And left you behind?"

"Yeah. I got a long, deep cut, too. Mine was on my calf." He pulled up his pant leg to show off a sizable bandage. "They stitched it up pretty good. Said it's deep enough that they need to make sure it heals before sending me back up the line." He unrolled the pant leg and pressed out a pucker. "I hear they're sending you back to the States when you're strong enough to travel."

"I heard the same thing. Disgusting, isn't it? Getting forced out because of an accident? What honor is there in that?"

"That wasn't just an accident, sir. It was sheer stupidity." He glanced again at the far bed and scowled. "I've got me a mind to clean that guy's clock. Has he said anything to you yet?"

"He's too gutless. Won't make eye contact. I catch him sneaking a peek every now and then though." Ole looked up at Buddy. "What do you say? How about if we pay our respects?"

"Why go through the trouble?"

Because of what the chaplain said. And it's really getting me down to see him so depressed. "Maybe we need to let him off the hook."

"Are you out of your ever-lovin' mind? He isn't worth it. Besides, we've both paid a hefty price for his idiocy."

Ole lifted his chin. "I'll bet you a supper in another one of those fancy French restaurants that in less than five minutes we can make that soldier weep."

"How do you plan to pull that off?" Buddy said with a glance at his watch.

Ole pointed a finger. "Get me that contraption over there, will you?"

"All right, but I still don't understand why you want to do this. He should be coming to us. On his knees."

With no small amount of effort, Ole slid onto the wheelchair. "Drive, Private, drive."

A couple of steps down the corridor, a nurse rushed up from behind. "Where are you going?" she demanded through pursed lips. "Get back to your bed right this instant."

"We'll be back in a few minutes," Ole said then looked up at Buddy. "Private, carry on."

The nurse took a reluctant though obedient step back, but not without a scowl.

"You certainly are authoritative," Buddy muttered in Ole's ear.

"A slog through Hades will do that to a man."

As they approached the far bed, Driver grimaced.

"We came to pay our respects," Ole said.

"Get outa' here. I don't want your respects."

"Hey, what is this?" Buddy said. "We coulda' been killed 'cuz of you and now you're downright rude on top of it."

Driver raised his voice. "I said get out of here."

Lightly seizing Buddy's forearm, Ole riveted his attention on the wounded soldier and waited him out.

"I don't want you here," Driver said, "now git."

Buddy grabbed the back of Ole's chair and started to pull it back. "Come on, sir. This guy's a jerk. Let's not waste any more of our precious time on him."

Ole signaled Buddy to wait. After an awkward moment, Driver said, "What are you waiting for? An apology? Well, you ain't getting one. I'm not a whimpering little sissy. Now get out of here."

Ole stared him down. Hard. And as he did, Driver appeared to grow increasingly agitated, so much so that his chest began to heave. After an excruciatingly long moment, Ole lowered his voice then said, "We're staying right where we are until you forgive yourself."

Driver gasped and after a long moment of what appeared to be shock, tears welled.

Buddy drew up a wrist and glanced at his watch. His eyes widened. He held up two fingers and winked.

Maintaining a steady calm, Ole reached for Driver's hand and gave it a sincere pump. "You take care of yourself now, you hear?"

Buddy quickly maneuvered the wheelchair out into the corridor and as he pushed Ole down the aisle, a light whimpering from behind surrendered to uncontrollable sobs.

A moment later, Ole eased back onto his bed, both emotionally and physically spent.

"You lanced a boil," Buddy said and with tears welling in his owns eyes, he glanced back at Driver. "Kind of makes it easier to forgive a jerk like that, doesn't it?"

Ole scowled. "Suck it up, Buddy. One man crying is about all I can take on in a good day's work."

"Sorry, sir. Oh, and about our bet. You know how crazy things are these days. The powers that be can haul you, me, or anyone else off in a heartbeat. If that happens, what do you say? Can I buy you that fancy supper when we get back to the States? I'm a man who pays his debts."

Why couldn't this kid pay better attention? Ole was holding on emotionally by nothing more than a thin and rotting thread.

"Be looking forward to it, son," he said then quickly looked away.

CHAPTER FIFTY-FOUR

Gretta stepped out of the post office and woefully shook her head. But then as she got into the Model T, she tacked on a pleased-with-herself grin. "You didn't get that letter from the ship yet, but you did get this." She passed an envelope to Olivia. "It's from your friend Jeremy."

Too excited to wait, Olivia tore open the letter and read as the car clipped along.

"Don't keep me in suspense," Gretta said. "What does he say?"

Olivia's cheeks drew pain from grinning so wide. "He says he misses me immeasurably."

"He used that word?"

"Yes, he did ... oh dear."

"What?"

"He's thinking about dropping out of college. Possibly joining the military." Olivia smoothed the letter on her lap as she eyed the passing shops along the way though she didn't really see them. What was it that Brute had said about college boys signing up so they could show off their uniforms to the girls? Not Jeremy. He was above that. His character exemplary. But the fighting. What if he ...

She picked up the letter again and read on. "He says he can't wait for me to come to New York. Insists that I stay at his parents' home when I'm on my way back to England. If he does venture off to war, he wants me to continue to write to him." She looked up. "I feel as if I'm straddling two worlds," she said thoughtfully. "The manner in which I was raised, I've one foot firmly planted in a world of poverty and now the other in a world of luxury. What if I find I'm not comfortable around his parents? What if they have difficulty accepting me?" she said, gripping the door as the car rounded a corner too fast.

After giving her a sidelong glance, Gretta looked back up the road. "How could anyone possibly have difficulty accepting you?"

"His father is a senator, you must not forget. I'm unaccustomed to mingling with the elite class and attending high society events. I doubt very much that I'd fit in. Suppose I picked up the wrong fork? Used the wrong plate? I'm certain they will inquire about my family? What might I say? My grandmother was a pauper and on her deathbed she told me she'd deceived me all these years, telling me that my father was alive and well after all and that's why I journeyed to America? I loved my grand-mum dearly, but what sort of person is capable of doing such a thing?"

"If and when the time comes, simply tell the truth." Gretta stopped in the middle of the road and made a quick u-turn. "If they don't accept you, it will be their loss. Besides, we all know that true wealth is on the inside and that you have in spades."

"Where ..." Olivia said with a glance up and down the road.

"We're going back to Skinner Chamberlain's. You're going to need new clothes for when you return to New York."

"But ..."

"It's a very nice store. You'll love it. They've even got an elevator. Only one around for miles." She laughed. "Is there no end to the things they come up with these days? Now that they've invented elevators, next thing you know they'll start building higher buildings so people can get better views. I wouldn't be surprised to find them one day inventing moving stairs and moving sidewalks. And so it goes." Gretta gave her a sidelong glance. "I've been holding out on you. Got something I wanted to spring on you at suppertime, but I can't wait."

"This sounds most interesting."

"It is. Wonderfully interesting. Your father. He telephoned earlier today …"

Olivia gulped.

"While you were out on the porch reading. He's back in the States now and is being transferred to a hospital up at Fort Snelling."

Olivia needed to pinch herself. She was about to meet her father? "I believe I've heard of it. In Minneapolis?"

"St. Paul. Let's catch an early morning train. I'd like for us to be at the hospital waiting for him when he arrives."

Olivia inhaled a deep breath. "This is all happening so quickly."

"Important things appear to do that, don't they?" Gretta stopped at a crossroads and studied her. "I don't know that I've seen a puppy look sadder than you. What is it, dear? I thought you'd be thrilled to know the two of you are finally going to meet."

"I am," she said.

Delighted.

Relieved.

Frightened.

"However, I feel rather inadequate meeting him without that letter in hand."

"Don't be silly. It will come."

"Do you still believe that likely?"

THE HOURS PASSED SWIFTLY. THE HOURS passed slowly. Olivia played with her breakfast, barely able to choke down a swallow. "I'm frightfully nervous," she said. "What if he finds he's disappointed when he meets me?"

Gretta laughed. "I think I'd be far more concerned about him loving you so much he won't want to let you go."

"I got little sleep last night."

"I didn't either," Gretta said. "Can't stop worrying about him. Can't help wondering how he looks. How much pain he's in. If he's lost weight. I just hope he isn't depressed. That dear, dear man."

Their train arrived in St. Paul at ten past one. Within minutes, they climbed into a taxi bound for Fort Snelling. As they drew close, time seemed to slip past faster, the houses and trees seemed to whiz past more swiftly, and Olivia's pulse quickened, her breathing growing shallow. And then the taxi pulled up in front of the building.

"You'll find him in a ward, down the hall, first door to the left, third bed on the right," a pleasant nurse said.

Gretta gasped. "You mean he's here already?"

Their footsteps echoed down the pristine corridor. He was here. In the same building as Olivia. But just a few short steps away. She hugged herself as she followed Gretta into the room, and stopped immediately inside the door.

There he lay.

After all this time.

A living, breathing creature. Commanding in appearance though snuggly tucked in bed, fast asleep.

Gretta hurried to his side. Not Olivia. She watched from afar, enraptured as Gretta kissed him lightly on the cheek. He stirred then opened tired eyes and gulped. "Gretta?" he said. From a distance his amazing baritone voice boomed, coarse with feeling. "My dear, darling Gretta." He then eyed the corridor and slowly traced it until his gaze reached the door.

Might it be Olivia's imagination or did moisture gather in his confused eyes as they found hers?

And what was it that he said?

Emily?

CHAPTER FIFTY-FIVE

Olivia continued to huddle near the doorway. Who was this great big wonderful man? she wondered. Though helpless in a hospital bed, he bore the demeanor of nobility. Strong. Confident. Appearing keenly aware.

Had he really mentioned her mother Emily's name? Did Olivia bear that strong of a resemblance to her? Could it be that all after all this time the man still grieved his loss?

Gretta turned back. "That's Olivia, Ole. Your daughter. Isn't she beautiful?"

He motioned to her. "Olivia? Come."

She didn't walk, she floated to his bedside. "Mister ..."

"Father."

"Father," she repeated softly.

He held out large, strong hands and drew her into a warm bear hug, patting her lightly as if she would too easily break. "Let me take a good long look at you," he said.

And for a prolonged while they sat in reverent silence, only their eyes talking. Olivia felt a surreal connectedness, a beautiful connectedness she had never before experienced, a connectedness that made her feel whole and wonderfully complete.

"I want to know all there is to know about you," he said finally, holding her hand, as if holding on to never let go. "And yet I feel as if I already do. Your eyes. The precise image of your mother's. Kind and candid."

They spent the entirety of the rest of the afternoon making pleasantries—Ole, Gretta, and Olivia, conversing about her trip to America, about England, about Amber Leaf, about his voyage back to the States, though strangely nothing about serving on the Western Front. Might there be an acute awareness he felt a need to withhold? As he spoke, his gaze kept returning to her as though he were completely lost and she was north on his life's compass.

"Tell us all about France," Gretta said. "How were you wounded?"

"My dearest darlings." Ole took on a mortified-looking grin. "I'll leave you with the fantasy that I was wounded with glorious honor having fallen on my sword fighting to the death for your freedom." He shifted his sheet as if looking for a place to hide. "Enough said."

Gretta shared an amused smile with Olivia then said to Ole. "Then tell us about the war, about your stay in France."

He shook his head. "My, how things have changed. In less than two decades we've progressed from a traditional war to a modernized war … if one could call that progress, that is."

"Why wouldn't we?" Gretta said.

"Because instead of fighting on horseback with rifles and bayonets and killing hundreds if not thousands, we've gone from land to air and sea using airplanes and submarines and bombs and torpedoes and tanks. Now we don't kill hundreds and thousands, we're killing hundreds of thousands and millions."

"I see what you mean," Gretta said thoughtfully.

He hesitated then turned to Olivia. "Enough of that unpleasant talk. What are your plans? How long can you stay with us?"

When she drew back, he studied her with eyes that appeared to be filled with pure raw love. But then he said, "You appear troubled. Is anything wrong?"

She looked to Gretta and then at her father. "I must return to England sooner than I had hoped," she said, unable to conceal the sheer agony in her tone.

He sat up with a start and flinched from what appeared to be a stab of excruciating pain. "You're not …"

She choked down a lump that strangled her throat. "That letter from my grandmum? I fear I've misplaced it … while aboard ship. We've been waiting for it to come in the mail. If they were able to find it, we should have received it by now. I need to journey back to New York. I must see if I can still retrieve it."

"But it's too dangerous for you to—"

"I'll be fine. I met a young man aboard ship. He's invited me to be a guest at his parents' home."

"This young man, are you sure you can trust him?"

"I assure you he has a quality about him. From what I've seen, he seems very much like you. And I've found him to be the consummate gentleman. I'm certain you would approve."

"The letter. I don't understand. How could your grandmother keep you from me … or me from you?"

That thought unnerved her as well. "I don't know," she said. "It makes no sense. It's unfair for us to merely assume I'm your daughter and you're my father on her word alone. There's nothing I wish more than to learn that it's true. But until I can provide proof … if I can't produce that letter, which at this point seems most unlikely, I must return to England to begin a thorough search. I would have done so before, but never felt the need until I misplaced the letter. I'm still wretched about losing it."

She watched helplessly as Ole looked to Gretta with eyes steeped in what appeared to be disappointment, a wave of insecurity washing over her like a swell on a stormy sea. Was he changing his mind after having met her? Might he possibly be wondering if she's an impostor?

"If you'll excuse me," she said, "I feel I'm in need of a cup of tea."

"I DIDN'T KNOW WHAT TO SAY, Gretta," Ole said. "Did you see that pained look on her face? I didn't know what to say," he repeated.

"What could you say? You were just caught off guard."

"But still …"

"How is the pain? Ole?"

"What?" he said as if he hadn't heard her.

"I said how is the pain? Do you need help with anything? Are you hungry? Can I feed you anything?"

He fiddled with his covers. "I only need you to love me."

Her eyes sparkled. "That's far too easy. I'm a sucker for an amazing man."

"Such a wonderful flatterer," he said distractedly. "I can't wait to get back home to your cooking. And I certainly can't thank you enough for all of your letters and cookies and candies. The comforts of home mean a lot to man when he can't have them." He hesitated. "Tell me, Gretta. Do you believe her?"

"Olivia, you mean? About the letter?"

"About everything."

"If she's lying, she's the best little liar in the whole wide world. And in answer to your question, yes, I definitely believe her. But what I believe isn't important. Do you believe her?"

He thought for a moment. "Strangely, yes," he said. "I can only hope I'm not being a fool."

Gretta smoothed his hand. "You didn't fight her when she said she wanted to return to England. Why is that?"

"If I were her, that's precisely what I would have needed to do."

Gretta's countenance grew troubled. "I only hope she can produce that letter."

CHAPTER FIFTY-SIX

"**N**ineteen eighteen. What an unbelievable year." Gretta peered past the paper. "This is wonderful. Listen to this. On the eleventh hour of the eleventh day of the eleventh month, the armistice is signed. Ole ... the war is over!" She glanced at his wheelchair. "We'll have to celebrate as soon as you can get around better."

He gave his head a woeful shake. "One killing machine winds down and another one winds up," he said. "I think we'd better stay away from the masses until the Spanish flu is over and done with. That stuff is lethal." He looked over his shoulder. "Say, what's Olivia up to?"

Gretta grinned. "She's in the kitchen baking an apple cobbler. Seems she loves spoiling you, too."

Several days later, Ole sat upright in bed gazing about the too familiar room then at Olivia who studied a number of pictures on the dresser as if she were either memorizing them or, having gone back in time, imagining herself a part of them.

"Your mother back from the post office yet?" he said.

She swiveled on her heel and grinned. "I'm still not used to hearing the word mother, stepmother though she may be. But I am thoroughly enjoying the adjustment. And in answer to your question, she should be back soon." Olivia plucked the crutches from the wall. "Shall we begin your morning exercises?"

"I can think of a few things I'd rather do," he said with a shrug, "but let's get on with it. Where to? The kitchen this time?" Seizing the crutches, he drew himself up as if doing so required no effort whatsoever while swallowing the pain of the slightest movement.

"Excellent," Olivia said.

"Thank you, dear. Been practicing in my sleep." He nodded for her to take the lead.

"No." Olivia held her ground. "You go first. I want to make sure you don't fall."

A grin broke as he maneuvered through the bedroom door that at the moment could use significant widening and then headed out into the hallway. "Are you sure you haven't missed your life's calling?" he said. "You'd make an exceptional nurse."

She slipped out ahead and drew open the door to the kitchen. A few steps later she pulled a chair out by the table. "You sit here," she said. "I'll fetch some coffee and join you for a few minutes if you don't mind the company." A short while later she placed a cup and saucer on the table and with a flick of her wrist slid it in front of him, positioning it just so.

He looked up. "Your mother used to do that."

"My mother?" she said appearing taken aback.

"She was fastidious about her handiwork, too. Paid the greatest attention to the minutest detail. You laugh like her. Talk like her. Walk like her. I never realized what a strong role genetics play until you came into our lives."

"What was she like?" Olivia lowered onto the chair next to his and like an elegant lady folded her hands on her lap. "Grandmum never said much about her. I think she found it too painful."

"She was much the same as you. Decent. Principled. Kind." He warmed at the memories. "Playful. A tremendous amount of fun. And her weakness? That was her strength. She never felt she quite measured up because her father was so poor. Didn't realize how unspoiled that made her. She was never demanding. Took nothing for granted. Certainly made life easier for me."

"Sounds like Gretta," Olivia said.

"She was. Much the same. And speaking of your mother ..."

Just then Gretta backed in the door, her arms piled high with mail, eyes wrought with concern.

"Why the long face?" Ole said.

She gave Olivia a sidelong glance. "By the sound of things, you won't be going to New York for a while."

"Why not?"

Gretta presented the daily paper to Ole. "Take a good look at the headlines. I stopped by the store and picked up a few of these." She held up a small quantity of facemasks. "Seems we've been too isolated. Spanish influenza has gotten bad, really bad. Theatres, churches, schools, everything's been ordered to close to fight it."

Ole unfolded the paper. "With so many soldiers home from the front and everyone out celebrating the end of the war the way they did, it's no wonder the flu took off like a wildfire." He scanned a few headlines then set the paper down. "By the time this is all over, I don't doubt we'll have lost more people to the flu than to the war ... forget what I said about you making a good nurse, Olivia. It's far too dangerous a profession with epidemics like this breaking out."

"I should have gone to New York before the flu got out of control," she said thoughtfully. "I must return to England. That, and Jeremy wishes to see me again before I leave."

Ole shook his head. "It's better that you stay here. By the look of things, this wave is far deadlier than the one last spring. You'd expose yourself more if you traveled. Besides, if they're closing churches and schools, we all need to stay put until the threat subsides."

"I fear becoming a burden."

"You are family," Ole said in a no-nonsense tone. "You are forbidden to ever think of yourself as being a burden."

"I second that," Gretta said, but then her voice softened as she turned to Ole. "I found out something else."

"By the sound of your voice, you make it sound worse then the flu. What is it, dear?"

"Nelson's home."

"Already?"

"From what I hear, he's in pretty bad shape."

"The flu? Or was he wounded?"

"Mustard gas."

Ole let those gruesome words sink in for a moment. "How bad is it, or do I even want to know?"

"Second- and third-degree burns."

"Where?"

She paused as if holding back words too despicable to speak.

"His face."

CHAPTER FIFTY-SEVEN

The afternoon half spent, Ole picked up a pawn. "Checkmate," he said then raised a mischievous brow. "Ready to get beat again?"

Olivia lightly patted his hand and with a smirk said, "You've just won five games in a row."

"Checkers then?"

"As I recall, you've won the last seven games in a row, not that I've been putting it to the count." She got up. "Now if you'll excuse me, I believe I hear my knitting calling."

What was a father to do? "And here I was so enjoying our bonding time."

"I'm feeling far more beaten than bonded at the moment."

"Now that hurt," Ole said. "How will you ever learn to respect me if I always let you win?"

"Correction. You never let me win. How will you ever learn to respect me if I continue to lose?"

He smirked. "That's a rather shallow point, is it not? You aren't going to leave your poor father here in the parlor all by himself, are you? The isolation is killing me."

Olivia burst into laughter. "You enjoy your own company far too much for me to be manipulated. Perhaps you might read some of your motor magazines. And on second thought, rather than knitting, would you prefer that I bake something for you? At least you'll have a mortal within shouting distance."

"That all depends. What are you planning to bake?"

"An apple pie."

"Well, maybe I can handle the alone time then."

Ole involved himself in thought as Olivia walked away. Though the world about them suffered, they had been working hard to form warm memories—breakfasts, dinners, and suppers at the table, chats before the fire, parlor games, Ole reading while Gretta and Olivia knitted, and the three of them together had celebrated Olivia's first Thanksgiving dinner in America.

One morning several weeks later, Ole announced, "Since the epidemic is finally falling to the wayside, I don't know about the two of you, but I'm weary of being boarded up at home. I'm ready to venture out into the world. Anyone care to join me?"

Gretta slipped a bowl of oatmeal in front of him. "You're not going anywhere until you eat something that'll stick to your ribs, my love."

He dutifully scooped a generous spoonful of brown sugar onto the cereal and gave it a thorough stir. "Been meaning to tell you, I talked to Deacon yesterday afternoon … you know, when the two of you were off in an upstairs room abandoning me."

"We would never abandon you. We were up there sewing."

"Like I said … that aside, he invited us out to the farm."

"When did we get his letter?"

"He telephoned when he was in town." Ole turned to Olivia who nibbled at a slice of toast. "Don't you think it's high time for you to meet your great uncle? Sounds like your great aunt Maude could possibly be there, too. It might be good for you to see his farm and wander around in the country for a few hours."

Her eyes lit up. "When do we go?"

"Thought maybe this afternoon." He glanced at his crutches. "Would you mind driving us, Gretta? Oh yes, and Pastor Collver is planning to stop by, too. We thought it might be fun for all of us to get caught up."

Olivia returned her uneaten toast to her plate with too much care.

"About Pastor Collver," Ole said. "I do believe my bride mentioned something about your concern to me, Olivia. Meeting him and his wife on the train certainly was strange, wasn't it?"

"That's what I thought," she said. "One thing led to another and before I knew it, I told him you were my father."

Was that fear Ole perceived in her eyes?

"I don't know why I feel so guilty," she continued. "Maybe it's because he gave his wife such a shocked look. Then they both got quiet. Too quiet. I felt as if I'd said something horribly wrong. Perhaps I did. It wasn't necessarily my place to tell him."

"Olivia, Olivia," Ole said with a shake of his head. "It's not your fault or mine that our relationship is filled with mystery. That's the problem, not you, not me. And one other thing. Around this house, feeling comfortable talking about even the most disagreeable things is compulsory." He glanced at Gretta, "Isn't it Mama?" and then to Olivia. "You're safe here. Always."

He got up. "Now if you ladies will excuse me, I think I'd like to get in a little exercise. Trudge up and down the basement steps a few times. Got to get in shape if I want to go back to Addison & Crowley first thing come Monday morning. Stairs there are plenty steep."

"Are you sure you're ready?" Gretta said. "If you fell ..."

"If I fell, you'd be blessed with my presence for more endless days than you could possibly feel comfortable enduring." With a laugh, he gave her shoulder a reassuring pat. "Don't worry. I'll be careful. It's not fair to put you through that kind of torture."

In the early afternoon, Ole peered over his shoulder and into the backseat. "You're awfully quiet, Olivia. Are you nervous?"

She continued to stare out at the countryside. "Enjoying the scenery," she said.

Minutes later they arrived at the farm. Deacon hurried out to meet them, first opening Gretta's door and giving her a bear hug, then Olivia's. As she climbed out, however, he drew back, appearing hesitant, almost guarded.

"That's my little girl there," Ole said with pride.

Deacon clasped her hand, though briefly. "She does bear a striking resemblance to Emily, I'll give you that."

I'll give you that? What an insensitive thing to say.

Maude, beautifully dressed in blue satin, stood on the porch with a warm though uncertain look. When Ole introduced her to her grand-niece, however, she transformed into the gracious lady Ole knew her to be.

After making small talk in the farmhouse over cake and coffee for the better part of an hour, Ole caught Deacon's eye and with raised brow, signaled the door. "If you'll excuse us, ladies, Deacon and I would like to go outside for a smoke."

But as they strolled out onto the porch, Deacon started to lower onto a rocking chair, then stopped halfway and said, "Where are you going?"

"As far away from the house as we can get. Let's go."

Ole didn't stop until he reached a fencepost alongside the field. Deacon hobbled along behind. "Something on your mind?"

"You bet there is," he said. "My little girl hasn't stopped squirming since you laid eyes on her. Maude's kind enough, but she keeps looking at Olivia like she's trying to figure out who she is, and you've been ignoring her."

Deacon drew a toothpick from a bib overall pocket and let out a sigh. "It shows that bad, does it? I'm sorry, Ole. I'll make it a point to be more gracious."

"Thank you. She may not be your grandniece by blood, but she certainly is through adoption."

"I know, but there's more to it than that. Truth be known, I've been holding out on you."

"About what?"

"Amelia. Maude and I never had much to do with her. She was the one who cut ties, not us. I figured she'd gone into a depression or something after Em died. Kept writing for a while, but she never responded. Takes two to make a relationship, so I finally gave up. After all, she had a right to live her life her way. Sure we'd exchange a card come Christmas, but that was about the extent of it. Like I told you before, she was twelve years my senior when she left home. We never really got a chance to know her. And we never did care much for that louse she married. He had a mean streak in him. Seemed kind of full of himself. After Pa died, Ma got married again, and we went through that rough patch. Maude and I were left pretty much on our own. Deep down I think we both resented Amelia for leaving us, for moving to England with that good-for-nothing and never bothering to come back. Can't blame her really for not saying anything about Olivia. Like I said, we didn't have enough of a relationship for it to matter."

"But why the cold shoulder toward Olivia, Deacon? That's not like you."

He shrugged. "I'm not doing it on purpose. Seeing her, I see Amelia. Feel some resentment I didn't know I've been harboring. It'll be okay. Just need a little time to make peace with it."

Ole stared out at the barren field, out where dirt was unearthed, out where what a man saw was what a man got. "When we go back inside …"

"Don't worry. I'll be kind."

"Thanks, Deacon. Blood relative or not, she's alone in this world now. Needs all the support she can get."

Off in the distance, a cloud of dust chased Pastor Collver's car up the gravel road and dissipated as he pulled into the driveway. "Looks like we got company." Deacon flicked his toothpick to the ground, and they walked off to meet him.

After a bout of happy backslapping, Deacon, Pastor Collver, and Ole sauntered into the house. Olivia still sat in the same chair at the table appearing relatively uneasy. Ole smiled at her reassuringly then turned to the pastor. "I believe you've met my daughter."

Pastor Collver broke out into relieved laughter. "Oliver Harrington, why did you hide such a precious treasure?"

Though Olivia blushed, she seemed to relax for the first time since they arrived.

"There's still a mystery behind it, but we plan to find out what that's all about."

"I don't understand," Pastor Collver said. "You really had us worried there. How could you not know you had a daughter? And such a lovely one at that?"

"Kind of makes one wonder, doesn't it?" He gave Deacon a forlorn glance. "Therein lies the mystery."

CHAPTER FIFTY-EIGHT

Twilight descended like a veil. After they gathered at Deacon's table for an early supper, Pastor Collver led a recitation of *The Lord's Prayer*. When they reached 'forgive us our trespasses as we forgive those who trespass against us,' Ole snuck a peek at Deacon. The man's lack of relationship with his departed sister and his subsequent resistance to Olivia, though bordering subtle, cut like a knife. That should not be.

After saying "amen" in unison, steamy bowls bobbed along counter to the conversation. "I sure will be happy to put this miserable year behind us," the pastor said. "Is there a soul on this great earth who hasn't borne a loss?"

Ole flashed on Nelson, on the loss inflicted on him—on their lack of relationship. There was far more to war than losing a life. As he lifted his fork to take a bite, his conscience bit him back. In the end, he was no different than Deacon. His unfinished business with Nelson wasn't grievous, but it was wrong nonetheless. Though he pitied the man, Ole harbored resentment. That needed addressing.

On their way home, Gretta said, "Lost in thought, are you?"

"A little, I guess. Would you mind stopping by the Prixton place? I think it's high time for me to pay a visit."

Gretta stared at the ever-changing road, then glancing back at him, she said, "Not at all."

Long minutes later, she pulled up in front of the Prixton's home. "Take your time," she said. "Olivia and I will wait for you out here in the car."

Ole hesitated at Nelson's door, his hand poised to knock. What kind of reception would he get? What would he say? Would the man even speak to him? And what about Gretta? How did she really feel about stopping by here?

The door opened wide. Nelson's wife, Aggie, greeted Ole with a surprised grin and stepped back in invitation. "How wonderful to finally get company," she said. "We've been beside ourselves with no company for weeks on end."

"The flu epidemic has been confining." Ole stepped inside and drew off his hat.

Aggie appeared different, more relaxed. Was that confidence she exuded? Whatever it was, it looked good on her, softening her already lovely features.

"Maybe things can start to get back to normal now." She paused. "Feel free to take off your mask. Since you've been holed up, too, you can't be contagious. Come in," she said. "You'll find Nelson in the parlor."

How was it that a few short steps could feel so terribly long and slow? Ole peered into the cozy room with windows on either side of the hearth and a floor-to-ceiling wall lined with shelves of books arranged fastidiously according to size and color. That could not be a man's doing. In the glow of a sputtering fire, the top of Nelson's impeccably combed hair shimmered above a wingback chair, a puff of smoke rising from his pipe like steam from a smokestack. What would Ole find when he rounded the chair? Were the rumors true? Would he be strong enough to hide his shock? He certainly needed to try.

To his further surprise, Nelson's voice not only emanated uncharacteristic warmth, but also a complete lack of mocking when he said, "Harrington, to what do I owe this great pleasure?" He stood and turning, he grasped Ole's hand, a black patch concealing one eye, which Ole didn't particularly care to see beneath for he'd heard it was blind. But to his surprise, a quizzical look manifested in Nelson's uncovered eye.

Ole flinched. He couldn't stop himself. The scars were far worse than he had anticipated. First- and second-degree burns made a pale patchwork of Nelson's cheek and chin leaving them ugly and too pink. Part of his discolored lower lip lacked form.

Nelson eyed Ole's cane and chuckled. "Aren't we a pair?"

"I've been wanting to stop by to say hello," Ole said as they lowered onto matching wingbacks before the fire. Feeling awkward, he gazed about the homey room. What could he say? What could he do? How could he begin to converse with a wounded enemy who had inferred Ole was a coward, who had mocked him for being childless? "Nice place," he said after an awkward quiet.

"Not too bad, I guess. I hear your daughter is here for a visit. Word's gotten around she's quite the looker." Nelson got up again and squatted before the fire where he stoked a few dying embers. "I'm happy for you," he said, his tone continuing to sound sincere, as if he meant it. "How long before she heads back to England?"

"Any day now, but there's nothing I'd like more than for her to stay on."

Nelson turned and looked Ole directly in the eye. "I apologize for being so cruel … about your daughter, I mean. Jealousy is an awful thing." His eyes then lowered to Ole's cane again. "What happened?"

"Soldier drinking on duty. Looks like a night on the town for him is ending up to be a lifetime of agony for me. But the toughest part was not getting a chance to stay in the thick of things long enough to find a way to play war hero. Guess I've got a pride problem."

Nelson looked up. "You were driving tanks, right?"

"Gunner, not driver."

"All the same. You've got guts, Harrington. A soldier with claustrophobia doesn't volunteer for tank duty."

Ole's forehead twitched involuntarily. "How'd you know about that?"

"That you volunteered for tank duty? Or that you had claustrophobia?" He laughed. "Is there actually someone who doesn't know? You think the attorneys at Addison & Crowley are dummies? You stood head and shoulders above the rest of us. We had no choice but to find your Achilles heel. Our pride depended on it."

That was a backhanded compliment Ole rather enjoyed. "How about you?" he said. "How are you doing?"

"Been better, but not too bad under the circumstances."

"I'm sorry about the …" Ole couldn't bring himself to say the word.

"Disfigurement? Don't be," Nelson said. "I've been learning a lot from this affliction. There's a part of me that wishes I could have learned it long ago."

Was it Ole's imagination or was Nelson being humble? "I'm afraid I don't understand."

"Want a cigar? Cup of coffee?"

"No thanks. Can't stay long. The girls are waiting in the car."

He brightened. "Invite 'em in."

"That might be kind of hard for—"

"Say no more. I wasn't thinking."

Nelson lightly stoked the fire again, nudging glowing embers as if prodding his thoughts. He turned back to Ole and fingered a scar lining his cheek. "My wife actually likes me now. Seems we've become good friends. That's worth something."

"But didn't she … like you before?"

He shook his head. "Loved me maybe, but you knew me, Ole. There wasn't much to like. I feel like a brand new automobile that's finally gotten its first ding. These scars are miserable and painful, but they're more of a relief than anything."

"Too much pressure needing to be perfect all the time, is that it?"

"You nailed it. It's bondage. I still care, sure, but I'm not as mean or demanding or obsessed any more. Being wounded did that for me. What about you? What did you learn? What good has come out of your crushed hip?"

Ole reflected on the question, feeling hard-pressed to come up with an answer. What had he learned? Wounds hurt? Never get into a truck with a drunk driver? Mobility has limitations now that it never had before?

When Ole didn't answer, Nelson said with a smirk, "I may have had a problem with pride, but so did you. Come on. Admit it. All of our feet are made of clay."

Feeling a chill from being emotionally undressed, Ole hesitated, but then let out a relieved chuckle. "Not all pride is bad ... you've changed, Nelson. I like it. You wear candor well."

"Just sorry I had to learn the hard way what is and isn't important."

Ole thought for a moment before choking out, "What are you going to do now?"

"We're living off an early inheritance these days," he said with a shrug. "My dad's taken pity. I don't like it, but we need his help, that is until I can make my own way. Not sure how to do that yet. You've probably already surmised that my business ran into the ground before I went overseas. That's why I signed up. I could try to start up the practice again, but who wants to hire a scar face?"

Ole pondered that thought, though briefly. "Aren't you being a little hard on yourself?"

"Take a look at me and ask that question again."

"Come back to Addison & Crowley."

"I don't think so."

"Why not? Boss has an opening."

"I've burned my bridges. And like I said, who would want to hire or work with someone with an ugly disfigurement?"

"We've all suffered, Nelson. People identify with scars. Knowing you've suffered, too, mark my word they'll feel more comfortable around you. Trust you more."

Nelson's Adam's apple dipped. "Why are you trying to help me?" he said. "After all I've done to you and Gretta, what's in it for you?"

"I want to help."

"But ..."

"Neither Gretta or I hold a grudge."

"You mean to tell me that after that accident ... I mean, she can't have kids because of me. And jerk that I can be, I rubbed it in your face."

"I have a daughter now," Ole said. "And I'm not meaning to be unkind, but if Gretta had married you, she would have been miserable. What was it that you said about your wife? She finally likes you now? As for Gretta and me, you've done us a favor."

"You can't be serious."

"Oh, but I am. Not only did you make it possible for her to get over you, it isn't possible for us to be happier."

Nelson returned to his chair and inhaled a drag from his pipe, the scent of cherry tobacco filling the room. "What about Boss? What about breaking trust with him? Why would he bother to take me back? He doesn't owe me a thing."

"You know him. He's all about business. He's looking for talent, and that you've got plenty of. You know the law. You know the firm. You know Amber Leaf. Think about it. While you do, I'll be sure to put a bug in his ear. I've got a feeling he'll be in touch with you sooner rather than later." Ole got up. "Thanks for the talk. I really am pleased to see you're doing well."

"You never did tell me why you came."

"Seemed like the decent thing to do."

Nelson appeared to study Ole for a moment. "I can't figure you out, Harrington. What makes you tick? How are you always able to take the high road, no matter what?"

Ole looked up, grateful to the One who made it possible to walk tall, to thrive in a bigger and far more honorable world. "I've learned to follow an amazing lead."

"I envy you."

"Why? There's plenty of room for us all." He reached for Nelson's hand. "I'll be looking forward to seeing you at the office again. Hopefully this time we'll play on the same team."

"Ole?"

Not Harrington? "Yes?"

"Give your bride my best."

Ole wasn't sure he wanted to. This was a Nelson that Gretta could very well have fallen in love with.

CHAPTER FIFTY-NINE

Olivia curled up in an overstuffed armchair near the bedroom window, positioning it at an angle to absorb as much of the sun's warmth as possible, for this afternoon required it. Days growing cooler. Nights growing longer. Hope doing a sad little dance as it lured her down a steep descending spiral. Two letters from Jeremy today, yet no word from the ship.

Fortunately, Jeremy's letters had grown longer and more heartfelt. Yet with them came pressure for her to return to the East Coast. Which meant leaving Oliver M. Harrington and his bride. Leaving Amber Leaf. Between Jeremy's studies and family commitments, holiday weekends would be best, he'd said. After kissing his signature then pressing the latest letter lovingly to her cheek, she tucked it back into its envelope, eased it into the fattening bundle, and slipped it into her dresser drawer along with the rest of her permanent items, which at present reminded her of her not-so-permanent stay.

At half past two, the familiar aroma of fresh-baked bread drew her back to the kitchen where Gretta upended a loaf pan onto the breadboard. "Where's—"

She spun around. "Your father is out for a walk."

"But he went earlier."

"He needed to go again." Something appeared amiss as Gretta generously slathered butter over the steamy crust. "What did your Jeremy have to say?"

He is beyond himself with excitement to see me once again. "He is happily anticipating my return to New York."

Gretta slid a loaf to the side and started slathering a second loaf as if distracted, one ear on Olivia, the other on something that appeared far more compelling. "When does he want you to come, did he say?"

"For Christmas."

Gretta swiveled around again, this time as if stung by a wasp, the pitch of her voice louder and higher than usual. "But we're going to Deacon's then."

"I'm uncertain as to what to do."

"Do you mean you're actually entertaining the idea of leaving?"

"I intend not to be unkind, but I am. I must. Yesterday I found it difficult to relax around Deacon. The thought of spending any part of the Holidays at their home makes me feel rather wary. I have the feeling he wants to approve of me, yet he doesn't. At least not yet."

"That's silly. How could anyone not approve of you?"

"You didn't feel it?" Olivia said. "The tension, I mean? It may have been subtle, but it was there."

Gretta appeared lost in thought as she carefully sliced several slices of hot bread and placed them on a plate. "Yes, I did," she muttered. "I don't understand it. He's one of the most decent men I've ever known. Doesn't have it in him to be unkind. At least I didn't think he did."

Olivia reached for a warm crust, her eyes fixed on it as she slathered it with butter as well. "He and my grandmum were never close. She rarely mentioned him. Something must have happened between the two of them somewhere along the way. I find it difficult to believe that she never told him about me. Perhaps I'm a reminder of something he'd rather forget."

"But that isn't fair to you."

"I don't find life particularly fair. It just is. He must not believe I'm the blood daughter of your husband, that I'm his grandniece. Why blame him, though? For all we know, he could think I'm nothing more than a money—"

"Please don't."

"But I can't prove—"

"It doesn't matter." Gretta swallowed her first bite of warm bread and quickly washed it down with a gulp of tea. "Even if you aren't a blood relative, which I don't believe for a minute, Amelia adopted you. That makes you family, regardless. And we want you here. As for Christmas, maybe we'd better rethink that. Maybe the three of us should celebrate it here by ourselves."

"You would do that for me?"

"I would do that for us."

Olivia spun on her heal, maddening moisture gathering only too quickly, blurring her vision, but not enough to blur a letter lying face up on the table. "What might that be?" she said, feeling a need to change the subject.

"That's why your father decided he needed to take another walk. I've got a feeling this will be a long one." She hesitated. "Do you remember him telling us about a boy named Buddy?"

"The one who saved his life?"

"That's him."

"Certainly I do. Their supper date sounds marvelous, but where might they find a French restaurant in this part of the country?"

Olivia found it odd that Gretta didn't answer.

"It would be wonderful if I could still be here to meet him," Olivia prattled on. "The letter is from him then?"

A woebegone expression crumpled up Gretta's face as she shook her head. "It's from his mother."

"Why her?" Olivia said.

"It about killed me to watch Ole read it. His lips trembled. He got up after he finished it. Shoved it at me. Said he needed to go out for a while. By the look on his face, I knew that meant a long while."

"What did the letter say? Or dare I ask?"

Gretta set her plate to the side with too much care. "His mother told Ole she wasn't sure how to reach him, but that Buddy had written to her a number of times about an amazing man named Oliver Harrington from Amber Leaf, Minnesota, so she guessed at the address and hoped he'd get her letter. According to her, Buddy was extremely close to his uncle. He died some time back from a freak accident. Seems Ole unwittingly took his place in Buddy's heart. The saddest thing is, the boy never made it home from the war."

"He got killed?"

"No."

Olivia let out a lungful of spent air. "What a relief."

Now tears welled in Gretta's eyes. "He came down with influenza, Olivia. Couldn't beat it. His mother said she was sure Ole would want to know. She thanked him for being such a positive influence on Buddy's short life ... for being a perfect father figure to him."

Olivia pinched her eyes closed.

Making up for the son he never had an opportunity to know. Another son figure that he lost in death.

CHAPTER SIXTY

In the December arctic cold, Olivia drew the covers tight to her chin. Icy sheets. Chattering teeth. A silvery sliver of a moon gleaming bright through frosted windowpanes. All served to compound that unsettling feeling of cold. Her toes chose not to warm no matter how much effort she expended. Perhaps a hot water bottle might be of help. She quickly donned a bathrobe and scurried down the stairs in woolen socks, the kitchen much too far away.

Soft voices drifted from the living room. Good. Perhaps her new-found parents might wish to join her in a cup of hot cocoa before turning in for the evening. She peered through the door and was about to enter, but hesitated instead. Though warmed at the sight of their closeness as they cuddled near the fire, something about their tone indicated this was a private conversation that lent itself to respect, not interruption.

However, as she turned on tiptoes determined to return upstairs and crawl back into bed to endure the bitter cold, she couldn't help overhearing the content of their exchange, content that triggered an entire new kind of chill. Respect for privacy no longer repelled her to her room. In its place, a quest for naked truth enticed her like a honeybee to a blossom. With her back to the wall and an ear tilted toward the doorway she lingered—listening.

It sounded as though Ole had spent the better part of the day out at Deacon's farm. Earlier in the afternoon when Olivia had inquired about his whereabouts, when he'd return, Gretta had indicated that he'd taken a ride out into the country. It was no wonder she hadn't said more. The longer Olivia listened, the more her stomach churned as Ole shared the troublesome details of their conversation.

"He asked if Olivia had produced that letter yet," Ole said.

Was that disappointment that issued from his voice?

"After he met her," Gretta said, "I thought he was okay with things the way they were."

"He was, but then he said he gave that letter more thought. Can't seem to get peace about it."

Olivia leaned in and listened harder to hear Gretta's nearly inaudible voice.

"What did you say?"

"What could I say? I had to tell him the truth … no, she hasn't."

Olivia's head swirled. Of all of the witless things in the world, why did that precious letter have to disappear?

"Deacon asked if that didn't strike me as being strange," Ole continued.

"What did you to say to that?" Gretta said.

"With Amelia dying, and Olivia having been adopted, I asked him who else she could turn to." Ole's tone hardened. "In the kindest way possible, he said he was concerned that we might be so determined to have a child of our own that we aren't willing to listen to reason. Said we were vulnerable and far too eager to accept her without question. He can't understand why I would still hold out hope that she could be my daughter by birthright."

For the next long moment, the only sounds emanating from the room were the hissing and sputtering from the fireplace … and from the hallway, Olivia's shallow intake of breath.

"I'd be disappointed to the bone to find out she isn't your daughter," Gretta said. "You would be, too, and you know it. If she isn't, I don't want to know. I'm happy with our fantasy."

Olivia's heart sank. How could she blame either of them for how they felt? Feelings were neither right nor wrong—they merely were.

"We've been wanting to adopt anyway," Ole said. "Since her grandmother took care of that, at least she is still my adopted child and to me that means the world."

"Our adopted child," Gretta corrected emphatically, but then her tone took a downturn. "You look troubled, Ole. What is it?"

"Deacon. He has a nose like a bloodhound. I've never known him to be wrong."

"About what?"

"Extortion. What if he ends up being right about that?"

Devastated by the exchange, Olivia padded back up to her room. The last thing she wanted was for them to hear stifled whimpering.

Lightly closing the door behind her, she eyed her suitcase. She hadn't their trust. Why should she? How could they? She wasn't sure she trusted herself.

"Did you hear something?" Gretta said.

"I think so." Ole got up and peered down the hallway. "Must be our imagination. No one's there," he said on his way back to the sofa. "No matter you slice it, too many things add up," he said. "She's not extorting. She *is* my daughter. I know she is. Duly concerned though Deacon may be, nothing overrides that."

"I feel it, too."

He pressed his back hard against a cushion. "I have to admit what he says does make sense, though."

"Which is?"

He pulled Gretta close and leaned his forehead against hers. "Where are the facts? I'm an attorney. Attorneys deal with facts. But a good attorney also needs to listen to his gut. I know Deacon believes himself, and I appreciate his sticking his neck out for us, trying to protect us. But we won't ever come to an agreement on this, not without proof on either side … I only hope our side wins." He stared into the flames for a long moment. "What's the matter with us, Gretta? Why are we waiting for a stupid letter that we know will never come? Let's reassure her. She needs us. Amelia already adopted her, so she's every bit as much family as any in-law." His gaze found its way back to the hearth. "Fire's dying. What do you say? Time to call it a night?"

"You go ahead. I want to go upstairs and throw another quilt over Olivia first. Make sure she stays warm enough. Nights are getting a lot colder now."

A short while later, Gretta entered their bedroom wide-eyed.

"Is she asleep?" Ole said.

"Seems to be. But her suitcase … it's sitting beside the wall, wide open, and half filled."

He gulped. "It was dark in her bedroom. Are you sure you aren't imagining things?"

"There was enough moonlight for me to know it wasn't my imagination. You don't think this could be because of Deacon, do you? She did mention that she didn't feel comfortable around him. And Jeremy did invite her to the East Coast. Told her the best time for a visit would be during a holiday. I hope she isn't planning to take off for New York without a word of goodbye."

Ole gave his pillow a punch. "I don't know what to think. What I do know is that the first thing in the morning we need to reassure her that like it or not, she is family and she belongs with us."

Gretta's shoulders slouched.

"I only hope we have that long," she said.

CHAPTER SIXTY-ONE

Olivia drew the quilt to her chin not wanting to get up. Last night's comments replayed in her mind. Relentlessly. "Extortion," her father had said. "What if Deacon is right?"

Extortion? That word mortified her. How could it not? Until able to prove without a doubt that she's her father's daughter, she must leave him in peace, allow him and Gretta to carry on with their lives without distraction.

Go, she told herself. You mustn't look back. Be on the next train bound for New York. Spend several days with Jeremy and his family. Then board the next ship back to England.

That's the decent thing to do.

Shivering, she rolled out of bed and tucked her toes into cold slippers, all the while eyeing her partially filled luggage.

Time alone would tell if this would be her one and only visit to America.

Time alone would tell who her real father might be.

Time alone.

If then.

"Of all of the mornings for Olivia to be late for breakfast," Ole said while swirling what little was left of his coffee, "why does it have to be today?"

Gretta patted his shoulder in passing. "Would you care for another slice of French toast, dear?"

"Better not. I've got to get to the office." He glanced at the clock for the fourth time in as many minutes. "She's never late for breakfast. She should have been down here by now."

"I think I hear her stirring. I'll go check."

As Gretta hurried off, he carried his plate and utensils to the sink, pleased with himself for being a dutiful husband, then peered out the window where he gazed at the crisp winter's morning. A squirrel skittered in and out of the branches of a bare oak. A fawn and its mother idly grazed in the thicket at the edge of the woods. Bright sunlight glistened off the ice-glazed lake. What an idyllic way to start the day.

Just then the tramping of swift-moving feet intruded into his reverie. His world was about to turn upside down. He sensed it.

Gretta rushed back into the kitchen. "She's leaving, Ole! Our Olivia, she's leaving."

"She's what?"

"She'll be down in a minute. Said she'll tell you all about it. Last night, I told you I had a bad feeling."

He rested a heavy hand on the sink as if steadying himself might stabilize his thinking. "The extortion. Do you think she overheard us talking about it?"

"Must have."

"We've got to talk her out of going."

The look in Olivia's eyes as she entered the kitchen ... Ole had seen that look before. In the hospital ward up at Fort Snelling. The apprehension. The vulnerability.

"Gretta told you then?" she said.

"Why, Olivia? Why now?"

She squared her shoulders. "I'm not extorting. Honest, I'm not."

Ole's breath rushed out in a whoosh. "You heard us then … last night? Olivia, you must believe us. You only heard part of the conversation. We don't believe for a minute that you are capable of that."

Please say something. Anything.

"I must go back to England. I must prove myself. I need you to believe in me. But mostly, I wish to find out who I really am." She hesitated. "I need to believe in me, too."

"Adopted or not, you are my daughter."

"Our daughter," Gretta corrected again. "Olivia, you are all we could have hoped for and more."

"I know. It is not possible for your sentiment to be more mutual," she said. "I fear you've ruined me. I believed I was wonderfully happy, but now I'm no longer certain. Returning to England, living there, will be like stepping back in time. Back to the humdrum of a small dress shop. Back to the old neighborhood. Little to look forward to. I doubt I will ever enjoy contentment again, not after experiencing heaven right here on earth with the two of you."

"Then stay."

"No. I must go. I need to have peace in my heart. Until then, I will spend several days with Jeremy and his parents first then board the first ship back. I plan to check the train and ship schedules today and leave as soon as possible."

A helpless feeling of dread overwhelmed Ole. That same feeling that crushed his insides each time Gretta had lost a child. That same feeling that sucked the life out of him when he learned a tumor had cast their fate.

But this time he wasn't helpless.

"I will hire a private detective in England. See what he can sniff out."

"Thank you kindly, but no. This is something I wish to do for myself."

"Then I'm going with you," Ole said.

Olivia's eyes swelled. "But ..."

"No buts about it. Go to New York as soon as you can work things out with your friend Jeremy. I'll book passage. After you spend a few days with him, I'll meet up with you at the Port of New York."

Gretta reached for Ole's elbow. "We'd better get you to the office. You're running late."

Ole kissed Olivia lightly atop the head then hobbled behind Gretta to the car on one crutch. Before hopping in, though, he gazed back at the house.

"What if we do find out who her real father is, Mama? And what if he isn't me?"

"You are her father by adoption, Ole, and no one can ever take that away from you."

CHAPTER SIXTY-TWO

Gretta shook out a dishtowel, spanking the air with a pop.

Ole looked up. "That certainly was subtle."

"We got a letter from Deacon today," she said.

"How I wish that man had a telephone."

"But he doesn't."

Olivia stopped scrubbing a pot. Was that in response to hearing Deacon's name? After a thoughtful moment, she resumed scrubbing, though over-zealously.

"Invited himself to dinner on Sunday," Gretta said.

"What about his wife?"

"Didn't say."

Olivia's quiet grew loud in its own way. How could it not? Deacon had inadvertently fueled the flames of rejection with what he assumed was good cause.

At Olivia's expense.

At Ole's expense.

Even at Gretta's expense.

Though he had meant no harm, with hope as fragile as it was around this household, his vigilance had done so just the same.

"I'm sure she'll come, too," Ole said. "Are you okay with that, Olivia?"

She shrugged then said, "That's fine."

"Is it?" he said in a caring tone. "In time, you'll learn to love Deacon. From the sound of things, he never developed a healthy relationship with your grandmum."

"That relationship does not concern me."

"I know. That's my point. He's been trying to do right by us to get at the truth. But knowing him, I'm sure he's been examining his motives at every turn. He doesn't have it in him to be unkind."

Olivia turned and rested her back against the sink. "Of that I'm sure, but I felt rather debased. As if I were a thief. I'm having difficulty ridding myself of that feeling. I've tried, but it clings and won't let go. Perhaps he's done me a favor. I feel a need to try even harder to prove that I'm your daughter."

Ole got up, and willfully ignoring a blistering pain shooting down his leg, he crossed the kitchen and drew her into a warm embrace. "The wound will heal. You just need a little time and a few good overriding memories."

At half past one on Sunday afternoon, Ole drew back the curtain. The clatter of Deacon's buckboard sounded louder as he approached the house. "What in the world!"

Gretta peered over his shoulder. "What is it?"

"Would you take a look at that? It's Deacon. He has something on his wagon. It's covered … and it's big. That's not true. It's huge. I'm not sure what it is, but by the look of things, we're about to find out."

"He came alone," Gretta said bouncing to her toes and peering again over Ole's shoulder. "I wonder why he didn't bring his wife along."

As Deacon eased the strange looking object off the wagon, it dropped to the ground with a thud. "I'd better help him." Ole then hurried outside. "Need help with that?" he said.

"I've got it. Be grateful if you held the door for me, though."

"What is it?"

"Just a little something I carved for Olivia."

Ole chuckled. "A *little* something."

Immediately inside the entry, Deacon peered into the kitchen. "Gretta, Olivia," he said. "May I come in?"

Gretta grinned an easy grin. "You're always welcome here. You know that."

He stood with cap in hand as if needing a moment to gather himself then took a step forward. "Olivia, though I didn't mean to, I'm worried that I may have made you feel as if you'd done something wrong, and for that I couldn't be more sorry."

"Please. I'm okay."

"But I'm not. Not knowing you existed until Ole got your letter out of the blue the way he did, I didn't know what to make of it. I would have thought your grandmum would have mentioned something about you, but she never did. That doesn't excuse my being overly protective of Ole and Gretta or my probing behind your back. I don't know how I could have been so thickheaded trying to protect them from you the way I did. Suddenly one day it dawns on me. You are my grandniece, too, adopted or not."

"But I wasn't adopted," Olivia insisted.

No, please, not the adoption again, Ole mused. Can we just let it go?

Deacon winced before continuing. "I believe Ole did mention something about that. I can only ask your forgiveness and hope you'll accept this gift and the spirit in which I made it." Deacon glanced back at Ole. "For my penance, I did for you what you've never had the time to perfect on your own. I've been looking for a way to pay you back, too, for all those times you've helped me with the harvest and the times you've helped me fix up the farm. I only hope that I haven't overstepped your boundaries by doing so."

What could this aging old buzzard have done that Ole could possibly take offense? Could this be what he hoped? Would Deacon actually go through all of that painstaking work for Olivia? If so, that was one amazing work of love.

Deacon drew a sheet off the strange-looking gift that lay thickly padded under layers of newspaper. "This is for you, Olivia," he said. "Go ahead. Tear off the rest of the paper."

After a moment's hesitation, she dutifully peeled back layer upon layer until a nose broke through. Then a head. "What …" She tore the paper off faster, Ole and Gretta sweeping the discards to the side as swiftly as they fell to the floor. As she continued, a shoulder appeared, a flank, a hoof until the entirety of the beautiful craftsmanship was revealed.

Olivia's hands flew to her lips, her eyes brimming with wonder. "A rocking horse? Tall as a Shetland pony."

Ole ran a light finger over the horse's nose, over its mane. "Beautiful job, Deacon. Absolutely beautiful. We can set it in front of your bedroom window, Olivia. You mentioned that you wanted to become a writer one day. What better place for you to get inspiration than to don your pony while you stare out across the lake."

"But …"

"You'll have plenty of time to enjoy it. After our trip to England, you'll be back. This is your home. You and me, we'll both be back."

"Trip to England?" Deacon said.

"Olivia is leaving in a couple of days. I'm going with her. We're going to find out …" Ole paused. The trip to England. Knocking on doors. Probing the past. Again that dreadful thought hit him. What if he and Olivia find out who her real father is and she no longer has time for Ole and Gretta?

Don't think, Ole. Don't think.

"No matter what," Deacon said, "Olivia, you are my grandniece, and you are Ole and Gretta's daughter."

Oh that that could be true.

LATER THAT EVENING WITH OLIVIA ALREADY having gone to bed, Ole sauntered into the parlor. The thought of her having been an orphan still gnawed at him. At least he'd put on a good pretense in front of Olivia when Deacon brought the adoption up again. That's your hurt talking, he'd told himself. That's your I-want-my-own-child-so-badly-I-can-taste-it talking. That's jealousy ... of some strange man who didn't know he was Olivia's real father, her own flesh and blood.

He placed several logs on the grate and enough kindling to get a good flame going and then struck a match, but it wouldn't light. He struck another and another, each a reminder of a child, his child, that had been conceived yet not allowed an opportunity to breathe its first breath. He drew out one more match. This one for Olivia. He struck it and it burst into flame. But fizzled out as quickly.

Meanwhile, Gretta busied herself in the kitchen as he continued to absently stoke the dying embers. A man who settled for nothing less than a satisfying relationship, he shared everything with her. Everything, that is, except how he really felt about her barrenness. He could never share that. The truth would crush her. Though it was not her fault, it grieved him. Deeply.

He returned his attention to the hearth. Trying to lose himself in nature's wonder. Trying desperately to empty himself of thought. To empty himself of feeling. Yet the thoughts came. Tormenting thoughts. Thoughts of loss and grief. Thoughts of a dream that kept coming and going and coming again. A dream that refused to stop playing torturous games with his heart.

He didn't care to strike another match. Why put more effort into something that drained him dry? Something as simple as lighting a fire had become as painful as being burned by one. Yet bent on overcoming his feelings whether he wanted to or not, bent on defying reality whether he wanted to or not, he struck yet another match. This time it burst into flame and a bright fire blazed.

As he stared into the dancing flames, Gretta came up from behind and placed a tray with a steamy cup and an overflowing bowl of popcorn on his lap. "Fire is beautiful," she said. "Careful with the chocolate. It's awfully hot."

She remained at his side eating and drinking and staring quietly into the flames as well, then finally broke the quiet. "I felt so badly for Olivia today when Deacon mentioned the adoption word. Did you notice how defensive she got?"

Coming from Gretta, that word struck Ole differently this time. In its own way, it was a good word, wasn't it? Orphans need love. Orphans are unspoiled. Orphans don't have it in them to take love for granted. Like anything in short supply, they understand and appreciate its value.

"You're too quiet," Gretta said. "I need to hear your voice, even if it's no more than a grunt."

He glanced at her. "No. I noticed it, too. I'm being tested, Gretta. When I was in the hospital, a chaplain there preached to me about that 'in everything give thanks' scripture. It worked for a while, but now it's turning bitter in my mouth. Anyone can give thanks when things are going well, but when they aren't, it's no easy task."

Not having a little girl of his own? Ole's heart shattered at the thought.

"No matter what, Olivia is still family," Gretta said. "And being an orphan, she needs us more."

Was that what it meant to be obedient? Ole wondered. To have to settle for second best? But if Ole wasn't Olivia's father by birth then wasn't she having to settle for second best, too? If that was the lesson, so be it.

"I'm afraid, Gretta," Ole said. "What if we find out who her true father is? Will she look for the man? What if she finds him? What if he wants her? And she wants him? What if she turns her back on us completely?"

"She won't. She's not capable of that."

He shook his head as if that could shake off the dreadful concern. "I wish she was mine, Gretta. I want her to be ours. If only we could change reality."

"The last chapter hasn't been written yet. She still very well could be. You need to hold onto that."

"And if you're wrong?"

"Stranger things have happened. But, Ole? What worries me most is, what if you do find out that you really aren't her father and you learn she's known all along?"

That troubling thought had crossed his mind. He swirled his chocolate and took a sip. It had grown cold while flames once again dwindled in the darkening hearth.

"Then I'd say we've lost all the way around. Haven't we?"

CHAPTER SIXTY-THREE

Through the train's window, Olivia waved another good-bye to Ole and Gretta.

And so the journey began.

The whistle blew a final warning and off she went, the most treasured part of her life already in the past.

She spent the majority of her time in the sleeper car until the train pulled into Grand Central Station. Though tired from a long and exhausting ride, she dusted herself off and quickly, though tentatively, headed straight for the man in a chauffeur's uniform holding up a sign that read 'Miss Olivia De Haven.' With gruff demeanor, he said, "Afternoon, miss," then seized her bag and swiftly led her to a waiting car.

Feeling as valued as her baggage, she sat quietly in the back seat and peered out the window. Dreary sky. Snow-dusted streets. Large houses huddled closely together. Ramshackle tenements resembling those one would find in the older sections of London.

Soon the driver pulled up in front of a house, the best of the lot, which was located in the middle of a long city block. He got out and opened Olivia's door. "This way, Miss."

She hesitated, uncertain what to think. What were they doing here?

In this neighborhood? Why hadn't the chauffeur retrieved her suitcase? Surely this wasn't the home of a senator. "Allow me to me fetch my—"

"I'll get that for you later," the driver said in a tone that would not be challenged.

The front door of the house creaked open and an elderly woman appeared. Her eyes radiated warmth, her tender voice quivering with age. "Come in, my dear. I've been expecting you."

Relieved by the welcome reception, Olivia gladly entered, but as she did, the telephone rang. The old woman excused herself, leaving Olivia alone at the entry. As she waited, she eyed the unfamiliar surroundings. The house smelled of old things, of dust, of mold, of moth crystals. Though tidy and large, it appeared wanting of daylight.

The wrinkled woman with measured gait returned a moment later reached up and lovingly touched Olivia's cheek. "I certainly didn't mean to be rude and leave you here alone," she said. "Let me introduce myself. I'm Jeremy's grandmother. That telephone call was from him. He asked that I offer his apologies. Said he had gotten tied up in a class of some sort that lasted too long. He'll meet us within the hour at his parents' estate. While I gather my things, please tell the driver we'll be out in just a few minutes." A knowing grin formed. "And feel free to call him Henry. He's a little hard to get to know at first, but when you do, you'll learn to love him." She chuckled. "A real softie thrives beneath that gruff demeanor."

Having barely met this woman, Olivia already adored her. It was more than her manner and kindness. The implication of getting to know Henry implied serious intentions that instilled comfort. A short while later, the car eased over rolling hills and along winding roads. A cool winter sun broke through and glistened through bare trees, the view much more inviting than that of the darkened streets and run-down tenement houses they'd left behind.

"Are you nervous, dear?" the old woman said.

"Quite."

"Don't be." She patted Olivia's forearm. "You will find Jeremy's parents quite entertaining."

"As they well may be," she said, determined to face a conflicting reality, "but I'm certain they're also rather accomplished. As for me, I'm no debutante."

"I know," the old woman said. "Jeremy tells me you've been going through a rather difficult time, that there's some confusion about your parentage. Do you know anything at all about your real parents?"

"We continue to seek answers. As for Jeremy, I'm not certain I shall feel comfortable in his world. You see, my grandmum raised me … we didn't have much."

The old woman rearranged her shawl, draping it just so about her thin shoulders. "I understand how you must feel, but don't be deceived. My dearly departed husband came from old money." She laughed. "You'd never know it to look at the house I live in. You see, the more you have, the more you have to lose. We found that out the hard way."

"You suffered a tragedy?" Olivia said. "I hope you don't mind my asking what happened."

"Not at all. The thing that sustained a privileged lifestyle for us was the very thing that did us in. We made a dreadful mistake. Tied up all of our assets into one place and then one day, poof, it was gone. We lost it all." Her gaze appeared contented as she stared off. "But we were happy. We had each other. And we learned that money is nice, but it certainly isn't everything."

The car rounded a curve through a heavily wooded area and then through a clearing. "What a marvelous building," Olivia said. "I gather that's the country club? Jeremy mentioned that he enjoys spending time there."

"Oh no, dear. That's not the country club. That's my son's home … where Jeremy was raised."

Olivia held a gasp in check.

It is?

CHAPTER SIXTY-FOUR

Like a prince standing at a portal, Jeremy awaited Olivia with an expectant grin. He offered his arm and led her inside the massive estate. Overwhelmed by the surroundings, of course, Olivia then went on to greet his parents with a pleasant "good morning" rather than "good afternoon," her show of nervousness appearing to break the ice. Though the Harrington home was lovely, the Lang home was palatial in comparison, Olivia's guest room larger than the entirety of her flat back in England. After dressing for dinner, they went on to spend an elegant evening at a banquet table. So engaged in fascinating discourse from politics to the war in Europe were they that they stayed put until time to retire for the evening. From the Harringtons to the Langs ... life far exceeded Olivia's imaginings, which had seemed far too grandiose to ever achieve.

The next morning, however, depression settled over the Lang's breakfast table like low-hanging clouds. Though the buffet offered variety and aroma that would tempt royalty, Olivia's appetite dissipated. What was it that suddenly plagued this household?

Jeremy wiped a telltale stain of blueberry preserves from his lower lip. "Thought we might take a stroll through the garden before Henry drives me to classes this morning," he said. "Perhaps I can be of help with planning your day."

Speaking, at the moment, felt as inappropriate as talking out loud during a Sunday morning sermon so she answered with a thoughtful nod.

And yet the quiet remained.

Glancing at his watch, he swilled the last of his orange juice and downed it with a gulp. "Time marches on. We'd best get going."

They drew on their overcoats and when they reached the garden, Olivia finally relaxed. This was the only place on the property that didn't lend itself to perfect order. As a matter of fact, it was an absolute mess. "You chose this setting because?"

He looked about and chuckled. "Wasn't thinking, I guess."

"I rather felt a strain at the breakfast table. Everyone appeared unusually quiet."

"Oh, that. After you retired to your room last evening," he said, drawing an arm about her waist and guiding her as they strolled along, "we received word about a favorite cousin of ours. We thought he had made it through the war unscathed. He'd been fighting on the Western Front. We were anxious for him to come home, but when he insisted on staying in France a while longer, we assumed all was well. What we didn't know was that he had consumption. Or should I say it had him?"

"I'm sor—" She pinched her eyes closed. "No wonder the wretchedness." What a relief that the war was finally over, and Jeremy's life would no longer be at risk.

"Enough about sad," he said. "For now, let's think of some fun things for you to do today." He stopped and looked toward a riding stable. "Even though it could be a trifle warmer, if you love the outdoors, you are welcome to go horseback riding if you'd like, play croquet, or go hiking. We have some amazing walking trails in our back woods. Or you can spend your day inside painting, sketching, or reading. Our library is filled with great books. Our servants are at your disposal. When you decide what you would like to do, let them know. Then I thought you might want to ride along with Henry later when he comes to fetch me. I'll meet you in front of the campus at two o'clock straight up."

Facing the day with no Jeremy at her side, Olivia said, "How I wish you would be here enjoying the day with me."

"I do as well. You and my grandmother are kindred spirits. She'll stay around for another day or two. You can always draw up a chair and have a nice chat. Knowing her, she'd love it."

After waving good-bye, Olivia followed the sound of music until she reached his mother's parlor. Jeremy's grandmother sat at the grand piano playing a favorite Mozart piece. The dear woman looked up, and seeing Olivia enter, she smiled and invited Olivia to join her on the piano bench. After several tunes, they took a long stroll, read books together in the library, played several games of chess, and then enjoyed tea, drawing an end to an idyllic morning and early afternoon.

At two o'clock Henry pulled up in front of the campus. Surrounded by a group of starry-eyed co-eds, Jeremy didn't appear to notice their arrival at first.

"We'll give him a moment," Henry said.

A bright-eyed blond glanced at the car, at Henry ... at Olivia ... and her eyes shot icicles. Jeremy appeared taken aback when he followed her gaze to the car. After bidding farewell to the retreating girls, he hopped in the back seat with Olivia. A stolen kiss and a few miles of idle chatter later, he said, "I'm worried about this man named Oliver Harrington. Can't get him out of my mind. I find it amazing that he is committed to going all of the way to England because of you. How could the poor man not be devastated if he learns he isn't your father?"

"That's precisely the problem." She stroked the handle of her handbag. "We must find out and sooner rather than later. Should he not be my biological father, I wish not to subject him to any more hurt or confusion. That he does not deserve. But no matter what the outcome, he is and always will be my adopted father. I will always want him to be a significant part of my life."

"Did you try contacting the ship again?"

"No. What good might that do?"

Jeremy sat quiet for a long moment, thinking. "Do you remember the name of that young man you spoke with?"

"It was Horace, but he no longer works there."

"Are you sure?"

"I recall him telling me I was fortunate … that I'd caught him on his last day. Said he was signing up for the war … It won't be possible to make contact with him now. If anything, a cleaning person may have found the letter in my cabin, but I'm certain they've tossed it out by now." She stared deeply into the passing forest. "I fear this deep dark mystery has me tied in knots."

"You know," Jeremy said, his countenance turning hopeful, "I've done some checking. Our ship. It was due to arrive earlier this morning. It must be in port now. Maybe they'll let us forage through the cabin you stayed in, let us try to find the letter ourselves. We need to get there sooner than soon."

She brightened at the thought.

"You know what they say, if you want to get something done right …" he turned to the chauffeur.

"Henry … to the pier."

CHAPTER SIXTY-FIVE

On the boardwalk at the Port of New York, Olivia gazed up at the massive ocean liner and reeled. This great big wonderful vessel had served as a springboard, propelling her into an amazing world where the past seemed distant and the present surpassed her wildest imaginings. But what about her future?

"The ship almost feels hallowed," Jeremy said, his voice warm with feeling.

She'd met him aboard this ship. Now he stood with her and gazed at it, too. Ready to walk in step up that long gangplank. Eager to search for an elusive letter that in and of itself contained the power to anchor her in this strange and wonderful new world. Yet she remained steadfastly torn between hope and despair for what were the chances of finding it? Again that feeling of apprehension swept in and it grieved her for those chances remained slight.

"Every night during our voyage when I returned to my stateroom," he said, "I laid in bed and stared at the ceiling praying for morning to come so I could spend more time with you. I didn't want our journey to end."

Dizzied by the sentiment, she nuzzled close to him, resting her head lightly against his shoulder. "Neither did I. I wish with my entire being that I could remain here in America with you and with my grandmum-appointed father and stepmother." She fixed her gaze at the top of the ramp. "They must allow us on board."

"All we need to do is be polite, make our request compelling, and show respect." He guided her forward lightly by the elbow and winked. "Come. I'll show you how it's done."

Not only did she find Jeremy's confidence refreshing, he was correct. She found herself increasingly hopeful when in a matter of minutes they happily boarded ship and foraged about inside the cabin. The stateroom in perfect order as before, they searched every drawer, checked beneath and behind all furnishings, under the bedding, and in and under the wastebasket.

Please, please be here.

Minutes later, her greatest fear paid an unwelcome visit. No letter. Her shoulders drooped and her spirits plummeted. She felt more vacant inside than the stark cabin, if that were possible.

Jeremy held her tight. "Don't worry," he cooed. "We won't give up. We'll go home and get in touch with the corporate office one last time."

"But Horace is no longer there. I've already attempted to reach him several times, remember? No one else will know." She hesitated. This was not an appropriate time to retreat. "You're right. We mustn't allow Grandmum's secret to remain buried with her forever."

Back at the estate, Olivia made one final telephone call to the ship's headquarters, Jeremy smiling confidently at her side. She reminded the kind gentleman of her plight. She pressed, she urged, and she pressed again, fighting the obvious with her entire being. But it did no good. Still no letter. No knowledge of a letter having been found. No Horace. With the young man having enlisted in the Army, there was no way of knowing whether or not he'd found it. As for the cabin, it had been occupied several times since their voyage, so the letter was definitely lost. If it hadn't arrived in Amber Leaf by now, it was hopeless. Nothing further could be done. Hope after all this time … forever denied.

During the course of their evening meal, she drew inside herself, absently poking at the roast beef on her dinner plate, cutting it in small chunks, moving it around, and cutting it again.

"Is the food alright, dear?" Mrs. Lang said.

"I'm afraid we've received some rather disappointing news," Jeremy said, answering for Olivia. "We need time to work things out."

As his mother, who appeared confused, looked to his father, Jeremy turned to Olivia. "Let's retire to the parlor," he said. "We can always come back later for a midnight snack."

With a warm fire sputtering on the hearth, they huddled near the window and stared at a heavy snowfall. "It's lovely out there," Olivia said after a long quiet.

"And I'm feeling restless." A warm smile stretched across his preppy face. "How adventurous do you feel? Want to bundle up and take a stroll out into winter's icebox?"

His suggestion precisely what she needed, they stuffed their hands through the sleeves of their coats and headed outside. Gentle brisk breeze. Snowflakes pelting their cheeks, glomming onto their lashes. Muted steps on a virgin white blanket. The great outdoors felt wonderful.

But the further they walked, the more Jeremy appeared to crawl inside of himself. He stopped at the wrought iron gate and looked to the other side as if hoping to find comfort there. "What now?" he said.

She looked deep into his eyes.

What now?

He knew.

"We're leaving in several days as planned," she said. "I must have peace. If I am to go forward with the relationship with Oliver and Gretta Harrington, I must know who I'm giving to them." She paused then said, "I must be certain who I'm giving to you as well."

He squeezed her hands until they hurt. "You mean the world to me."

"Miss Olivia?" a voice cried from the mansion. "You have a long distance person-to-person telephone call."

Jeremy slipped an arm around her shoulder and guided her in. "Must be Oliver Harrington."

Minutes later, it was as though she were walking on air as she said, "He's meeting me the day after tomorrow at the Port of New York at ten in the morning ... Jeremy? He said he loves me."

"What's not to love?"

But do I love him? Olivia wondered. Or is it the mere thought of him that I love? The thought of having a father? A real father? And might it well be that the thought of his having his own child is what has captured his heart?

Was it even possible for either of us to one day know that truth for certain?

CHAPTER SIXTY-SIX

O le stared at his bowl. The stew smelled flavorful, but the thought of eating? Revolting. A healthy appetite was the least of his concerns.

"You've barely touched your supper again," Gretta said.

"I'm not hungry."

"But you need to keep up your strength. You've barely eaten since she left."

"Olivia. Her name is Olivia." He winced. "I'm sorry," he said. "I didn't mean to raise my voice. It's just that I feel so helpless. Most things I can fix, but not this one. It's too big."

"You've got to get hold of yourself, Ole. I heard you up walking around again in the middle of the night."

"I was reading her letter."

"Which one?"

"The first one …" His voice broke. "The one telling me …"

"You've got to fight this thing. Don't let it destroy you."

He mindlessly smoothed his napkin. "Olivia needs me," he said. "I know she does." He looked up. "Have you ever experienced anything like that, Gretta? Someone being so close that they feel as if they're a part of you?"

"I think we all do from time to time," she said. "I guess my question would be, does she need you? Or is it you who needs her? ... Ole?" Gretta looked deep into his eyes. "And speaking of needing people, do you plan to see your father during this trip?"

"I can't go all of the way to England and not pay a visit."

"Do you think he'll ..."

"He'll be decent. Cold, but decent."

OLIVIA CLUTCHED HER PILLOW, NOT WANTING to get up. Not yet. She had but one more day to enjoy this elegant home, this magnificent setting, but more importantly, the welcoming feeling of being close to Jeremy, of getting to know him better, of inhaling in his marvelous air. If only it might be possible to stop time. If nothing else, simply slowing it down would be a tremendous help.

The last to rise, she dined alone on bacon and French toast. Jeremy and his parents had flitted off to attend to overly busy lives. Only the servants milled about, meeting her needs in every way imaginable as if she were their only charge. Somehow she felt more comfortable in their company. Their lives seemed simpler, more manageable, more caring, less demanding.

During the morning hours she reconfirmed passage to England, caught up on a bit of reading in the library, and then spent the rest of the day readying herself for a special date with Jeremy.

"You are beyond beautiful," he said that evening as he helped her into the awaiting Roadster.

As they rode along winding roads to the country club, she felt like Cinderella on her way to the ball. Jeremy couldn't have been a more well-mannered or striking young prince. When they arrived, music from a chamber orchestra played softly in the background of the elegantly decorated dining hall. Formally set tables. Flickering candlelight. And when the waiter appeared tableside, Jeremy ordered Châteaubriand. She could easily adapt to living in grand style such as this.

After the main course, the orchestra played *I'm Always Chasing Rainbows*. Jeremy stood. "May I have the honor?"

Gliding about the dance floor with him was pure heaven. Each move smooth, confident, calculated. And then he whispered in her ear, "We need to talk about our future."

Her heart fluttered. "Our—"

"That's right. When you and Oliver Harrington return from England, I'm making you mine, even if it means nothing more than making a trip to the justice of the peace."

How was it possible that Jeremy might set his affections on her? To be thoroughly smitten, and so quickly? But what did it matter? Reeling in the wonder of it all, she could have danced until dawn, but rather they returned to their table to conclude dinner with a delicious slice of lemon layer cake and coffee.

She presumed it impossible for this evening to go better.

Though the possibility remained for it to grow worse.

Having finished dessert, Jeremy reached for her hand as the waiter seated several young ladies at a neighboring table. Several beautiful young ladies. One, in particular, appeared to catch Jeremy's eye, holding it too long. As they continued to gaze at one another, he let go his grip of Olivia's hand. As he did, she drew her wrap over shoulders as if to stave off a light chill.

"I presume you know her?" Olivia ventured.

"No," he said without meeting her gaze. "She must be new to the area."

"Perhaps you would do well to introduce yourself."

He turned to Olivia, appearing sheepish, as if to have been pricked by conscience. "Why would I do that?"

Not allowing herself to indulge in a bout of jealousy, she shrugged. She needed to pay closer attention. Jeremy may be the man of her dreams in many ways, but he also may be ahead of himself in matters of the heart.

Later that evening as they motored back to the estate, she found it difficult to stop reliving the evening from beginning to end and back again. All was picture perfect with the exception of one inappropriate slip of a look. One subtle releasing of a hand.

And Jeremy's intimating he would marry her ... without asking ... without mentioning those three small, though absolutely essential, words.

"You're awfully quiet," he said. "Is it something I've done? Something I've said?"

As if he needed to ask.

She took note of the hairpin curves in the road up ahead. This was not an appropriate venue for serious conversation. "I'm fine. Really I am. Doing a little thinking is all. Formulating my thoughts. Might we have a chat in the parlor before we turn in for the evening?"

"Look, if it's about ..."

She mouthed *shhh* accompanied by an encouraging smile, which seemed to relax him.

A short while later, walking into the parlor felt akin to walking into a funeral. Her funeral—that is, the funeral of her future. She knew full well what needed to be said, but had no clue as to how it might be received.

"Would you care for tea?" Jeremy said.

"No, thank you. I'm really quite sated. I must say the dinner was delicious. Thank you so much."

"Do we sit together on the divan, or might it be more appropriate to face one another on the overstuffed chairs?"

"Either is fine," she said. "I promise this shall not be painful."

"How did you know I feared that?"

"I believe it's referred to as woman's intuition."

"This wouldn't happen to be about those strangers at the country club, would it?"

"Correction. Stranger. And indeed it would."

Pink rose from his neck, crawling up to his cheeks, to the tips of his ears. "I don't know why I did what I did. It didn't feel right. I embarrassed myself, and I fear I may have hurt you in the process. I'm not sure what to say. I can only hope my character isn't that lacking and that it won't happen again."

"Perhaps you aren't ready for a relationship. You prefer to be, but you aren't." She reached up and touched his cheek. "That's neither right nor wrong, Jeremy. It merely is. Perhaps it's that our relationship has moved too swiftly too soon. After all, we barely know one another."

"I don't want to be that way." He looked as if he were about to weep. "But what can I do about it?"

"Feel free to take whatever time you need."

"Time for what? Time to grow up? That's too risky. The moment I laid eyes on you, it was love at first sight. That's never happened to me before. I don't want to take the chance of losing you."

They sat quietly for a long while, she reaching for words, he for the first time since they'd met appearing to feel miserable in his own skin.

"I've never met anyone quite like you before," he said.

"Nor I you. It would be dreadful to lose you, but neither would I feel comfortable facing a future of suspicion and doubt. If we are to enjoy a lasting relationship, it must be solid. It must be all or nothing. If you aren't yet able to make that commitment, I won't judge you. But I must know up front," she said, a growing ache giving her cause for concern, "so we both might move on with our lives in the most mature way possible.

CHAPTER SIXTY-SEVEN

Olivia sat before the mirror and brushed her hair until her scalp hurt. Whatever had happened this evening? Why must life hurt so? Her perfect world felt as if it were ripping apart from the outside in and she felt helpless, incapable of stopping it. Fortunately she and Oliver Harrington would be off for England first thing in the morning, which at the moment seemed far too many hours away. She wished to have those hours behind her.

She carefully placed the brush on the dresser as if it were fragile and might easily break. As she did, to her surprise the word "father" slipped from her lips, softly as if a prayer. Not grandmum, but father. He was the link to her past, the link that anchored her, that made sense of everything. Before knowing him, she would never have had the strength of character to speak to Jeremy the way she had this evening. She would never have had the strength of character to face that sudden and relationship-ending conflict brought on by the introduction of another possible suitor, nor would she have possessed the willingness to so easily release him. Her father was the solid anchor she'd searched for her entire life. It was his respect that she coveted whether he was here to witness it or not. It was his love of which she desired to be worthy.

She lightly stroked the bristles. Appropriate or not, she had bonded with Oliver M. Harrington. Deeply. How wonderful if he were to sweep her up in his embrace now, to hold and console her. Yet that remained a fantasy for she must not allow herself to take advantage of his great big heart, not until she knew for certain that it belonged to her. No, she must not do wrong by him. And to think she'd only gotten to know him for a few short months. A few short wonderful months.

She awakened the next morning with more resolve than she'd thought possible. What happened? Though clouds shielded a dismal sky, it was as if the sun had risen in her heart.

"Good morning, father." She looked curiously toward the door. The voices, though moderated in the early dawn, were easily distinguishable.

"Good morning, son. How was the big date last night?"

"We had a fabulous time," Jeremy said without hesitation, "and I aired my intentions," he added with a lilt in his voice.

Drawing the sheet to her chin, she listened harder, but the footsteps grew faint, the voices too low to decipher.

How might it be that an innocent violation could turn around on her, growing her heart toward Jeremy rather than repelling it away? His decency perhaps? The fact that he cared deeply, that he owned his transgression, and was in his own way repentant? He owed her nothing and wasn't required to respond to her in a mature and loving manner, yet he had.

She tore out of bed, hurriedly got ready, and while stuffing her arms through the sleeves of a cardigan, descended the stairs to breakfast two at a time.

Jeremy followed a last bite of waffle with a gulp of tea. "Well good morning," he said, the glint in his eye unmistakable. "Did you get enough sleep?"

A smile blossomed. "I believe so, and you?" She looked to Jeremy's father who sat beaming as well. "Good morning, sir," she said.

"Good morning."

"Definitely." Jeremy appeared all teeth.

The chair opposite his father sat empty, the place setting removed. "Where's your mother?"

His father answered for him. "Early morning meeting. Honestly, if there's a planning committee within a two-hundred mile radius of our fair town and you had bet she's on it, you'd win every time."

"I'm seeing you to your ship today," Jeremy said, suddenly appearing impatient.

"That's so lovely of you." A servant nudged her chair closer to the table as she lowered onto it. "I feel rather guilty, though, that my returning to England is luring you away from your studies even if only for several hours." She paused. "I find it curious that I referred to it as England rather than home."

"You're heading back overseas so soon?" his father said, appearing confused.

Olivia considered for a moment the significance of this trip, how her future hung in the balance. "I must solve a lifelong mystery."

"What mystery, if you don't mind my asking?"

"About my father."

His bright eyes faded. "But I thought he was—"

"A nobleman?"

A creased brow accompanied Jeremy's father's question. "Do you mean your parentage is still in question?"

What had happened to this man? He'd been consistently welcoming. Why the change? "It has always been in question." She glanced at Jeremy. "Have you not told him?"

Mr. Lang shot Jeremy a cross look. "No, I don't believe he did."

Though a servant slipped a warm plate in front of Olivia containing an artfully prepared waffle slathered in maple syrup sandwiched between several thick strips of bacon, her appetite evaporated.

"She had the proof, Father," Jeremy said in a halting voice. "It was in that letter she lost."

"How could anyone possibly lose a document that important?"

Taken aback by the accusing tone and its underlying implication, she moved to the side for the servant as he poured fresh coffee into her cup. She then looked to Jeremy for help.

But he looked away.

CHAPTER SIXTY-EIGHT

The ride to the Port of New York seemed to take forever. When they arrived, Olivia rushed out of the car then stopped short.

There he stood. Oliver M. Harrington. The mere sight of him a comfort standing as he did on the boardwalk. Leaning heavily on his cane. His intense gaze riveted on the giant ship. His thoughts appearing thousands of miles away. What was he thinking? Why would a man of his stature so readily venture so far so soon with no guarantee of a positive outcome? Could his love for her mother have been so intense that he would go to such lengths to prove Olivia was their one and only daughter?

She dizzied at the thought, gooseflesh prickling from head to toe. At the moment, she couldn't feel more proud. His presence alone made all that was wrong with her world seem right. With Jeremy looking on, she wanted to call him father, to shout it, but that would be presumptuous.

Then Ole turned and eyes brimming with love coupled with uncertainty locked onto hers.

"Good morning," she said, taking a tentative step forward. "I presume your journey went well?"

He chuckled. "It was too long, I'm afraid. I fear I couldn't wait to get here."

Nor could I wait to have you here. "I wish for you to meet Jeremy."

Ole extended a hand. "Jeremy, my boy, how very nice to meet you."

Was it Olivia's imagination or might Jeremy actually have felt awe-struck with Ole's powerful presence? Whatever she sensed, it felt wonderfully reassuring—from having felt slighted to feeling invaluable in a short span of just under two hours.

After a pleasant exchange of light banter, Ole reached again for Jeremy's hand. "It was a pleasure talking with you. Now if you'll excuse me, I'll leave the two of you to say your good-byes in private."

Jeremy gave him a polite nod then seized Olivia's hands and looked deeply into her eyes. "I regret the bumps in the road these past couple of days," he said.

Ask him, Olivia. Always clean up behind you. "You looked away this morning at your father's accusing tone. That troubled me."

"I believe in you … and we have nothing to defend." He stared off for a brief moment then returned his gaze. "I can't seem to get on track these days. Can't seem to get things right. While you're away, I will to tend to my character. Promise me you'll write every day. I doubt I'll be able sleep until I meet you here again on the boardwalk."

She pecked him lightly on the cheek followed with a quick hug good-bye. Turning, she seized Ole's arm and with a skip in her step they ascended the gangway. When they reached the top, she glanced back and waved. A fleeting pang of guilt swept through her for Jeremy looked forlorn. Why the absence of sadness in her own heart? That might come later, she mused, though she sensed it doubtful.

She and Ole settled into their cabins then met on deck as the horn sounded and the ship set sail. Strangely, the long voyage back to England paled in comparison to her original journey to America. Once again rich with camaraderie and fine food, Olivia reveled in a marvelous present. But to her surprise, she enjoyed very little alone time with

Ole for wherever they went, people appeared drawn to him, to his wisdom and confidence. As she enjoyed his easy laughter and easier ways, she realized that these were days far too meaningful to end. But sooner than she wanted, the shores of England appeared on the horizon. It was then that an unexpected feeling of apprehension overtook her. Ole must have felt it, too, for his laughter gave way to a sad sort of quiet.

"There is something we haven't discussed," she said.

He drew her close. "There's no need to discuss it. Whatever the outcome, whatever we find, you are and will always be my daughter. Understood?"

She felt the truth to those words as solidly as she stood. Nothing else mattered.

After disembarking, they gathered their luggage. Olivia accompanied him as he checked into a hotel, and then together they journeyed to her flat several blocks away. No words spoken. The sound of light breathing. The rhythmic cadence of foot drops. A gnawing hint of trepidation growing ever stronger.

Until they stopped in front of her flat and looked up.

CHAPTER SIXTY-NINE

Ole looked about the flat. It felt strange to stand here, as if time had somehow stood still. How long had it been?

"Place still looks the same," he said finally. But then his sweeping gaze met with the alcove—and stopped. His breathing grew shallow.

"That's where Grandmum kept my crib when I was little," Olivia said as if sensing his discomfort. "Are you well?"

"I'm fine." I think.

"May I take your coat?"

He shook his head. He needed to get out of here. "Why don't I go back to the hotel? Give you a chance to unpack. That will also give me time to plan our course for the next several days. You must be getting hungry, though. I know I am. I'll return in a couple of hours. Take you out for a bite to eat. Are you up for that?"

"I am happy to run down to the cellar. We have canned goods …"

"No. We'll dine out. I insist."

"As you wish."

OLIVIA GLANCED AT THE ALCOVE. WHAT happened? Why had Ole balked at the sight of that small space? And why the need to leave so quickly? Might he have had second thoughts about returning to England?

Forcing concern aside, she quickly emptied her trunk, tossing soiled clothing into the wicker basket, placing toiletries back in the cabinet where they belonged. In short order, she was bathed, brushed, and wearing fresh clothing.

Ole returned several hours later appearing forlorn. "The war certainly has taken a toll on Fritz," he said.

"You've seen him then?"

"Ran into him out in the hallway. Caught up a bit."

She thought for a moment. "Perhaps he would be a good one to inquire about the past."

"I brought it up," Ole said. "Couldn't let a good opportunity slip past. Seems he was surprised, too. Knew nothing about it."

Now what!

Ole escorted her back to his hotel where they dined in the hotel's dining room.

"You will visit your parents while you're here, I presume," Olivia said as she set her menu to the side.

"Your grandparents, you mean? I was hoping you might accompany me."

"I would be honored," she said. "I noticed you've made little mention of them. I'm terribly curious. What are they like?"

He shrugged. "They're just people ... so tell me. Any thoughts about who to approach next?"

By the manner in which he dismissed his parents, whatever had transpired between them must not have been pleasant.

"What about the Fletchers?" she said. "I'm certain Anne knows something. When I spoke with her about you, she appeared strangely troubled."

"Where do they live?"

"In the flat above mine."

"They've never moved? After all this time?"

Olivia shook her head.

After being comfortably sated, they appeared at the Fletchers' uninvited. After a single knock, the door opened and a stunned Anne Fletcher stood with mouth agape. "Oliver? Ollie Harrington?"

"One in the same," he said and his grin grew wonderfully warm.

"Come in, come in, come in. Oh my, look at you." She grasped his hands and looked him up and down. "You've not changed in the slightest. Still handsome as ever." She gave a quick glance over her shoulder. "George, you must come. You'll never believe who's here."

Olivia stepped back and watched as though they were on stage and she comfortably seated in the audience. Should they find that Ole is not her real father, he is at the least her adopted father, they now share a common bond to the past, and to her that meant the world.

Anne glanced at Olivia as if finally noticing her presence. She then gave Ole an apprehensive look. "Olivia tells me you're her father?"

"That's why we've come. We're hoping that to be the case, but aren't certain as to how to prove it. Did Amelia ever share any information with you that might be of help?"

"No," Anne said tentatively. "Never mentioned a word. Did she, George?"

As he shook his head in agreement, she turned to Olivia. "That's why I was taken aback when you said Ollie here is your father."

"Might you have any suggestions as to who else might know then?" Olivia said.

"None whatsoever."

George turned to Ole. "What about your parents? Certainly they would know."

"They've never mentioned a word. We're planning to stop by to see them tomorrow."

"Have matters improved with them?" George reddened. "I'm sorry. It's rude for me to ask."

"No." Ole let out an exasperated sigh. "They never did."

"By the way, Olivia," Anne said, abruptly changing the subject. Who could blame her? This family dialogue was becoming terribly wretched. "I have your mail. Mary's mother dropped it by. Asked if I might be so kind as to give it to you since Mary …"

Olivia flinched at the foreboding tone. "Since Mary what?"

"You didn't know then?"

"Not the flu." She took a step back. "No. Please don't tell me that."

Anne scurried into a far room and returned with a large stack of mail and handed it to Olivia, her eyes fixed on it as if unable to face her. "I'm awfully sorry," she said. "It's a terrible loss. Mary was such a lovely young lady."

Strong arms drew Olivia into a tight embrace, girding her.

What if through no fault of her own she lost that support as well? No. Ole wouldn't do that to her. It wasn't in his character.

CHAPTER SEVENTY

A s Ole plopped on the side of the bed and tugged off his shoes, rushing footsteps intruded the quiet, rushing footsteps that stopped at his hotel room door, followed by an urgent knock. Some disgruntled guest must have found the wrong room, he surmised.

Exhausted from an emotionally-packed day, at the moment, there was nothing he desired more than a good night's rest. Oh, well. But when he got up and answered it, he looked into widened eyes. "Olivia? What on earth are you doing here this time of night?"

Sidestepping him, she pressed into his room. "I had to come."

"Couldn't this wait until morning? It's far too dangerous for you to be out and about, walking these streets alone at night."

"I sorted through my mail," she said as if she hadn't heard a word he'd said, and then she held up an envelope, waving it. "This came. The letter ... it came. It appears Horace wasn't thinking clearly. He undoubtedly had his mind fixed on the war. Silly boy sent it here to England rather than to Amber Leaf."

Not taking her attention off the envelope, it was as if Ole sensed in her vulnerable eyes a mingling of hope and fear.

In an instant, he tore open the envelope only to have another spill onto the floor. Olivia scooped it up and handed it to him. On the outside in strikingly familiar penmanship it read *To Oliver M. Harrington.* He scanned an accompanying letter of explanation, his heart pulsing madly in his throat. He then flopped onto a chair at a desk in his room and looked up at Olivia in disbelief. "You were right all along," he said. "The shipping company found this letter in your cabin."

"Hurry." Olivia's tone emanated urgency. "Open it … please."

Vacillating between anticipation and dread, he ripped open the second envelope, the salutation jarring. "It's definitely the letter from Amelia." He held it up. "Look. She still called me Ollie … my dearest Ollie, at that."

Olivia sat quietly as he read in reverent silence.

10 August 1916

My dearest Ollie:

I can only hope that this letter finds you most happy and well. Do know that I have been following your success over these many years through word of Deacon's rather sporadic correspondence with an acquaintance of ours and could not be more pleased to learn that you've prospered well. Of course, I would have been surprised to have learned otherwise.

Your choosing to venture to America could not have been wiser. The war has taken a heavy toll on England, the likes of which I could not have anticipated, not in a lifetime. And if that isn't enough to endure, consumption has taken its toll on my lungs. It appears that I won't be long for this world, which is the reason for this wretchedly long-overdue letter.

I am writing in the hope that you and Olivia will somehow find it in your hearts to forgive me when you realize how blatantly I have sinned against the two of you. I am encouraging this pardon for your sakes. To ask for that forgiveness for my sake would be unbefitting on my part for forgiveness is a blessing I do not deserve. I can only hope that sharing an understanding of the why of it all will help to soften your emotions.

By the time you read this letter, you will have met your beautiful daughter. She is exemplary in every way—unspoiled, honest, generous, thoughtful, hardworking, very much like Emily, very much like you.

Those many years ago when Emily was in that dreadful accident and lost your son, the doctors were able to save your daughter. Yes, Emily was carrying twins. While the child was still in hospital, I immediately visited your parents' estate. Not only did they insist that I stand outside their door in gloomy drizzle as though I were a common beggar, when I shared the dreadful news of the loss of our dear Emily and their grandson, a look of unmitigated relief washed over them. So stunned was I, that I fled before mentioning word of their granddaughter. The more I considered that transgression, with you off in the military, I feared that if they learned of Olivia's survival, they would claim her as their own. Though their outer wealth would have served her well, their inner wealth I found most inadequate.

That evening I returned home and in the wee hours of morning made a solemn promise to Emily's memory that I would never allow those dreadful people to have access to her child. I considered adopting Olivia, but that would have taken your signature and then you would have known. I did, however, take it upon myself to infer that I adopted her. How could I transgress you in that manner, you undoubtedly wonder? I in no way had any intention of violating you. But while you are a strong man, I fear your father is ever stronger. Do know that I had every intention of turning Olivia over to your tender care after you completed your service in the military.

There is no question that your parents felt nothing but disdain for my beloved Emily both before and during your marriage, and through no fault of her own. I hope you understand that my primary concern was protecting her, especially in death, from further violation.

You are undoubtedly wondering why I chose not turn Olivia over to your care when I learned you were leaving for America. That was where my altruistic nature took a back seat to shame. I had every intention of doing so, but kept telling myself I'd keep her for just a few more days. I promised myself I'd tell you the next time I heard from you, but that letter, that cablegram, that telephone call, it never did come. And it was as though you had deserted my Emily, too. Unfortunately, those few more days then turned into weeks, which turned into months, which turned into years. And for that I have forever paid a price. No one gets nothing. No one gets it all.

I only hope that after meeting your beautiful daughter, you will accept her into your home. She needs and is most worthy of a loving family.

Yours most sincerely,

Amelia De Haven

CHAPTER SEVENTY-ONE

Olivia reached for the letter, smoothed it open as if it were made from ancient and fragile parchment that would disintegrate from the slightest touch, and began to read. Her expression pivoted from curious to thoughtful to touched and finally to surprised, her lashes matting with plump tears. Having finished reading, she looked up.

Too emotionally spent to communicate other than nonverbally, Ole could not take his eyes off the letter. Though a grown man, a part of him felt a need to wail like a toddler at the violation he and Olivia had suffered at the whim of one Amelia De Haven. Another part of him felt as if he'd been locked in a cramped cage and finally set free. No silence he experienced in his ample lifetime had ever felt so fulfilling, had ever felt so complete … as pure and unadulterated love overflowed in the interior of this fine hotel suite.

He got up and drew Olivia into a warm and loving embrace, kissing her lightly atop her head as whimpering muffled against his chest. So this was what it felt like to hold a child, his own child, in his arms. This precious moment too long denied, though surreal, felt every bit as wonderful as he had hoped.

She felt delicate.

He felt complete.

Fulfilled.

Needed.

And as sure as night followed day, he could imagine nothing on the face of the earth more rewarding than to be able to meet that need and the many needs that would follow in the coming years ahead.

"I can't believe it," he said. "After all of this time … I finally have my very own child."

Olivia stepped back. "But Grandmum," she said with a telling ache in her voice, "how could she …"

Ole unclenched a tightening fist. "She did it for your mother, Olivia, your mother who had her own life and the lives of her children ripped away from her in the blink of an eye. We need to remember that. Both of us. Always."

Olivia could not have found comfort in unconvincing words for she looked as if she'd just choked down a tablespoon of castor oil.

"I'm taking you back to Amber Leaf with me," Ole said. "Your step-mother and I need more time to get to know you before that young man we left back in New York steals you away from us for good."

Ole hesitated. Was that a pang of jealousy that ripped through him? What did it matter? Sharing a priceless treasure would be difficult, he reasoned, but he had achieved his life's dream and that was all that mattered. He had a child. A daughter. His own flesh and blood. And she loved and cherished him, too. That was another inexplicable wonder he felt. That was another inexplicable wonder he strangely knew. And that was enough.

Olivia looked as if she wanted to say something, but chose not to.

"Come. I'll walk you back to your flat."

Shortly thereafter, they stood outside her flat for a final goodnight. "First thing in the morning," he said, "I'll send a cablegram off to your mother. You have no idea how thrilled she will be." He kissed Olivia again lightly atop her forehead. "Now go get some sleep."

Her eyes sparkled beneath the street lamp. "I rather doubt I'll find that a likelihood."

Ole chuckled. "Neither will I."

OLIVIA CLOSED THE DOOR AND LEANED the entire weight of her back against it. Her wildest dream a reality? And tomorrow she would meet her grandparents … Lord and Lady Harrington.

She thought of Jeremy and grinned as she tried to visualize his expression as he read the amazing news in her next letter. But then she remembered how she had felt when her father mentioned Jeremy's stealing her away for good. How unacceptable the exchange with Jeremy's father at the breakfast table that morning before she left. She replayed the scene in her mind—how unworthy he had inadvertently made her feel, how Jeremy chose not to defend her though he had insisted she didn't need defending. Whether Ole was or was not her biological father did nothing to alter her worth. How could Jeremy and his father not understand that? This man named Oliver M. Harrington, though, he had certainly understood and had chosen to value her regardless of her parentage.

And in the end … she grinned from ear to happy ear … she belonged to him.

Too awake to sleep, she rifled through her paltry wardrobe. What might she wear tomorrow that would make an excellent first impression on her grandparents? Her only appropriate garment was the dress Gretta had bought for her at Skinner Chamberlain's back in Amber Leaf.

Time to begin ironing.

As she ironed the creases into oblivion, thoughts of Jeremy

continued to vie for her attention. The more she thought, the more intently she ironed. It would not be wise to invest valuable time in someone whose affections were conditional. She wanted better than that. Besides, the unconditional love she received from her father filled her to overflowing. At the moment, she didn't need more.

She crawled into bed, pulled the covers to her chin, and looked up. "Please change your character, Jeremy, please. If you choose not to, the beautiful connection we've so enjoyed shall never last."

OLE RUSHED INTO WESTERN UNION, HIS chest swelled with pride. "I would like to send a cablegram to Gretta Harrington in Amber Leaf, Minnesota," he said.

"Wonderful news. Stop. The letter. Stop. It came. Stop." The instant he pronounced those words, it was as if something broke loose deep inside his soul and for the first time since he could remember he laughed with complete abandon.

The clerk looked at him strangely, as if he'd lost leave of his senses.

"Olivia is our daughter. Stop," he continued. "Our beautiful, beautiful daughter. Stop." He wanted to add 'and by blood, too,' but he refused to do that to Gretta. "In the end, everything falls perfectly into place. Stop. We will be home soon. Stop. All my love. Stop. No … all our love. Stop. Oliver."

CHAPTER SEVENTY-TWO

Since leaving England, Ole had returned for a visit but once. Briefly. Hadn't felt welcome.

Slowing the automobile, he looked up at the massive gate and a feeling of consternation overtook him—that same feeling he felt when he passed through his back door when Gretta had lost yet another child. It was as if he were again marching headlong into a prison rather than home.

Don't get wobbly, he chided himself.

Meanwhile, Olivia sat quietly at his side, eyes widening, a tremor revealing itself in her hand as it rose to meet her lips. "Is this ..."

"Yes. This is where I was raised."

She appeared to grow increasingly ill at ease as the automobile meandered along the sinuous road leading to the palatial estate. Ole was far too new to this father business. How might he offer comfort?

"Nervous?" he said.

She gazed about. "Terribly much so, I'm afraid ... and you?"

"I'm fine," he said, willing his feelings into being.

"I gather it's been a rather long while since last you've visited your parents."

That thought troubled him. "Your grandparents, do you mean? Actually, it has been."

"May that have been why you and my mother bonded as you did?"

Jarred by the assumption, Ole gave her a thoughtful look.

"I presume that which my mother's parents lacked in material wealth," she said with her gaze locked straight ahead, "your parents lacked in emotional wealth."

Such wisdom from one so young. "Your grandfather isn't what one would call a man given to emotion."

"Your mother, she remained aloof as well? … Forgive me. I'm rather beside myself with curiosity."

"She does follow his lead."

"You must have found that rather difficult."

"I didn't know any differently," he said as the forbidding mansion grew ever closer. "I never understood love, not until I met your mother, that is. When you haven't heard the words 'I love you,' you prefer not to hear them. They tend to feel dirty."

"You've not shared the sentiment with your father either then?"

"A man dare not do that to Lord Harrington, son included."

Olivia drew her wrap tighter as they pulled to a stop. "People suffering from poverty of the soul have the greatest need to hear those words, do they not?"

"How did you become so wise?"

She finally smiled. "It appears I've inherited the trait."

It felt surreal knocking on the door of the place Ole had once called home, but he also felt much like a stranger, and a stranger knocks. He squared his shoulders, and a moment later, a servant invited them in. "Good to see you again, Henry," Ole said.

"Marvelous to see you, too, sir. I am pleased to find you looking well."

Ole's mother and father gazed at them from a comfortable distance. Well dressed as always. Hair now white with age. Familiar-looking faces scored with wrinkles. And though shorter in stature, they stood erect with sharp unreadable eyes.

Though fire hissed and spat in the hearth, Ole felt incapable of shaking off a chill. To his chagrin, with Olivia at his side, he viewed his parents' home much the way he had when he'd first brought Amelia here to meet them. In contrast to her world, which had so lifted him, nothing had changed. The oppressing décor in muted colors. Paintings of landscapes and flowers, but none of people. The hard, cold sculpture of a horse with no rider. And though the great room bore but a hint of stale dust, inhaling a breath in the large chamber suffocated him then—it suffocated him now. The oppression. The dominance. His father's self-acclaimed prerogative to rule others' lives. To rule his life.

But that was from days long passed.

His father stretched forth a hand. "The prodigal has returned. How good to see you again, my boy."

"Don't be unkind, dear," his mother said and then turning to Ole, she reached up and pecked him lightly on the cheek. "It's wonderful to have you home again, Oliver."

Oliver? How does one grow close to one's mother and father when held back by physical distance and verbal formality? he wondered.

After an awkward moment, his father nodded at Olivia. "And who might this be?"

"I should like to introduce Olivia … your granddaughter."

"My … pardon me?"

Why did the only emotion the man seemed comfortable revealing have to be that of anger?

"How could you … I can't believe you capable of keeping our own flesh and blood from us … and for all this time."

"She's absolutely lovely," his mother said as she reached for Olivia's hand. "Our very own granddaughter. Oliver, why?"

"I just found out."

His father's brows snapped together. "You can't possibly expect us to believe ..."

"She's your grandson's twin."

That look.

As Ole stared down that sudden demeaning look, he recalled Amelia's letter, that look she described—and then he understood.

"You mean Emily's ..." his father said.

"That's right."

The frown deepened.

Ole's eyes met with Olivia's and in them were revealed an acute understanding of what he himself felt. The coldness. The rudeness. No wonder Amelia had felt a fervent need to protect her granddaughter.

"Oliver, why don't I show Olivia the garden while you and your father have a nice little chat?" his mother said.

When they disappeared from view, Ole stuffed a hand in a pocket and pivoted, giving his father his back. He still felt estranged from the man. Surely there must be a way to penetrate that barrier, but how?

Because of him, Ole had felt compelled to live in a far-away land where he was free to be his own man and not feel oppressed.

Because of him, he'd been denied a lifelong relationship with a beloved daughter he never knew he had.

Because of him, Olivia experienced the same rejection Ole's dearly departed Emily had suffered.

Or was it because of him? Ole had made his own choice. Amelia had made a choice as well, albeit a painful choice accompanied with devastating consequences. His father had merely been himself. There was nothing Ole could do to correct the past, but he could attempt to correct the future. What was it that Olivia had so eloquently implied? Those suffering poverty of the soul need love the most? "I'm pleased to see that you and Mother look well," he ventured.

His father approached the bar. "Care for a drink?"

"No, thank you," Ole said tentatively. "You've done a marvelous job of managing the estate, I see."

"Not without our challenges."

"But still, you are to be commended."

"How's the wife? Gretta? That's her name, is it not?"

"She's well, thank you. It would be good for you to one day meet."

His father appeared to stiffen at the suggestion.

Which irritated Ole. "I'm concerned about your granddaughter," he said, "that she might feel rather unwelcome."

His father lifted his nose. "You married a pauper … against our wishes. Now you bring this girl into our home and expect us to accept your choices again. What do you expect from us?"

"That pauper's daughter is your granddaughter. She has your blood."

His eyes took on a hard quality. "How could you possibly believe she's your child? You as good as admitted that she popped up out of the blue. How can you be certain she isn't after your wealth?"

"Because of a letter I received from Amelia," Ole said with strength of tone. "She wrote it on her deathbed."

His father dropped several ice cubes in a crystal goblet and poured in a golden-hewed liquid, swirling it as if swirling around his thoughts.

"She said that when she told you of the passing of Emily and our son, you appeared relieved." Ole looked away for a brief moment, catching himself. "No, that isn't true. She called it a look of unmitigated relief."

"Surely, you don't mean to hang that on me?"

"I don't need to. Amelia did that quite well herself …"

His father's jaw dropped.

"… so much so that she couldn't bring herself to announce the birth of your granddaughter … or should I say of my daughter? You being a man of power, she feared you would take Olivia away from her. She refused to allow that to happen to Emily or to her memory."

His father balked, stared off, looking ill at ease as if he had suffered a crippling blow to his solar plexus. What was worse? He appeared vulnerable in his old age.

To think that since a child Ole had felt intimidated by the man. Now he felt as if he were the intimidator ... and that realization brought him no pleasure. How could it be that the honesty of mere words could wield that much power?

"She wrote that? In a letter on her deathbed?" His father strolled to the sofa and eased down. "What have I done?" he muttered.

A more relevant question might be, what are you continuing to do? "Do you honestly feel Olivia is unworthy of being your grandchild simply because her mother was a pauper? Please tell me it's not possible for you to value her that little."

"I don't know what I feel any more," he said absently. "I only know what I was taught." His father turned away, ran a hand through his hair, and then turned back again with an unreadable look. "Why America, Oliver? And why would you choose to marry beneath your class?"

Though his father had eyes, clearly he did not see nor did he understand. "I guess you might say that I needed to find fulfillment in my own right."

Creases lined his father's forehead. "But you could have lived a life of plenty. You turned your back on it. You turned your back on us."

"You're wrong. I turned my back on that easy life of plenty. And in doing so, I received more than I could have hoped ... but not until after I left England."

"You must be mistaken."

"No, sir. Love, honor, and respect? They trump all of the money and power in the world any and every day of the week."

His father got up, punched a hand in a pocket, and meandered about the room as if pondering what Ole had said, as if not knowing how to respond. After a long moment, he looked at him questioningly. "You are happy then?"

"Yes, sir. More so than I ever imagined possible."

"That's good, son," he said after another long moment, sounding as though he meant it. "That's good," he repeated.

Which left Ole pondering the fairness of life. Which is better? he wondered. To obtain one's heart's desire early on yet not appreciate its worth as did his father with him? Or to have that desire dangle at arm's length until one learns to value it more than life itself—as happened with Olivia and him? Perhaps having to wait for a dream's fulfillment had merit in its own right.

Forgive him, Ole.

But it's too hard.

Tell him. Don't think. Just blurt it out.

"I've missed being your son," he finally offered in a voice coarse with emotion.

"You …"

The sentiment barely spoken, Olivia's words about people suffering from poverty of the soul revisited him. *Say it Ole. Take courage. You're on a roll. But make sure you soften it. Be indirect.* "And you love us, too."

His father paused as if stung, then nodded slowly, shattering a lifetime of tension. "Thank you for having the courage to say it, son." He put a hand on Ole's shoulder then turned to the waiting servant. "Fetch my wife and granddaughter for us, would you, Henry?"

"If they appear hesitant to come," Ole added, "tell them my father here has a condition of the heart."

Footfalls echoed as the servant hurried away. A long moment later, Ole's mother rushed into the room, panting, with Olivia at her heels. "What's happened? … What … We were told we were needed immediately," she said, turning to Ole's father. "That you'd had a heart attack. But you? You're in perfectly good health."

"A condition of the heart." Ole's father projected an air of innocence. "I fear you must have been misled."

As Olivia steepled her hands to her mouth appearing to hide a grin, her sleeve slipped, exposing a pale birthmark on her forearm in the shape of a rose.

Gasping, his mother grasped her wrist and turning it, she examined it. "Olivia? That birthmark."

"Yes?" she said.

"My mother. Your great grandmother. I find this beyond belief. She had one as well. Precisely the same shape. In the same place on her arm." Her eyes widened, filling with what appeared to be absolute joy. She then turned to Ole, tears streaming down her cheeks.

After a long moment, Ole's father turned to him. "You and Olivia must get your belongings. I insist. You need to stay here. With us. Or should I say your mother and I need you and our granddaughter to stay here with us? To acquaint," he said with a warm eye cast on Olivia and then turned to Ole, "and to reacquaint before you go back to the States. We've missed you, son … more than you'll ever know."

So this was what it felt like to experience true parental love. Ole wasn't sure he liked it. Maddening moisture threatening to overtake his eyes. Unwelcome tightness choking his throat. Why did his father have to say that … now? Couldn't he appreciate Ole's need to guard his dignity? Honestly!

After a forceful yank on the leash of emotion, Ole glanced at Olivia questioningly.

In short order, they journeyed to London, to the hotel, to the flat, gathered their belongings and then returned to the estate where they spent the entirety of the next week sharing old memories, building new memories … as if restoring the years the locusts had eaten just as God's Word had promised.

Their visit filled with more joy than Ole could have imagined, at the end of the too-brief stay, he turned to Olivia and said, "I fear it's time to go."

"To my flat?"

With a thoughtful shake of his head, he said, "No. To Amber Leaf. Home … where we belong."

ACKNOWLEDGEMENTS

MY HEARTFELT THANKS TO BRETT BURNER, Publisher at Lamp Post Publishers, for seeing potential in this work and guiding me through the publishing process. Thanks also to Rebecca LuElla Miller for her excellent editorial assistance.

Thank you to members of my writers critique group (Felicia Cameron, Martha Gorris, Ann Larson, Jean Mader, Mary Kay Moody, and Diana Wallis Taylor) for their selfless input.

To Marilyn Damian, Pastor Richard Dresselhaus (for generously sharing his wisdom in his "One for the Road" devotionals), Anne Fletcher, Gene Hendrickson, Jeanne Holien, Lorraine Hooks, Lori Lobnitz, Sybil Obendrauf, Ardena Okland, Scott Okland, Shirley Ravenshorst, Bonnie Roach, Ellen Sheldon, and Nadine Washburn, among others, for your inspiration, input, and encouragement.

Last but definitely not least, my profound thanks to my readers, Elnora Dresselhaus and husband Fred, for your amazing input and support. I could not be more blessed.